Once More
With
Feeling

Also by Megan Crane

Once More With Feeling

MEGAN CRANE

Quercus

First published in Great Britain in 2012 by

Quercus
55 Baker Street
7th Floor, South Block
London
W1U 8EW

A CIP catalogue record for this book is available
from the British Library

ISBN 978 0 85738 000 5 (PB)
ISBN 978 0 85738 255 9 (EBOOK)

10 9 8 7 6 5 4 3 2 1

Typeset by Ellipsis Digital Limited, Glasgow

Printed and bound in Great Britain by
Clays Ltd, St Ives plc

This is not my life. These are not my cobwebs.
This is not the darkness I was designed for.

Colum McCann, *Let the Great World Spin*

1

It could be worse.

I made the words my mantra. A daily chant, an affirmation – and the best part was that it was true. It could, in fact, always be worse. *Pestilence. Famine. Disease. Death.*

Any of those were much worse, obviously, than my own puny little grief.

There were so many people who got divorced. Many of them had no idea that their marriages were even in trouble until it was all over, just like me. I wasn't the only one, the only fool. I couldn't be. Just like I couldn't possibly be the only one with the great misfortune to come home unexpectedly and find her spouse in bed with someone else.

It could be worse. Couldn't it?

But I was getting ahead of myself.

I got out of court surprisingly early that day, thanks to a 'sewage issue' in the local courthouse I wanted to know as little about as possible, thank you, which meant I had to take a break from fruitlessly arguing Benjy Stratton's latest DWI charge before the granite-jawed and perpetually outraged Judge Fennimore – who was as unamused by Benjy's antics as I was now that we were on round three and Benjy was not yet twenty-two. I headed for my car, breathing in the perfectly blue, early September afternoon, and made the command decision not to go back to the little law office that Tim and I had spent the last few years building into a fairly robust practice for Rivermark, New York, if I did say so myself.

I knew that if I showed my face in our converted little Victorian offices of Lowery & Lowery, a few steps from Rivermark's picturesque town square, the overtly busty and only intermittently helpful office manager Annette would bury me beneath the reams of paperwork she always claimed to need help in deciphering.

Help from me, I thought, expertly roaring along the back roads out of the centre of town and up toward the ridge where our house stood sentry. *Never help from Tim.*

Instead of dealing with another conversation about why it wasn't appropriate for Annette to ask me to 'check her work' when both she and I knew perfectly well that always meant I ended up doing it for her and then paying her for the privilege, I decided to stage my own, personal revolution and go home. Even though it was barely 2 p.m.

I could catch a yoga class, I thought giddily, kicking off my appropriate court heels the moment I walked through the door of the house Tim and I had spent so much time making into the perfect refuge, up high on the ridge overlooking the pretty valley that was Rivermark, my home town.

I tossed my jacket on the bench in the front hallway, and debated whether or not to go down the hall into the kitchen to grab something to eat. I went over the shopping lists in my head – different ones for the local supermarket, Trader Joe's and Whole Foods, of course, because we needed different things from all three – and decided that if I hurried, I could make the yoga class I liked and then treat myself to something delicious at the little coffee place next door afterwards, when I would feel lithe and long and more inclined to choose fruit over the chocolate-drenched pastry I actually wanted.

I started upstairs, thinking about pastries and chocolate and how virtuous yoga would make me feel, and how very much I wanted to feel virtuous after another day spent listening to Benjy Stratton spew out his entitled rich-boy views on his own poor decision-making skills. I also noticed how cool the bare wood was beneath my feet as I walked up the stairs, like some kind of massage.

There was no sense of foreboding. At all.

The sad reality is that I simply walked down the upstairs hall, completely unaware, as I'd been doing every day for all three years Tim and I had lived here. Right past the carefully framed photographs that captured choice moments from Tim's and my life in all their candid glory. Our first trip together to his favourite beach down in

Delaware. That first Christmas at his parents' place in Maryland, when he'd proposed out in their woods surrounded by all that quiet and snow, a whole eighteen months before they'd died so suddenly and heartbreakingly, one right after the other. And our wedding, of course, that slick and spare affair in a modern loft in Manhattan, filled with all of our New York City friends, so few of whom we saw now that we'd moved way out into suburbia.

I'd put all of those photos together myself, picking and choosing our memories, making a certain group of three pictures real and representative of who we were, of our life together, while casting another set into dusty purgatory in a box beneath the bed. I'd had them all framed in complementary distressed woods, looking at once elegant and inviting between the built-in bookcases that lined the long hallway. I had always been the custodian of Tim's and my relationship mythology – I even thought of myself that way with some measure of pride – but that day, I didn't look at any of those pictures. Why would I? They had long since become a part of the décor. Just colourful parts of the wall I *really* looked at only when suffering from some kind of melancholy. Or P.M.S. Or, as was too often the case, both.

I walked down the hallway and into our bedroom. I didn't hear anything. I didn't sense anything. I thought I was alone in the house, as I should have been, at two o'clock on a random Tuesday.

I was already pulling my blouse off as I went. I'd dumped

the dregs of my coffee on myself earlier that morning on my way into court, and was fuming slightly about our outrageous dry cleaning bill. But I'd pulled the blouse up and over my face as I walked through the doorway, just as I'd done a million times before, and as I finished yanking it over my head I automatically tossed it toward the bed, the way I always did—

Which was when everything slowed down. Turned to glue. Stuck.

It was as if the blouse stayed in the air for a long, long time. I watched it float in a graceful sort of arc, a silken scrap of royal blue, suspended there before me. I focused on the blouse because what was on the other side of it, what was happening right there on my bed, pale-yellow sheets and crisp white comforter strewn this way and that, was impossible.

Disgusting.

Impossible.

They had their eyes closed. *Of course they did*, I thought, from some kind of paralysed distance. You'd want your eyes closed if you were going at it the way they were. With all of that intensity. With so much *physicality*. I felt as if I were some kind of alien research scientist flown in from an outlying planet to make notes on this strange couple, who could not have anything at all to do with me.

Who could not be who I thought they were.

She was on her hands and knees, both hands braced hard against the mattress, making deep grooves in it with her palms. *He* was behind her, his body curved over hers, one hand on the mattress beside her and the other wrapped around her slender hip, slamming her back against him. Again and again.

This must be what it's like to watch porn on mute, I thought dimly. I'd always meant to get my porn on as part of the supposed sex-positive third wave of feminism or whatever, but had never got around to actually doing it. My consequently uneducated impression of porn was that it was supposed to be very loud, filled with all of that desperate moaning and shrieking and *oh baby*-ing I'd glimpsed in brief moments in sad hotel rooms, but this was not. They were both breathing hard, their sex-reddened faces screwed up with all of that taut, silent, terrible *focus*. And beyond that, there was the faint sound of flesh slapping against flesh.

My blouse hung in the air.

I stood there, frozen solid, not breathing at all.

Until the blouse landed, right on *her* face, and everything came to a screeching halt.

I realized then that I was half-naked, for all intents and purposes.

This horrified me so much that it was almost as if the rest disappeared. *Almost*. I wanted to cover myself, but I couldn't seem to move, and the fact that I was partly naked too, that I was *exposed* like that in only my raggedy old bra with the slightly stained straps I kept meaning to replace – well – that was what finally sent me over the edge.

I screamed.

Because there was, it turned out, no other adequate way to process the fact that I had just walked into my bedroom to find my husband fucking my sister. *My sister.* There was only the screaming.

It could be worse. I knew it could. *Amputated limbs. Suppurating sores. Cancer of everything.*

There were other thirty-three-year-old women who woke up on a Tuesday morning feeling comfortable – even, dare I remember the hubris, *pleased* – in their little worlds, only to find the whole of it in shattered pieces by nightfall. Tim was out of the house – a touch dramatically, I could admit, but it turned out that it *felt good* to throw his fucking clothes out of second-storey windows on to the driveway below, especially his shoes as they made so much noise – that very same night.

I couldn't think about my sister Carolyn and the things she'd screamed back at me without shaking violently and nearly vomiting, so I didn't. I couldn't.

My situation wasn't even anything special, I told myself as I sat where I'd eventually collapsed, in stunned silence in the empty living room, staring at nothing and still wearing the skirt and pantyhose I'd worn to court beneath the sweatshirt I'd shrugged on to cover myself. People went through things like this all the time. Hadn't someone I hardly remembered from high school posted three different articles on facebook in the last few months about how infidelity strengthened a marriage? It was all about *weathering the storm*, I told myself piously. Desperately.

That, I could do. And did.

I assumed that the abrupt and horrible discovery of his tawdry affair would shock Tim back to reality. I expected that without me in his daily life, he would notice that Carolyn, my faithless sister, older by two years and heretofore obsessed only with herself and the marketing career she'd been let go from eight months ago, was a complete disaster in every possible domestic department. She'd always been very vocal and *proud* of her inability to do her own laundry, for God's sake. She'd always claimed loudly that her refusal to perform domestic tasks was *a feminist act*, while I rather thought it had less to do with ideology and more to do with Carolyn not feeling like washing a dish or her own socks and underwear.

Tim had always rolled his eyes and agreed. But that was before.

While Carolyn could perform doggy-style sex enthusiastically – an image I would now be forced to carry with me to my grave – could she make the dinners Tim liked to have ready for him when he got home? Buy groceries and keep the house stocked so that she could toss together a dinner for two, six, or eight clients or friends at a moment's notice? Make the bed every morning or take care of the house so that an unexpected visit by anyone would never embarrass us? Do any of the hundreds of things I did daily, none of which Tim even necessarily specifically noticed, yet all of which kept his life running smoothly, prettily and competently?

All while also maintaining my own career as one half of the practice?

I didn't think so.

I didn't even attempt to process what had happened. What would be the point? It was unprocessable. It was impossible, and yet it had happened. I simply sat there on the plush sofa, surrounded by all the things Tim and I had gathered over the course of our seven years together, two years of dating and five years of marriage. All the detritus of more than half a decade. The by-products of intimacy. I threw out all the sheets they'd touched and put that mattress on the kerb. I sat. I waited.

But Tim did not call. Carolyn did. And not with the expected grovelling, prostrate, tearing of hair and rending of garments sort of apology either.

'I am so sorry,' she said. Her voice did not sound rough with shame. Or grief. Or horror at her own behaviour and the pain she'd caused. She sounded the way she always did. 'I really am. I never meant to hurt you.'

I was unable to speak. I wasn't sure why I'd picked up in the first place. Anger and betrayal and something else that hollowed out my lungs and sent acid coursing through my belly stole my breath, my words. I could only stand there at the island in my kitchen, frozen into place with my cell phone clamped to my ear and the refrigerator door swung wide open and abandoned behind me, unable to process what I was hearing.

'I love him,' Carolyn said in that same perfectly normal

way of hers. But it was impossible. Absurd. And yet she said it as if in her world there was a cresting soundtrack and all the right kind of lighting, making her the heroine of this moment instead of its villainess. 'And he loves me. I'm sorry. I really am.'

But she wasn't sorry enough to stop. She wasn't sorry enough to give me back my husband, who, she told me, was staying in one of the bed and breakfasts in town.

With her.

She wasn't, I recognized, sorry at all. Not in any meaningful way. Not really.

It could be worse, I told myself bitterly as, over the next few weeks, I was forced to come to terms with the fact that Tim appeared to be remaining in that bed and breakfast. *With her.* A step up for Carolyn, who had been riding out her unemployment at my parents' house. A step down for Tim, I told myself. *It had to be.*

I attempted to work from home because I didn't want to go into the office and face him. Or, worse, the judgemental Annette. Her inability to ever treat me with one iota of the deference she'd slathered all over Tim struck me now, in retrospect, as a clue I should have heeded. There I'd been, furious that she wasn't respecting me as she should, and meanwhile, had she known the whole time that Tim was sneaking around behind my back? Was that why she'd steadfastly refused to do what I wanted her to do? Had she assumed that I simply didn't matter enough – to anyone?

Because that was certainly how it felt. Even from my parents.

'Oh, Sarah,' my mother said in that sad way of hers that always made me feel as if she thought she was the victim, no matter what the issue was. She patted my hand as it lay between us on her kitchen table, the house free of Carolyn's presence, but only because she was currently tucked up in bed *with my husband*, and sighed heavily. 'We don't condone what Carolyn did, of course, but we don't want to get involved. We don't want to be in the middle.'

I didn't understand how there was a middle of this to be in, when it seemed like there was a very clear side to choose here – that this was one of the very few situations in life that was not grey at all. But I had never had any success figuring out what went on in my mother's head before, so the fact that I couldn't now? Not a huge surprise.

I told myself it didn't even hurt.

And *it could be worse*, I reminded myself when Tim sat me down for a 'friendly chat' about six weeks after he'd moved out, and long after I'd figured out how to navigate going in and out of the office without having to see him – i.e., monitoring his calendar to see when he was in court or out with clients. It was strange to see him again, after so much had happened. It was stranger to note that our 'friendly chat' had a clear agenda. It was all about what was fair and what we both knew to be true about our marriage (except I hadn't known anything, a point he glossed over) and the best way for everyone (by which, it became clear, he meant himself and Carolyn) to get what they wanted out of 'this unpleasantness'.

I slouched there in the deceptively uncomfortable faux-leather Starbucks armchair, wearing my post-sister-in-bed-with-husband uniform of ancient grey sweats and a navy-blue zip-up hooded sweatshirt, breathing in the competing scents of burnt coffee beans and warm milk, while staring at my husband, the man I had chosen to *spend the rest of my life with*, forced to contemplate the possibility that he was a complete and total stranger to me. Or, alternatively, a zombie in Carolyn's evil thrall.

I preferred the latter explanation, if I was honest.

'I'm sorry,' I said. I felt as if I choked on the words, but my voice sounded normal enough, if a little unhealthily high. Also, I wasn't sorry. I cleared my throat. 'Did you just call sleeping with my sister "this unpleasantness"?' I laughed slightly. It felt like a saw and sounded worse. 'Because I can think of other words.'

Tim sighed. I knew every line of his boyishly handsome face, every single expression he was capable of producing, and I knew that one, too. I assured myself I was reading him wrong. Because if anyone had the right to look *resigned*, it was not him.

'Don't make this more difficult than it has to be, Sarah,' he said. Gently, but with that undercurrent of exasperation to which he was not in the least bit entitled. Then he smiled. 'We're better than that, aren't we?'

I was ashamed of how much I clung to that, how much

my heart swelled and my breath caught. His use of the word *we*.

Long after we'd separated with an awkward almost-hug in the chilly parking lot, long after I had returned to the empty house on the hill and got back to the important work of hollowing out the perfect position on the sofa cushions to hold me as I brooded and shoved things in my mouth without thought, I still turned it over and over in my head. *We*. A word that did not, could not, had never, included Carolyn. *We*.

Tim did not call or stop by to reiterate any of the things I felt sure were lurking there in that one, meaningful syllable. *We*. But I still thought it was only a matter of time before the impossibility of living with Carolyn – because he'd told me that, too, that the two of them were now *living together* in that damned bed and breakfast, right there in the centre of town where every single person we knew would be sure to see them – became clear to him. How could it not? No one could live with Carolyn. In the sixth grade I had moved down into the largely unfinished basement of our parents' house so that I would no longer have to share the upstairs bedroom with her mood swings and melodramatic demands. College and post-college roommates, boyfriends, even that insufferable hippy she'd been engaged to briefly during her strange period in Portland, Oregon – everyone agreed that Carolyn was too selfish, too immature, too *adolescent* to live with.

I held onto that when Tim asked to meet again, about

two months after he'd moved out, to discuss the quick, no-fault divorce he thought we should get. As if it were something we could just pick up downtown together from one of the specialty shops, as easy as that.

'It seems to me that there is a fault,' I said after Tim presented me with all the paperwork and explained that this was the best way out of what he called *the situation*. As if our marriage were a preposterous guy from New Jersey, all steroids and terrible hair, soon to be discarded and forgotten. He sat there as if his own faux-leather Starbucks chair were perfectly comfortable, and I had the near-uncontainable urge to throw my not-nearly-foamy-enough pumpkin spice Halloween latte at his head. 'Your fault, in fact.'

I actually thought it was Carolyn's fault, but I also thought that there was a lot of grovelling Tim could do – like, any – before I let him know I understood that. I had elaborate fantasies of his extended apologies, all of which I would eventually, graciously, accept with varying degrees of longsuffering *goodness*, and all of which involved him on his knees. Or prostrate before me on a public street. In tears, of course. *Begging me to take him back—*

'Do we really want to drag all this out?' Tim asked, interrupting my favourite fantasy, which featured him somewhat bruised and battered and writhing on his stomach in the driveway. In the rain.

He smiled in that way that made his blue eyes dance and his dimples show. He reached over and put his hand over mine, right there in front of half of the town, and I thawed a little bit, like a fool. *See?* I wanted to shout at all the pricked ears and averted eyes that surrounded us. *See? We are still a we! We are!*

'Are we *those* people?' he asked softly.

And I still wanted to impress him. I still wanted to show him that *I* wasn't the one who was unreasonable, who made impossible demands. *I* could never be *those people*, whoever they were. Just like I could never be the notoriously demanding, high-maintenance, haughty and sister-betraying Carolyn.

A week or so after that, Tim and I met to discuss the *shape* our divorce would take. It could be so much worse, I told myself, as we sat there awkwardly in a more secluded mid-range restaurant this time, a gesture that I found suspicious at best, as Tim was not the sort to think of such things. I was the partner in our marriage responsible for *gestures*. I could feel the controlling, deceitful hand of Carolyn hovering over everything, and told myself *that* was why I couldn't bring myself to so much as pick at the warm bread the waiter had delivered to the table in a big, fragrant basket.

We would save ourselves the trauma of a long, drawn-out, agonizing divorce proceeding, Tim said. I wouldn't fight him for anything, he said, *right, Sarah*? Because *we* weren't like that. *We* were reasonable, logical people, and a big battle over hurt feelings – well, who did that serve? *We* could share everything. The law practice too, of course!

Why should our careers take a hit simply because our marriage hadn't worked out as we'd planned?

We, we, we. I felt *noble.* I nodded along, earnestly. He'd cheated on me, *in my own bed, with my sister,* and yet I sat at the tiny table too close to the busy kitchen and felt *gracious. I'll show him how reasonable and logical I am,* I thought fiercely, as if our divorce were a competition and I could actually win it.

And I was sure that when this insanity with Carolyn died down, Tim would wake up from this spell he was under and remember just how easy I'd made all of this. He might even *thank* me, I thought smugly. I drove back to our dark, empty home with visions of Tim's thanks dancing in my head, like bloated pre-Thanksgiving sugarplums.

Shockingly, the thanks didn't come.

But . . . it could be worse, right? Luckily, everyone I knew was appalled. Scandalized and horrified. They told me so at the supermarket, at stoplights. The joys of living in a mid-sized village in the Hudson Valley were that everyone I met in the course of my day knew the whole of my business. More to the point, they also knew all there was to know about Carolyn. And there was so much to know. Carolyn's entire history of shocking, self-obsessed, her-needs-above-all-else behaviour, was laid out and dissected in detail over the produce section in the grocery or in the shampoo aisle at the drugstore, and, everyone agreed, no one could possibly trust that Tim now that he'd proved himself to be such a terrible judge of character . . .

Until Carolyn announced their wedding plans, to take place in roughly six months, which was, I couldn't help but note, just about how long it took to get a no-contest divorce in the state of New York. *The minute the divorce goes through*, is what she meant when she waxed rhapsodic about a June wedding. I wondered if there was fancy wording for that sentiment that she could include on the invitations.

If so, I felt certain that Carolyn would find it. And use it, with as much shame as she'd exhibited thus far: none.

'I know that somewhere deep inside of you – even if it's buried right now – you'll understand that we just want to be happy,' Carolyn confided to my voicemail, as I had stopped taking her calls after that first, horrible one. 'And we want you to be happy too, Sarah. We really do.'

Which was when I started to think hard about plagues. *AIDS*, I thought fiercely as I considered the laborious process of making a new life for myself when I'd had no hand in dismantling the old one. *Bubonic plague. Tuberculosis.* I thought about insects. Locusts and bird flu. *Ebola*, I chanted to myself as I navigated a home town, a court-house, a gauntlet of clients filled with all those knowing, pitying stares. *Mad cow. SARS. Necrotizing fasciitis.*

Because it was getting harder and harder to convince myself that there was anything at all worse than this.

'I think we have to start considering the fact that this is really happening,' Lianne said, carefully, as if I were inordinately fragile and might shatter if she used the wrong tone. As Lianne was my best and, really *only*, remaining friend from high school, and had thus known me since we were both infants, I had to consider the possibility that, in fact, I might. 'I don't think he's coming back.'

We stood together in Lianne's bright and inviting kitchen, drinking coffee out of charmingly mismatched ceramic cups that somehow seemed perfectly grown-up and *planned*, like everything else in her happy life with Billy, whom she'd started dating way back in the eighth grade. We were having our longstanding Wednesday midday coffee date that we'd instituted not long after I'd moved back to town three years ago. I couldn't remember the last time either one of us had cancelled it. These days I considered it my lifeline – to a degree I was afraid would make Lianne a bit uncomfortable were I to tell her.

'It's okay,' Lianne said in that same gentle way, such a far cry from the usual matter-of-fact briskness that made her such a good nurse in the OBGYN practice where she'd worked for years. 'We'll get through this. We'll be just fine. I promise.'

Her use of *we*, I noted in a kind of dazed amazement, was even more comforting than Tim's had been. And also meant exactly what I wanted it to mean – no contortions of reality required.

'It's fine,' I said. It wasn't. It was any number of things, many of them in direct opposition to each other and all of them changeable and contradictory, but it certainly wasn't *fine*. And yet I found myself producing a smile, however faint. 'I mean,' I heard myself say. 'It's not like we're *those people*.'

Lianne poured some more coffee into my mug even though, after thirty-three years of friendship and the fact that she had given me my first cup of coffee in her parents' house when we were twelve, she was well aware that I was not the kind of person who liked 'topping up' my coffee. I preferred to fix the whole cup myself, so that it had the perfect ratio of coffee to creamer to sugar. But Lianne's brand of nurturing wasn't about coddling. It never had been.

'Which people?' she asked, not looking at me. 'The people who argue about every last detail because they're heartbroken and hurt and trying to fight back the only way they can?'

'Tim and I aren't like that,' I said with a certain loftiness that I suspected was simply because I looked for any excuse at all to say that these days. *Tim and I*. 'We're not going to make a big circus out of this, whatever happens.'

Lianne blew on her coffee as if she expected it to be scalding. 'Why not?' She looked at me, then away. 'This is the end of a marriage. Maybe it deserves a circus.' She shrugged. 'Doesn't have to be the full three rings, but maybe a clown or two? Some trapeze artists? A parade of elephants?'

Thinking of trapeze artists made me think of Carolyn's

rather impressive contortions in bed. In *my* bed. Contortions, I couldn't help but think, that my body simply wouldn't perform, yoga or no yoga. Carolyn was built willowy and bendable. I was curvier and shorter and significantly less flexible. I thought of myself as *solid*. I wasn't flashy, like Carolyn. I kept my more-dirty-than-blonde hair in a sharp, professional bob that I hadn't cut since That Day. I wore professional suits that had to pass muster in court. I didn't lounge around in tattoos and kohl, like Carolyn.

'Is this supposed to be helpful?' I asked, and I could hear the rage in my voice, but knowing it was unfairly directed at Lianne did nothing at all to dampen it. 'Don't you think this is humiliating enough? My fucking *sister* is sleeping with my husband, planning a June wedding *to my husband—*'

'I have one question for you,' Lianne said in a calm, wholly unperturbed way that was more effective than slapping a hand across my mouth. She met my gaze, her own steady and sure. 'And I really want you to think about your answer.'

'Am I tired of you talking to me like I'm a crazy person?' I asked dryly. 'The answer is yes.'

'Are you upset that you lost Tim?' Somehow, her very calmness made it worse. 'Or are you upset that Carolyn took him?'

I spent a lot of time spinning that question around and around in my head. Luckily, I had nothing *but* time. It was increasingly more humiliating to leave the house and see anyone, because every single person in this town knew what had happened to me – what was still happening to me, right this very minute in the bed and breakfast in the centre of the village – which meant I had a lot of time to sit alone and *brood* when I wasn't working, explaining to Rivermark's drunk and wealthy why the state of New York was not going to be impressed with their pedigrees.

It was getting harder and harder to cling to my belief that Tim would shake this madness off one day, and come back to me, the way I knew he should. But I was nothing if not tenacious, hide it though I might beneath the veneer of pathetic despair and questionable dietary choices. My belief in what should happen, what had to happen, only grew as the days passed – took root and spread wide, created whole forests. I knew, I just *knew*, that Tim would come back to me. He had to.

He had to.

And then came the lovely day two weeks before Thanksgiving when nosy, gossipy Mrs Duckworth, who had always been such a stalwart supporter of mine, always eager to talk about Carolyn's numerous trespasses with relish and glee, made that awkward, embarrassed face in the bread and cereal aisle at the supermarket where I had never, not once, seen the faintest hint of my sister. I had been secretly regarding that as *incontrovertible proof* that Carolyn's unholy alliance with Tim was therefore doomed. Because I knew the earth would be well into another ice age before it occurred to *Tim* to do the shopping.

'These things do get complicated,' Mrs Duckworth clucked, holding a family-sized loaf of multigrain bread between her pudgy hands. I looked down, dazed, to see I'd clenched great big grooves into my own skinny, newly-single-person's baguette. I forced myself to loosen my grip. Mrs Duckworth shrugged. Guiltily, I thought. 'But it's different when it's love, isn't it?'

Which was when I accepted the fact that maybe it couldn't actually get much worse, after all.

But, of course, I was wrong about that, too.

2

'I can't hear a word you're saying, Mom,' I said, frowning, barely able to hear my mother's voice over the sound of Lianne's family's noisy Thanksgiving evening game of running charades – which mostly involved her kids careening into walls and their boisterous accusations of cheating. 'Are you in a wind tunnel?'

I made an apologetic face at Lianne, who had just handed me her house cordless phone, and took myself out into the slightly quieter front hall. Behind me, her oldest girl screamed out a condemnation of her nine-year-old sister, with the kind of high-pitched outrage only a thirteen-year-old girl could manage to produce. I was smiling when I finally concentrated again on the phone call.

Not that I *wanted* to concentrate on this phone call. I'd boycotted my own family's Thanksgiving dinner this year, and my mother had made her displeasure about that abundantly clear. *I can't make you change your mind about coming to Thanksgiving dinner with your family, Sarah*, she'd said with a sniff, *but it seems you're determined to lash out and hurt your father and me as much as you've been hurt, and I can't support that.*

I imagined she was calling now, at almost ten o'clock at night, to rub a little more salt in that festering wound.

'Are you there?' I asked, girding my loins for the usual mother–daughter battle of wills. And, if I was totally honest, kind of anticipating it, too. Mom would be sad and wounded and often cold; I would, I swore, be calm and rational and not too 'lawyery', as she liked to accuse me of being. I'd been practising my speech all day in Lianne's downstairs bathroom mirror.

'I am not in a wind tunnel,' came my mother's frosty reply.

As far as I could tell, my mother had been this particular level of quietly angry with me ever since I'd thrown Tim out of the marital home, thereby, quote, *sharing your private business with the whole town*. Carolyn's flaunting of said private business in a bed and breakfast in the centre of the village, subject to the eyes and ears and gossiping mouths of all our neighbours? Apparently not as grave a violation of the family honour. Thanksgiving had only made it worse: my 'choice' to 'abandon the family' and 'force us to choose between you and your sister' being confirmation that I was 'determined to punish' her. I checked the weary sigh that threatened to come out.

'I'm at the hospital,' she said. 'You need to come at once.'

I felt a single greasy punch of nauseating fear, hard and incapacitating.

'Is it Dad?' I gasped, as terrible scenarios chased through my head.

I wrapped my free arm around my waist. I should have gotten over my damned self and gone to Thanksgiving at my parents' house, the way she'd wanted me to do. I shouldn't have taken a stand and refused to attend simply because they'd invited Tim and Carolyn as well. *We can't take sides*, Mom had said, in that surprised, somewhat affronted way as if I'd suggested she shiv her firstborn in the shower. *She's our daughter too.* I shouldn't have replied with such ferocity. *Pretending not to notice the problem is actually taking sides, Mom*, I'd snapped back. Was it worth it now?

'What happened?' I gasped out.

'Your father is fine,' Mom said, her voice thawing slightly, but only slightly. 'It's not him. I'm afraid it's Tim.'

I stared out the glass panel in the front door at the dark November night beyond. Something frighteningly large yawned open inside of me, too dark for me to look at directly.

'I think you called the wrong daughter, Mom,' I said evenly. When I could speak.

'Carolyn is already here.' Mom let out a small noise too sharp to be a sigh. 'She tried to call you herself, repeatedly, but said you refused to answer her calls.'

I pressed my fingers hard against my forehead and told

myself this was not the time to address all the problems I had with that statement.

'What happened to Tim, Mom? Is he all right?'

'We don't know yet,' she said. 'He went out after dinner to pick up some beer. When he didn't come back and he didn't come back, Carolyn called him and an EMT answered his phone. Apparently the roads were icy and his car spun out. He crashed into a tree a few blocks down from the supermarket.'

I was outside of myself. My mother's disembodied voice was in my ear, stringing together nonsensical words. The sounds of Lianne's family shouting and laughing down the hall floated around me but didn't touch me. The cold of the November night was a shock against my palm when I pressed it against the glass panel in the door, but I pressed harder, as if that could make it real somehow. Make me real, right here, living in this terrible moment. I saw that scrap of bright-blue silk, flying through the air, making as little sense as this. I struggled to pull in a breath.

'Is . . . ?' I couldn't form the necessary words. My throat felt as if there was a hand wrapped tight around it, crushing me. 'Is he . . . ?'

'We don't know anything yet.' That was not the immediate refutation that I wanted. It solved nothing, least of all that choking sensation. 'He's in surgery now.'

'But what do they think?' I whispered. 'What did they say? How bad is it?'

Mom was quiet for what was probably only a moment

but felt like years. Long, iced-over ages, and I was suspended there in silence, waiting. Only waiting, as if there had never been and would never be anything but this moment. This telephone call. I was aware of the breath moving in and out of my chest, the seeping cold against the skin of my palm, the heat pricking at the back of my eyes, and that constriction in my throat like some kind of instant onset of strep. My mind raced and raced, but came up with nothing, and in the darkest part of me, that great emptiness seemed to stretch. Grow. Take over. I didn't know how I could survive it. How anyone could.

'You have to come, Sarah,' Mom said then, finally. 'You're still his wife.'

I had been in the town hospital far too many times over the years, and didn't like the fact I was back now.

I'd been born here, and had the pictures to prove it. But those pictures were the only happy memories connected to the place. The rest involved pain, of one sort or another. The time I'd fallen off of my bike in the fifth grade, breaking two fingers and giving myself a minor concussion. When I'd gotten my tonsils removed in the sixth grade and was given only ice chips to soothe the burn, rather than the promised vats of ice cream. My cold-blooded attempt to add *good works* to my college résumé in high school as a candy striper, which had involved entirely too many tragically dying people and my reluctant acceptance of the fact that I was terrible with other people's physical pain and suffering.

When I'd had my appendix removed the summer after my junior year of college. When I'd visited Lianne's mother while she was dying of cancer, and nineteen-year-old, just-married Lianne was falling apart. When my father had had pneumonia that winter. All of those memories seemed to chase me, nipping at my ankles as I walked down the gleaming halls, my head swimming with the scent of the industrial-strength cleaning agents and that underlying, cloying smell of *unwell* that never seemed to go away no matter how much they scrubbed. The lights were always too bright here, the walls somehow too dingy.

It was not a happy place.

I followed the signs up to the ICU, aware that my body felt like someone else's as I walked. A borrowed body, one physically up to this task, somehow, despite the fact I felt as if I'd left the contents of my brain behind at Lianne's. Not that it mattered, because none of this felt real anyway. I thought I ought to *feel* any number of things, really, but I couldn't seem to get there. I just couldn't. I was numb everywhere I should have felt something. Just frozen all the way through. I'd driven across town in a daze, parked in the overpriced lot, marched across the cold asphalt as if on a mission, found my way inside . . . all without managing to form anything in the way of a coherent thought. I would have said that was impossible, had I not just done it.

I walked to the nurse's station in the ICU, identified

myself as Tim's next of kin, was told that Tim was still in surgery, and was then directed to the waiting room on the other side of the automatic glass doors, away from the low beeps and cloud of desperation that hung over the ward. The doctor would find me there when he came out of surgery, they said, with that dispassionate briskness that, I supposed, made medical personnel capable of doing their jobs in the midst of so much human misery. I swallowed and turned, wincing as my shoes squeaked against the floor, as if that might disturb the patients hooked up to their machines in all the curtained cubicles.

Obediently, I trudged down the hall to the room marked ICU Waiting Room, and walked inside.

And then immediately wished I hadn't.

Carolyn slumped in one of the jarringly cheerful blue chairs near the door like some kind of opera heroine, one arm thrown over her eyes, her other hand clenched around our mother's. Our mother who sat next to Carolyn as if she was personally holding her upright with her positive thoughts and boundless support. I couldn't help staring at them, just as I couldn't help the little bubble of anger and jealousy that seemed to pop inside my chest. *This* was my mother's version of not choosing sides?

I jumped slightly when a hand came down heavily on my shoulder, but I knew who it was almost in that same instant, and smiled slightly as I turned into my father's hug.

'Terrible night,' he said in an undertone, his low rumble of a voice like a small streak of comfort, lighting its way through me, making me feel that slightest bit less frozen. 'Just terrible.'

Carolyn shifted in her seat just then, dropped her arm, and opened her eyes to look directly at me.

It was the first time we'd seen each other since That Day, and I'd gone to a good deal of trouble to avoid thinking about That Day, thank you. But suddenly, right here in the waiting room, Tim already dead for all I knew, not that I could allow myself to dwell on that, I couldn't seem to think of anything else.

I concentrated on the blouse in the air, royal blue and frozen in flight. Better that than what lay behind it. Even now. Once again, I felt half-naked and exposed, dingy bra on display for all the world to see. My stomach twisted, then seemed to fold in on itself. Much like the rest of me wanted to do.

'Sarah.' She said my name and then seemed to think better of it. For the first time in my entire life, my sister looked like a complete stranger to me. I saw nothing I recognized in her familiar features – nothing I knew looking back at me from her eyes.

Or maybe I just wanted her to be a complete, unknowable alien. It made it so much easier to hate her.

I told myself she looked like Olive Oyl, that she looked out of place and absurd, but I suspected the real problem was that she made me feel so frumpy. Even in operatic upset, she still looked *interesting*. My still-untrimmed hair was definitely getting shaggy, and I hadn't bothered to dress for dinner at Lianne's, which meant I was in ratty jeans and a sweater which, I knew now, was far too staid and boring. I felt like someone's sad-sack Aunt Ethel. I felt like the kind of woman who couldn't hold on to her husband. Which, in fact, I was.

'Well,' I said, when I could no longer stand the uncomfortable silence, the surge of anxiety, the immediate and vicious dip into body hatred, 'At least this time you have your clothes on.'

Carolyn stared back at me for another long, tense moment. Like she didn't know me, either. I noticed her eyes were rimmed with red, and her dark hair was scraped back into a makeshift ponytail. She was too bony, as always, but tonight she actually looked fragile rather than chic. She bit her lower lip, as if she were physically biting back words, and dropped her gaze to the floor. My heart pounded in my chest, and I realized then that I wanted her to fight. Maybe I wanted the distraction. Or maybe I wanted the excuse to scream at her the way I had That Day – more proof that she was the kind of terrible, awful, reprehensible person who could do something like this to her own sister.

'The nurses told me he's still in surgery,' I said instead, irritated that my voice sounded so hoarse. As if I had anything to be ashamed of here. 'It looks like we're in for a long night.'

I felt foolish, suddenly, as if I were aping medical dramas I'd seen in the past. As if I were speaking the lines to some script, and I was a terrible actress. I still felt as if my body wasn't mine, as if none of this were real, as if I were somewhere else watching it all happen. What did it say about me that some part of me wished I really was?

But there was nothing to do but wait. And pretend that Carolyn wasn't in the room. If my husband's girlfriend had been anyone besides my sister, would I have allowed this? I knew I wouldn't have. I didn't know why I didn't throw her out, too. But I didn't. On some level, I was afraid that if I tried, she wouldn't go. And worse – that my parents would back her up.

And the truth I had to sit with – for hours – was that I was far too cowardly to test that theory.

They told us he made it through surgery some time before dawn. And that we could see him, one at a time and for very brief periods. I was up and on my feet without thinking about it, and only noticed that Carolyn stood too as I passed her on my way out of the waiting room. I saw her hands ball into fists, but she stayed quiet.

I'm still his wife! I thought furiously. *You haven't won yet!*

But then I hated myself that I could be so petty, even here. Even now.

I followed the nurse into his small, curtained space, and had to remind myself to breathe. No matter that I'd cautioned myself to expect the worst – and no matter that the doctor and nurse had made a point of mentioning that he was *a little bit worse for wear*. I still wasn't prepared.

The last time I'd seen Tim he'd been *Tim*. That big grin and bright eyes that made you believe that whatever he saw in front of him, he loved. But tonight Tim lay on the bed, covered in bandages and connected to machines, looking pale and fragile and not anything like himself in the middle of it. It took me long, frightening, wholly disorienting moments to find the things in him I recognized beneath the tubes and the lines, the machines and the bandages. This was the beaten-up, gaunt and sick version of a man I always thought of as smiling and sparkly. I had a hard time reconciling the two.

My breath came then, ragged and almost painful.

'You can talk to him,' the nurse encouraged me in her relentlessly cheerful voice. 'Some people think that patients in his condition can hear everything that's going on around them.'

'Do you believe that?' I asked, and my voice sounded wrong, too deep and too distant. I had to squint a little bit to focus on the nurse, who smiled impersonally though her expression was warm.

'The human body is a pretty amazing machine,' she said, with kindness. 'I believe almost anything is possible.'

That wasn't really an answer, but I took it.

I moved closer and settled myself gingerly into the chair next to his bed. I smiled as best as I could at the nurse, and then waited for her to leave before I turned my attention back to Tim. Should I take his hand? Should I leave him alone, untouched? Did he find my touch repulsive now or was it just that he preferred Carolyn's? There were so many details we hadn't gotten to yet in our brand-new talk of divorce. And there were so many times I hadn't been paying attention anyway – I'd been waiting him out. How was I supposed to know what to do in a situation like this?

I felt my breath catch in my throat, and realized with a mixture of shock and horror that I was *that close* to dissolving into sobs. The kind I'd steadfastly refused to allow myself since That Day, because giving in to the urge would be too much like surrendering, and I, by God, was not about to surrender. The kind I suspected might tear me limb from limb if I succumbed to them. I pinched the bridge of my nose, hard, and forced myself to breathe through it. In. Out. Until the worst of it passed.

I wanted a real adult to walk in here and tell me what to do. Not one of my parents, who were compromised and complicit simply by being a part of my dysfunctional family – and inexorably tied up in my feelings about my sister. A *real* adult, the kind who would exude competence and grace and know exactly what needed to happen. Even in a situation like this. It baffled me that I was supposed to be that adult right now. That I was supposed to be able to handle this, or at least survive it. Dignity and grace under these circumstances seemed like asking for far too much. Like for the sun and the moon maybe, when I was beginning to think I was lucky to be upright at all.

I straightened in my chair, and leaned forward onto the bed. The hospital mattress creaked like plastic beneath my elbows, and I rested one hand on Tim's arm, well away from the vicious-looking IV drip that was taped to the back of his left hand. I studied him, taking him in from much closer than I'd been to him in weeks. He looked different, as if my memory were starting to blur him a little bit around the edges now that I no longer saw him daily. He looked like someone else with his eyes closed, with the brutal architecture of medicine and potential healing all around him and in him, and with the bright pull of him dimmed, somehow, because of it. Here, he was just a man, just a body, no more than broken flesh and bone.

He's in what we call a medically induced coma, the doctor had said, looking as exhausted as I felt, *to encourage his brain to stop swelling, and the rest of him to keep healing. In a few days, if it all looks good, we'll take him off the drugs and wait for him to wake up.*

Looking at Tim now, I couldn't see his swollen brain, or any of the other sickening, dangerous, life-threatening things the doctor had mentioned so matter-of-factly. I could only see the hands that had held mine so tightly once, so small now against the white sheets and blankets, freckles and faint golden hairs dusting the backs of them like remnants of the life I remembered far too vividly. The jaw he always kept clean-shaven, even if that meant he had to shave twice a day, was shadowed tonight, making him look even more unlike himself. But this was him, and I was here, and I couldn't turn back time on any of the things that had happened in the last few months, not even this.

I opened my mouth to speak to him, but stopped myself. What could I say? Even if he really could hear me, which I somehow doubted, what was the right thing to say under the circumstances? What did a soon-to-be divorced wife say to the husband who had so cruelly and callously betrayed her, when he was himself so terribly hurt?

If I were a better person, I thought then, looking at Tim as I listened to the machines breathe for him, I would have allowed Carolyn to be his first visitor. However little I liked it, my sister was the one he wanted. How much more obvious did he have to make that?

But I wasn't a better person. That was perfectly clear to me, as I sat there hollow-eyed and with leftover adrenalin and fear churning around inside me. There was the part of me, I could admit, that saw this accident as an opportunity. Isn't that what near-death experiences were supposed to do? If Tim woke up from this, wasn't this exactly the sort of thing that should snap him out of his Carolyn Fever? I had resigned myself to waiting this out, because I knew it couldn't last. But maybe this accident would expedite the process. When he woke up, maybe he'd realize it was high time he came home.

He had to.

Carolyn, I knew, was just a distraction, and I was happy to do whatever it took to figure out why this had happened in the first place. Counselling. Marriage retreats. Whatever he wanted.

He just had to wake up so I could tell him so.

I had loved him first, and for longer, and I loved him enough to hold on through this insane affair of his. Surely that counted for something. Surely that *meant* something.

Maybe not to him, I thought, putting one hand next to the other on his arm and holding onto him as if there were some kind of skin-to-skin communication, as if my palms could beam healing warmth into his cool flesh, as if he could feel anything in the first place.

As if he would wake up from all of this the man I'd thought he was when I'd married him.

I bent my head over my hands instead, squeezed my eyes shut, and held on as hard as I dared.

3

When I walked back into the waiting room, I could see the faint tint of dark blue in the sky outside the windows, lightening the inky-black night. Dawn was well on its way, and there was no getting away from the fact that this was really happening. Tim was really, truly, lying in that hospital bed. I couldn't imagine that away.

I nodded as politely as possible at Carolyn, as if that would win me points. Her agitation was like a living thing, bright and hot, and it seemed to slap at me. I watched as she bolted from the room, and fought that same surge of bitterness all over again. I was alive with pettiness. It crawled over my skin like lice. I tamped it down and let her vanish down the hallway without comment.

But the words I didn't say, vicious and mean, clogged the back of my throat and lay on my tongue like metal.

'How does he look?' Dad asked quietly.

'Hurt,' I said, past the heaviness in my throat and chest,

and my own great disappointment with myself. 'He looks hurt.'

'Carolyn will feel much better once she sees him,' Mom murmured, as if there had been some concern on that score.

'For God's sake, Roberta!' Dad snapped, and I sensed more than saw the scowl he aimed at her, and her own tight little shrug in response.

'It's fine,' I managed to say, though I itched. *I itched.* I didn't look at my mother again.

I couldn't stand the strained silence, and I didn't want to stay there, stretched between my parents and all the weight and pull of my relationship with both of them. And their relationship with Carolyn, which ate at me, so unfair did I find it that they could find anything to support in what she was doing.

I didn't want any of this. I wanted my bright, cheerful life back. I wanted the comfortable familiarity and occasional surprises of my work, my days spent jostling for supremacy with Annette, and the shared, peaceful, contented evenings of my marriage. Comfort, companionship, and, yes, sex too. Did Carolyn know about that? Or did she think that Tim's and my sex life had stopped whenever it was theirs started, sometime in the last eight months since she'd come home jobless and apparently shameless?

But I didn't really want to know the answer to that question.

I wanted simply to rewind these last months away, because I had been happy back then. *Before*. Or if not happy, precisely – because who was *happy* these days? – I'd known exactly where I belonged and what my role was, and there was more comfort in that than I'd realized when it was just the way things were, when I hadn't ever really examined it.

I slipped from the airless waiting room, and made my way to the ladies room down the long, battered-white corridor. Inside, the industrial avocado-coloured walls beaming in the too-bright fluorescent lights made my head hurt, but I splashed water on my cheeks and tried to ignore the alarming contrast between the pallor of my skin, the hectic colour in my eyes, and what looked like full-on bruises beneath.

I just want my life back.

Somehow, that was the one thing I never dared say. I was afraid of the pitying looks, the patronizing comments, maybe. I was afraid that admitting that was wrong somehow, that I should be all about my anger over what had been done to me and less about what I'd lost. I had been so afraid that if I said it to Tim, he would shake his head like he'd done the night I'd thrown him out, and say something like he'd said then, staring up at me from the driveway below, his clothes and shoes strewn around him like a halo.

I wish there was a way to do this without hurting you, Sarah, he'd said, sounding very nearly apologetic, which wasn't, it had taken me long weeks to realize, the same thing as *actually* apologetic. *But there isn't.*

I wished, as I had then, and as fervently, that my pain – my loss – wasn't viewed as an acceptable risk to him. To Carolyn. That my feelings mattered so little, that their relationships with me were so meaningless, that they'd wanted each other more than they'd wanted to spare me this – I still couldn't think about any of that without getting a little dizzy.

I thought of Tim's still, sad body in that bed. I thought of the machines wheezing and beeping around him, of the IV punched through the pale skin of his hand. I felt that lump in my throat again, and that ache inside me that was far too complicated, far too messy, simply to be my feelings about what had happened to him tonight.

I want my life *back.*

Back out in the hallway, I kept my head down and stared at my shoes as I walked back towards the waiting room. One step, then another. My body still functioned, and part of me remained distantly amazed by that. No matter how much I hurt, no matter how unbearable life felt, I still kept on. I didn't fade off into the ether, or wither away on my couch. I was able to walk down this hallway, breathe, carry on. Maybe there was a kind of strength in this mindless survival. Perhaps the only thing to do in times like this was to concentrate on the small, necessary tasks. Like walking, for example. Or shoving my cold hands in the pockets of jeans I really should have washed weeks ago, so limp and baggy were they.

But when I glanced up to gauge my progress, Carolyn was coming towards me, her few minutes in Tim's room evidently over.

Be gracious, I cautioned myself, even as my stomach clenched and my shoulders tightened with another hard kick of that ever-present tension. Even as that other part of me protested, not wanting to be anything but exactly as mean and careless as Carolyn already had been. Was, in fact, still being. *Be the bigger person here.*

Carolyn drew closer, and there was no question that she was wildly, chaotically upset. Devastated, even. I could see the sheen of tears in her eyes, the moisture beneath, the way her mouth trembled. I could see and hear how her breath came too quickly, and I knew her well enough to know that this was her version of a complete and total panic attack. A breakdown.

On some level, I had to admit that I was surprised Carolyn cared this much about anything that wasn't Carolyn. That had certainly never happened before, and it made a kind of alarm go off deep within me. More than that, I wondered why she was putting on such a show – theatrical as always, even in a terrible situation like this where a little decorum would go a long way. That was certainly the thought guiding my own behaviour. But none of that changed the way Carolyn managed to focus on me then, her grief-stricken gaze narrowing into something else.

'This feels so unfair,' she said, her voice sounding strangled. I had the strangest notion that she was *trying*. To be polite? To be gracious, as I was trying to be myself? I didn't know. But she was definitely *trying*. 'He gets so little visiting time anyway and we have to chop it up into all these pieces.'

And I felt everything inside me, that whole great mess, spiral smaller and tighter, until I felt that I was nothing but one hard, concentrated ball of it, heavy and mean. And deeply, exultantly, petty.

Some part of me loved it. *Finally*, I thought. *Let's do this*.

'We?' I echoed, the strain in my voice washing through my limbs.

We? Really? Who the hell did she think *we* were in this scenario? I was Tim's wife. She was just his tawdry piece on the side. Did she really think that the fact we were related by blood made us connected somehow in this? Did she think it erased all the facts of this situation?

I could see that she did.

'Yes,' she said, wiping at her eyes. '*We*. I guess we'll have to share.'

Suddenly, the itchiness within me seemed to spill over into a swirl of questions. Why exactly should I be expected to cater to her many moods and panics, her upset here in the hospital where Tim lay in a coma, just because I was human and empathetic enough to notice them? Why had she never stopped and worried over my feelings while she was leaping into bed with my husband? Why was I beating myself up for being petty while Carolyn got to revel in it as much as she liked, in a bed and breakfast in the middle of town, where everyone who wanted to could hear them through the walls and probably did? Why did she so matter-of-factly imagine that she got to dictate the terms here – and why didn't she recognize that it had been an act of charity on my part to let her see Tim at all?

We would have to *share*? Was she insane?

'Did you enjoy seeing Tim, Carolyn?' I asked, in a super-naturally calm voice that I only recognized as my own because I could feel my mouth moving around the words. I was so angry it felt like I was electric – like I could power the whole town.

'Did I *enjoy* seeing the man I love laid out on a hospital bed, unaware that I was even there?' Carolyn asked unevenly, some new-for-her emotion making her voice waver. Her eyes flashed and her hands trembled, and I didn't care at all. 'What do you think?'

'I hope you got a good look,' I said in that same tone. I didn't shout. But it felt like I might have. Like the walls might have buckled with the force of it.

'What is that supposed to mean?' Carolyn asked, frowning at me.

'Tim and I haven't filed for divorce,' I pointed out, still so calmly. So deliberately. Almost kindly, in that detached, dispassionate way. I was aware of my parents coming out of the waiting room into the hallway, but I didn't turn to look at them directly. I didn't look away from Carolyn, not even for a second, as if that tight ball inside of me, darker and heavier by the second, might disappear if I did. 'We're not even formally separated. We've just had a few conversations.'

Carolyn seemed to realize belatedly that I wasn't simply narrating all of this, all things that everybody knew, just for fun. She froze in place, her gaze turning shrewd, as if finally, *finally*, she was *seeing* me.

It was almost enough.

'What's your point?' she asked, her voice still rough. She rubbed at her nose, her mouth. Then it seemed as if she were trying to be careful, but it was too late. 'Do you . . . do you think a near-death experience will change Tim's mind?'

Carolyn being careful was someone else's bullish rampage through the proverbial china shop. And I was tired of it. Of her. Of this entire situation.

'It's not Tim's mind you should be worried about.' I discovered that on some level, somewhere outside that focused core, I was very nearly enjoying myself. Close enough to count, surely. More than I had since September. 'It's mine.'

Carolyn only frowned and shook her head, as if I wasn't making sense. Yet I was aware that I was finally making the only kind of sense that mattered. The kind of sense I should have made from the start.

'I'm Tim's official next of kin,' I said, very distinctly. 'I get to tell the ICU who can visit Tim and who can't. And guess what, Carolyn? You just lost your visiting privileges.'

That lay there between us, crisp and uncompromising, as if I had demanded a duel in the old-fashioned way, like in all those movies I loved to watch on Masterpiece Theater. As if I'd thrown it down on the ground at her feet.

Carolyn seemed to stop breathing, her face paling. But I felt as if, finally, I were expanding. Taking up space. Claiming something, anything, as mine. Making this one thing in my life Carolyn couldn't violate, even if it was temporary. I heard one – maybe both – of my parents say my name in decidedly unhappy tones, but I ignored them. I watched Carolyn fight to process what I'd said, and for the first time since I'd walked into my bedroom and seen the end of my life as I knew it writhing on top of my favourite sheets, like two rutting, red-faced animals, I felt like myself again.

And I couldn't even bring myself to feel badly about it.

'You can't do this . . .' Carolyn's eyes searched mine, and widened at whatever she saw there. 'You're not really going to do this, Sarah?'

'It's done,' I said, with more satisfaction than I would have thought possible, welling up from all the hollow, empty spaces deep inside of me. Maybe that tight, hard ball wasn't meanness after all. Maybe it was my spine finally returning and doing its job. Whatever it was, I liked it. I more than liked it. 'But don't worry, Carolyn. I'm not like you. I wouldn't ruin your life on a whim and leave you no recourse. You can get back on that list anytime you like.'

'Let me guess.' Carolyn's voice was strangled, her face utterly devoid of colour. Her hands crept to her belly, as if she was nauseous. 'You want me to turn back time? Act like none of this ever happened? Go off somewhere and never come back?'

'All of that would be great,' I said, and had to bite back an inappropriate, probably incendiary smile. 'But nothing so dramatic is necessary.' I leaned forward slightly, made sure Carolyn was completely focused on me. 'All you have to do is apologize to me, Carolyn. And mean it.'

Carolyn's lips pressed together, hard. For a moment I thought I saw some kind of misery on her face – but, of course, that was impossible. That would mean she cared about me at all. That she had even a passing acquaintance with regret. And despite that small, almost forgotten part of me that wanted my big sister to act like a big sister for once, I knew she didn't. She simply didn't. She never had.

'I can't,' she said after a long moment, her voice curiously flat. Her hands moved as if she wanted to hold on to something, or, more likely, punch something. Like me, I assumed. There was a kind of anguish in her gaze then, but more than that, an implacable wall. She sighed. 'I'm not sorry.'

'I know,' I said, without a single drop of surprise. Or pity. I straightened, and shrugged. I felt lighter than I had in longer than I cared to remember. 'I guess that leaves you with quite the little quandary, doesn't it?'

She scrubbed her hands across her face again, as if

fighting to keep the tears back, but I couldn't let that bother me. I felt *free*. And if there was something dangerous in that, something hectic and a little bit crazed, I told myself I didn't care at all. That it was better by far than the numbness and inaction that had preceded it.

'Sarah.' She said my name like it hurt her, and if it did, I thought, it would be the first thing that ever had. 'You can't do this. You really can't. I'm not just saying that.'

'Girls . . .' Dad said from the doorway of the waiting room, in that gruff warning tone of his, and I hated it when he called us that. So dismissive and diminishing. So condescending. I was thirty-three and Carolyn was thirty-five, for God's sake. A little long in the tooth to be called *girls*. Not to mention the fact that I didn't wish to be thought of as part of any collective that involved Carolyn.

'This is no place to air all this family's dirty laundry,' Mom chimed in from beside him, her voice at its coldest. She glanced behind her as if she thought a phalanx of our friends and neighbours lurked there, judgements at the ready. 'We all need to concentrate on Tim. If you can't handle that' – and it was unclear which one of us she was talking to then, as she looked back and forth between us, and then at Dad, too, for good measure – 'I suggest you take a walk up around the halls or down into the lobby until you get yourself under control.'

I ignored them, and so did Carolyn, who was focused entirely on me. Too much so. As if she thought her attention alone could bend me to her will.

In her defence, I thought uncharitably, that had more or less worked with Tim, hadn't it?

'I understand that you're hurt, that *I* hurt you,' she said after a long moment or two, and if I hadn't been able to see the way her chest heaved, as if her emotions were fighting to get out, I might have been fooled by her calm tone. 'I understand that you feel betrayed and that you feel you have no choice but to get revenge on me this way. But this isn't just about me and Tim, and what happened between us.'

'Are you sure?' I asked. Dryly. 'Because I have to tell you, Carolyn, that's pretty much entirely what it's about for me.'

'A divorce is bound to bring up all kinds of bad feelings on all sides, obviously, but what happened last night has nothing to do with any of that,' she argued in the same rational, calm manner. I watched her take a deeper breath. A longer one. Her gaze was glued to mine, her eyes wide now, and the same hazel colour I knew I shared with her. I'd always hated that we had even that much in common. And I knew her tone of voice was all for show. I could see the panic lurking there, just beneath the skin, making her face seem tight. 'We have to concentrate on Tim now. On what *he* needs and what *he* would want if he could sit up and tell us himself.'

She sounded so reasonable. So calm and *adult*. If she had been talking about someone else's husband, who knows what I might have done? But she was talking about

Tim, and he was still mine. Legally, anyway. No matter how much she wanted that to be otherwise. No matter how much *he* might want it otherwise. She had no standing here, and he wasn't awake to argue about *the unpleasantness* any longer.

For once, in all of this mess, I was the one who got to make the decisions. I couldn't pretend that didn't make me happy.

'That was a pretty little speech,' I said, my voice soft in the quiet of the corridor. Almost kind. 'But I can't help but notice that you can't even bring yourself to apologize.' I lifted my shoulders and then dropped them. 'Saying that you *understand* why I might feel how I feel is really just a convoluted way of *not* apologizing for having made me feel that way in the first place.'

I shrugged again, as if I were done caring about any of this, and turned around. I thought maybe I'd head down to the cafeteria, which had to be serving breakfast any time now, surely. I could see light through the windows, indicating that morning had finally come, and instantly felt all the exhaustion I'd been holding at bay throughout the night slam into me. If not food, there had to be coffee . . .

'Sarah.'

I was tired of the way she said my name and I didn't stop, didn't turn back again. I didn't want to deal with her any more and I didn't see why I should have to. Another decision I got to make, and it felt just as good as the first.

'Sarah! You don't understand!' she cried out, as if the words were ripped from deep inside of her. She made a noise that was somewhere between a groan and a scream, and it made my stomach flip over in reaction. Or possibly foreboding. 'For God's sake,' she gritted out, her voice heavy with something I couldn't identify. 'I'm pregnant.'

And that was when it hit me, for the very first time, right there in the sterile corridor of the Rivermark hospital with my whole family looking on, that my marriage might really be over, after all.

4

The days passed, becoming a week of wholly interchange-able mornings, noons and nights. November gave way to December. It snowed, twice, and there were more and more holiday ornaments festooning the corners of things. There were happy blinking lights and relentless carols. Wherever I turned, there was the insistence of Christmas cheer when *cheerful* was the very last thing I felt.

Tim was better, the doctors said.

They said it every day, with varying degrees of qualifi-cation. He had been taken off the drugs that were keeping him in a medically induced coma a few days after the accident, but he hadn't woken up then as they'd expected him to do. He was now in a coma of his own making, the doctors told me, because there was so much healing he had yet to do inside, and because sometimes that's just how it was with patients with his kind of injuries. He would wake up in his own time, they said. They hoped.

And I sat there with him after they left each day, the

dutiful wife, while my head spun wildly and I wondered why I couldn't seem to feel anything but this great heaviness. It wasn't sharp enough to be grief, or not entirely, but nor was it flattening enough to be full-on depression. It simply sat on me, thick and suffocating, allowing me to move and breathe but never, ever escape its weight.

They were having a baby.

They might even have *planned* to have a baby. That meant they had a future together – that there would be no way to pretend otherwise. *They had a future.* And I had ...? I didn't know.

I hadn't wanted any further details that first night, when she'd told me. When, I supposed, I'd made her feel she had no choice but to tell me. I'd run in the opposite direction, in fact – had run so far through the slippery, antiseptic corridors and the dingy, forgotten stairwells that I'd found myself in the bowels of the hospital in some dim, forgotten radiology centre or other before I'd allowed myself to stop. There had been no one there to watch me collapse on the ground, bury my face in my hands, and sob. And sob. I could almost pretend it hadn't happened. That she hadn't said those words that changed everything, irrevocably.

I'd returned to the ICU waiting room when I could breathe again and the redness had gone down around my eyes. The baby Carolyn carried, the one that made all of the things I'd been thinking and hoping and holding onto so irretrievably, humiliatingly foolish, became one more thing we didn't discuss. Like my plan to bar her from Tim's room. That just ... disappeared. I might have been on fire with pettiness, but even I could see that banning the mother of a man's child from his hospital room while he was balanced somewhere between life and death was not the right thing to do.

Even if he did still happen to be married to me.

And because I was still his legal wife, his official next of kin, I had to sit in his little hospital cubicle when his team of doctors appeared every morning and involve myself in his care. I had to ask the right questions and make sure I absorbed and understood the answers, especially after Carolyn announced that she was too fragile to do so. I had to be strong for her and her child, too, no matter how nauseous the idea of either of those things made me. I had to sign all the forms, and give all the necessary permissions. I had to hold his hand when the nurses were watching, because I worried what they would say about me if I didn't, and then I hated myself for caring about something like that, something so small and vain. I had to act as if I hadn't finally noticed that everything that had ever mattered to me was gone, after all.

Had been gone, in fact. I just hadn't known it. Which, of course, made it that much worse.

But even worse than that was the part of me that liked the fact that I was the one who was Tim's caretaker. He might have slept with my sister, impregnated her. The two of them might have been planning a glorious, romantic future steeped in happy domesticity and a pack of kids. But I was his wife, and I was a good wife to him. Deep inside, I took a surprisingly fierce measure of pride in that. Perhaps because I knew that in the tending to his needs, in the navigation of the legalities and choices necessary to shepherd him through the tragedy that had befallen him, I got to spend long hours in that hospital pretending that he was still mine. The way he was supposed to be.

I lost track, somewhere in the whirl of endless days cooped up in the waiting room or in Tim's cubicle, back and forth between the two without end, of what I wanted. Of who I was, certainly. Of what had been happening before the accident and what was likely to happen on the other side of this, should we all make it through. It was as if, in the face of such a crisis, everything else that seemed so important when things were normal just melted away and allowed for the delicate act of crisis management to occur. Not that there was anything *delicate* about all of this sitting and waiting and *being there* in the brief stretches of visitation permitted under ICU regulations. It was a grim and exhausting act of endurance, complicated by worry and tension and, of course, Carolyn.

Who hovered. And cried. *And cried*. And who clearly felt better, now that she'd confessed her pregnancy to all of us and half the hospital. Or more secure in her position, anyway. She might not have been capable of subjecting herself to the messy medical details of Tim's care, but she took to her role as the soon-to-be mother of his child far too easily for my taste – a fact that alternately made me pity her and want to smack her.

'I feel much too pregnant,' she said one morning, shifting in her chair and holding her stomach, just to illustrate the point. 'Just . . . nauseous. And *thick*.'

It was clear to me that this statement was for my benefit, even though she was pretending to address my ever-frowning father. I glared down at the novel I'd been toting around as if I planned to get some reading done while my life shattered all around me, and pretended the sentences before me made some sense. In case I missed her reference, she clutched at her still-flat belly and let out a little moan. Next to her, my father looked disapproving, but, as always, remained silent.

'I haven't actually thrown up,' Carolyn confided to the stale air in the waiting room, polluted with the scent of old coffee and despair. The latter undoubtedly mine. 'But I feel like I might. Even though I'm *starving*. All the time.'

Was she labouring under the impression that her child – the one she'd made on my bed, with my husband – was an appropriately neutral topic? Knowing my sister, she probably did. I didn't know whether to laugh or cry. I found myself, for the first time in my adult life, actually taking my mother's advice. I got up, left the room without further comment, and walked.

In whatever direction I could go, as long as it was *away* from the pregnancy narrative I'd rather claw off my ears than listen to for a second more. Away from Carolyn and her inability to just stay quiet despite the fact that her very presence felt like an affront to me. Just – *away*.

I walked with no clear intention or direction. I loitered aimlessly in the gift shop, fingering the listless, insultingly bland gifts on display. I did a few laps around the glossy main lobby. Eventually I found myself heading towards one of the many glass entrances to the hospital. I wandered outside, and found the clear, shockingly cold December day crisp and bright and exactly what I needed. It was horribly, numbingly cold. But beautiful, even so. A hard sort of beauty, icy and inhospitable. Light bounced up from the hard-packed mounds of ploughed snow in the parking lot and along the walkways and danced from the ice left behind on the bare tree branches. I walked to the edge of the shovelled walkway and stood there, just breathing out clouds into the cold, staring out over one of the parking lots and into the glittering trees of the next block.

I had absolutely no idea what the hell I was doing here.

I was clinging so hard to my position as Tim's wife . . . for what? To what end? So I could deliver the remains of my marriage into Carolyn's hands the moment Tim woke up? What was my plan, exactly?

The baby thing killed me. It actually . . . ached. It hurt in ways that surprised me anew with each harsh breath. Because you don't know how much you want things until they're taken from you, do you? Until someone else takes them from you.

Tim and I had had a plan. We had always had plans. We'd made up a checklist for our life together and we'd taken great pleasure in ticking things off, one by one. Our own house – *check*. Our own practice – *check*. We'd planned to start trying for a baby in the next year or so, now that the practice was on its feet and doing well. It was the next chapter in our beautiful life, the one we'd plotted out together all those years ago in New York. I'd thought we were still on the same page. I'd thought we still wanted the same things.

I'd wanted his babies, if only in the abstract, and now I understood that would never happen. Not the way we'd planned it. Carolyn hadn't just stolen my man. She'd stolen my future children, too.

It was one thing to try to accept that he'd had the affair. Another to try to get past the fact that he'd had it with Carolyn, of all people. I thought I'd been doing a fairly good job with that – though Lianne had claimed only yesterday on the phone that I was in denial. But I'd been prepared to take him back when the infatuation passed. I'd been more than prepared. Then, that long first night here in the hospital, I'd assumed that the accident would serve as a wake-up call to him, as these things often did, according to myth and legend. I'd assumed that it would wrench him – *us* – back from this particular cliff.

But all the things I'd thought were based on the assumption that once he came back, everything would be as it was. That we could just . . . erase these past months. Pretend they'd never happened. Carry on as before.

A baby made that impossible, now and forever. Even if he and Carolyn were over. Even if he came back to me. There would always be *that child*. The physical manifestation of everything he'd thrown away, everything he'd done.

That poor kid, a voice inside me whispered.

And I had no idea what to do with that. What it meant. I only knew that I was cold straight down into my bones, in ways that had nothing to do with the December weather, and there was no hope, now, that I was ever going to thaw.

The waiting room was, happily, empty when I returned.

I took the opportunity to claim the most comfortable seat on the small sofa near the anaemic-looking potted plant in the corner. I had just settled into it and was trying to rub heat back into my hands when Carolyn walked in.

Alone.

It occurred to me that this was the first time we'd been alone since That Day.

I didn't have any idea how I should feel about that, and from the looks of it neither did Carolyn.

'Oh,' she said. She blinked as if seeing me threw her for a loop. Did she think I'd finally given up and gone home? Who knew what stories she told herself? I was sure they were epic. 'Dad just left. We didn't know where you were.'

I fingered the edge of my book's paperback cover, feeling

it thicken and round slightly. I looked back at her, but I didn't respond. She settled herself gingerly in one of the ubiquitous blue chairs, and I tried not to let myself concentrate on what seemed like such a deliberate attempt on her part to appear fragile. Maybe early pregnancy did that to you. I wouldn't know. And, thanks to her, probably never would. She was growing a brand-new life inside of her while my life had hit a wall . . .

I ordered myself to ease my death grip on my book, before I hurt myself. Or mangled the book itself into pulp.

'I really appreciate what you're doing,' she said in a low, deliberate voice. 'You're making this all go smoothly and I know you don't have to do that. I just want you to know that I'm grateful. I know Tim will be, too.'

I hated her so much in that moment that if she'd been even an inch closer to me I would have launched myself at her. I almost went ahead and did it anyway. I'd never raised my hand to another person in my life, but I wanted to pummel my sister's face in. I wanted to make her *hurt*. I could feel a throbbing sort of violence in me that I'd never suspected existed, flooding through me like wildfire, making my pulse race and my breathing go dangerously shallow.

'I know it doesn't seem like it now,' she continued in the same quiet way, clearly meaning every single word, wholly unaware of the danger she was in, 'but some day, all of this will be behind us and no matter how messy it all seems, I think we'll all agree that it was for the best. I really do believe that.'

I hated her so much I thought my head might explode from it. So much that my throat felt like it was on fire, as if I'd ripped it to shreds with all the screams that hadn't passed my lips. I felt consumed by it. Altered by it. I couldn't believe she couldn't see it distorting my face.

'Anyway,' she said, patting her own knees with her hands, as if to congratulate herself on such a good little speech, 'I wanted to make sure to thank you.'

I sat there, frozen into impotent, furious immobility, because I knew if I even blinked I would try to choke her to death. With my bare hands, the very ones that shook slightly now. I sat there and watched her settle back against the chair, and pull out some cheerful magazines to wile away the time. She didn't seem to have any trouble reading. She didn't seem to have any trouble at all. She was stealing every single thing I loved about my life – she'd done it before I'd even known to look, before I'd had any inkling there was any danger – and now she was thanking me for my witless help in letting her go right ahead and do it.

And I wasn't beating the life out of her because I was worried about making a scene. I was pathetic.

It was clear to me then, as all of that violence and fury sloshed around inside of me, making me feel sick to my stomach, that I knew nothing at all about my life. Not really. It had gone completely off track, and I hadn't even noticed it was happening. I'd been wandering around in some dream of what it should be for far longer than I wanted to admit. Clearly. Carolyn had been making babies with my husband while I had been ... what? Defending horrible, over-entitled rich kids like Benjy Stratton – arguing that they should be allowed to continue driving drunk through the streets? Fantasizing about winning the ongoing war with my office manager? About yoga classes and pastries? What kind of life was that? It seemed to me now, surrounded by the truth of it, of its sad detritus, that I was almost criminal in my own obliviousness.

How had this happened? How had I become ... *this*?

'I can't remember why I didn't go on that backpacking trip,' I found myself saying out loud as Tim lay there in his cubicle, still so unresponsive, the same machines still surrounding him, their little sounds almost like background music to me now. The beeps and sighs, the scrape and squeak of nursing shoes on the linoleum out in the hall. 'Do you remember? I was going to take a leave of absence and see the world. Just me and a backpack, and maybe a journal to write in.'

This was the first time I'd actually talked to him. Out loud.

I'd felt too self-conscious before – as if it would have been too forced, too much of a performance, too much the sort of dramatic thing I was sure Carolyn would both do and be really into, and what would I say, anyway? The wild need to harm Carolyn physically had faded somewhat, but my horror at how blind I'd been about my own life had only grown more intense as the hours ticked by in this latest endless day. I frowned, not sure why I was talking now, and folded my own hands hard against each other in my lap.

'I wanted to wander,' I told Tim, all my grand plans coming back to me in a rush, all the nights I'd spent poring over maps and guidebooks, all the websites I'd visited and travel journals I'd spent hours upon hours reading.

My college room-mate and I had taken a much less ambitious trip the summer after we'd graduated from NYU, before we started at the positions we'd been sure would lead us into our glorious futures – me as a legal assistant in the law firm I hoped would get me into a good law school and Brooke in the publishing house where she dreamed she'd one day be an editor. We'd spent a month wandering in Costa Rica, and it had been life-altering in ways I'd never been able to explain to anyone who hadn't had the same kind of experience themselves.

I'd planned my own, much more involved and intrepid journey, all through law school – all over Australia and New Zealand, then up into Africa and India, or maybe Japan and China to start, I could never quite decide – and even after I'd taken a job that no sane person could possibly have turned down in one of New York's top law firms, I'd told myself I was only putting it off for a little while, not cancelling it altogether. It had been the major defining dream of my twenties, that trip.

But in the end, I'd never taken it.

'I wanted to go on a safari in Botswana and sleep beneath the sky,' I said, as much to remind myself as to Tim's prone figure on the bed before me. 'I wanted to get lost in Hong Kong and eat foods I couldn't identify in Budapest. I wanted to drive the Great Ocean Road in Australia. I wanted to spend a Christmas in Prague.'

Tim's machines offered the only response, in wheezes and beeps. He stayed still. Silent.

When had I given up on that particular dream? I couldn't really remember. I couldn't recall making any kind of conscious decision to stop working towards my big trip. It was as if, once Tim and I had started dating when I was a brand-new junior associate, I'd just shifted all of that attention and blistering focus to Tim instead, and the trip had sort of stopped being important.

Not that I'd thought about it that way. Not in so many words. Not at all, really. But the more we'd spent time together, the more it seemed to make sense that I should focus on other things – like the careers we were building, rather than formless dreams of knocking around the planet by myself, for no other reason than I thought it would be fun.

And Tim and I took our own trips. Together. New England in the fall, to marvel at the autumn leaves. Napa. St Croix. To more on-the-beaten-path places, perhaps, but they were still places worth seeing. It was still *travel*. And then we'd gotten engaged, some six months after we'd started dating, and I'd thought it all made so much *sense*. We had *plans*. We were ambitious in exactly the same ways, for exactly the same things. We made a checklist and we both wanted every single thing on that list.

And we loved each other, of course. That most of all. We'd gotten married eight months after that, because, like I'd heard all my life, when you knew, you knew. And I knew. Tim was like a key finally turning in just the right lock.

I'd been so *sure*.

I let my eyes travel over Tim then, taking in every detail of his poor, struggling body. He was paler than I'd ever seen him, and the more he lay there, so quiet and so still, the more he seemed to diminish. Sometimes I sat right here, in this ever more uncomfortable chair, and wondered what would happen if he never woke up at all. Would he just disappear? Would the bed swallow him whole?

Would I disappear with him?

The fact that I didn't know how to answer that last question shook me. Hard.

'I wanted to be a public defender,' I said then, my voice sounding surprisingly loud in the small, curtained-off area. 'I can't remember if I ever told you that.'

I must have, surely. In the very beginning, if never again. I had never planned to stay at that fancy, high-blooded firm for long. I'd wanted to pay down my school loans, that was all, not surrender myself to the notorious 'golden handcuffs' that chained so many young lawyers to the big corporate firms. But it was as if I were reading him a story – as if I were talking about some fictional character, not myself. As if I had no emotional connection to my own memories.

'I wanted to save the world,' I whispered, and it was true, though it made me feel something too close to embarrassed to say it out loud, after all this time. Now that I was older. In my thirties. Settled. I should know better than to think there was anything one person could do to save the world. I could hardly think up a way to save myself.

But I remembered that wildness inside me, that feeling that the sky wasn't big enough to hold me, or all the things I wanted to do. I remembered when it seemed as if all the songs spoke to hidden pieces of my soul, and that deep-down conviction that there was greatness out there, waiting for me, if I could just find it. I couldn't remember the last time I'd felt that way. Or anything close to it.

I blew out a breath, and couldn't tell if the shake in it was laughter or something else, some emotion I was afraid to name.

'And here's the funny part.' I leaned closer to the bed, to Tim's ear – half of me feeling ridiculous because there was no one listening, not even the person I was supposedly talking to. But only half. 'I don't know when I stopped wanting that. When I started wanting only our life instead. Or why. Did you do that, Tim?'

I laughed then, a little bit, though I couldn't have said why. Nothing was funny. I was frozen right through, and I had no hope of that ever changing, not as that baby grew daily inside Carolyn. Not while all of this continued to be so grim and sad and true. And Tim only lay there, healing. Or dying.

I didn't know what it said about me that I couldn't tell which one I wanted more. Or that when I'd sobbed in that far-off, battered little corner of this terrible hospital, I'd been crying for the babies I would never carry and the life I hadn't really been living, after all. But not for him. What did that say about me? Did I really want to know?

But I worried that I already did.

'Did you do that?' I asked him again, tears in my voice if not on my cheeks. 'Or did I?'

5

'I'm really glad you came over tonight, Sarah,' my father said all of three bites into his signature lasagne, the one he usually slaved over for days, and which he only made on very special occasions.

The fact that this supposedly casual dinner, just me and my parents on an unremarkable Thursday evening in December, gathered around the cosy little round table in their kitchen like all the dinners of my childhood, qualified for the lasagne treatment alarmed me. To say the least. I mustered up a smile and tried to kerb the paranoia, without much success either way.

My mother, who notoriously didn't like to eat heavy meals in the evenings, even if the meal in question was Dad's famous lasagne – the recipe handed down from his Italian mother who had spoken only a few words of English – had been picking at her usual small bowl of salad, but she put her fork down abruptly then, as if she expected things to get ugly. It occurred to me that my assumption that this dinner – to which I'd been invited by my father in curiously formal language two days before – would involve any clearing of air, long-overdue apologies for the production of their first-born daughter, Ruiner of Lives that she was, or, at the very least, expressions of support from my parents was, perhaps, naïve.

I tried to tell myself that was just paranoia, too.

'Thanks for the invitation,' I said as lightly as I could, ignoring the clear signs that my parents were ready to *have a talk with me.* 'You know I love your lasagne, Dad.'

'We just want to check in with you,' he said, smiling warmly. The warmth was definitely alarming. 'See how you're doing. This must all be so hard on you. It's hard to believe it's been going on this long now. Three weeks, isn't it?'

I swallowed the forkful of lasagne I'd tossed into my mouth, though I hardly tasted a thing. Certainly not the explosion of flavour and cheesy goodness that this dish was supposed to deliver in spades.

'Something like that,' I muttered.

'This is such a terrible situation,' Dad continued, frowning down at his plate. At least the frown was more normal. The attempt at warmth only made me nervous. I loved my cerebral, professorial father, but he had never been much in the way of an arbiter of justice in the family. No one had. The Stone family motto was *Ignore, Repress, Pretend.* 'Just terrible.'

'A terrible situation all around,' Mom chimed in, shaking her head as if at the enormity of it all.

I waited, but nothing else seemed to be forthcoming. I wanted to ask what, exactly, Mom meant by *all around*. But maybe I was hearing support for Carolyn under every syllable when it wasn't necessarily there. It was possible, I could admit. I'd promised myself on the drive over that I wasn't going to pick a fight with them, and by *them* I mostly meant my mother, because what was the point? They were my parents. They didn't change – maybe they couldn't. And that meant it was the very definition of insanity to keep acting as if one day, left to their own devices and apropos of nothing, they might.

I was determined to stick to my plan. To any plan, at this point, just to prove that I could. That there was something left that couldn't be taken from me.

'Do you remember that I wanted to be a public defender?' I asked, deciding it was better to talk about other things. Safer things. Things so far in the past that they couldn't possibly hurt anybody now. 'I wanted to travel all over the place, save the world. I'd forgotten all about that.'

'Of course,' Mom said in her arch way. Or maybe it was just her innate chilliness. She let out a little laugh. 'All you ever talked about was this third world country, that social ill and *plights*.'

So much for my theory that nothing from the past could hurt me. I told myself that this was my mother being funny. Such a laugh riot, that Roberta Stone. Ha ha ha.

'Plights?' I echoed. All in good fun, etc., I thought. So I smiled as if I really believed that.

'The *plight* of the downtrodden. The *plight* of the lower classes. The *plight* of the rainforest.' Mom picked up her fork again and speared an anaemic-looking tomato with it, only to wave it in the air as she spoke. 'You had a great many *plights* and you were very concerned with all of them.' She let out another laugh, which I found a tad too thin to be entirely good-humoured. 'We were all so happy when you met Tim and grew out of it.'

I stared at my lasagne as if likely to see my own history play out in the meat sauce, the recipe for which Dad guarded as if it was a matter of national security, and realized that I'd lost my appetite. Mom – 1, me – 0. As usual.

'I don't know why I grew *completely* out of it, though,' I said, frowning at my plate. But determined, somehow, to continue having this conversation, however unlikely it seemed that my parents might possess any particular insight into my life choices. It was better than the alternative subject matter we had on hand, which was even now thundering about the room like a wild circus elephant, daring us to keep ignoring it. 'I mean, maybe it's a little self-indulgent to want to wander around the Kalahari Desert for a year, but why did I give up the kind of law I wanted to practise? I certainly never dreamed at night of being the go-to Rivermark DWI attorney.' I shook my head, baffled by my own choices. 'It's like I turned into someone else and I don't even remember doing it. Is that normal?'

'People change when they get married,' Dad said, in his

low, easy voice. So soothing. So supportive. So suspicious, really, when I thought about it. I tried to stop thinking about it. 'It's part of becoming a unit – of forming a partnership. Not only is it normal, I think it's necessary.'

But I wondered. There was a partnership, and then there was pretending to be someone you would have laughed at if you'd met them a few years earlier. Did everybody go through that? I didn't think they did. Lianne, for example, was exactly who she'd thought she would be when she grew up. That was one of the reasons she was so *solid*. She had worries and problems, like anyone, but she didn't have *doubts*. She wasn't racked with regret. I kind of thought this was a crucial distinction. Or should be.

'The public defender's office would never have been a good fit for you,' Mom said, with a dismissive wave of her fork that rubbed me the wrong way.

'You don't really know what would be a good fit for me.' I fought to keep my voice calm, light, easy. Because I knew points would be deducted if I got noticeably emotional. That was how my mother played this game. It was where Carolyn had learned that insulting *calmness* she'd used on me at the hospital the night of the accident. '*I* don't even know, so how could you? But who knows? Maybe this is the perfect opportunity to think about it again.'

I was surprised to feel that little *click* inside, as if something had finally fallen back into place. Or wanted to, anyway. Maybe this really was an opportunity, however unwanted. Or maybe the key point here was that I had to start thinking about it that way, or I'd go crazy. I was close enough to crazy as it was. No need to walk any further down that road.

'I think that's a wonderful idea,' Dad said, smiling as if he couldn't hear Mom or see her concerned frown. As if the conversation he was having was perfectly pleasant and lacking all murky undertones. 'It's never too late.'

'Of course it's never too late, and you should do anything you set your mind to,' Mom said then, sounding almost impatient. She shrugged. 'But do you really want to start a new career at thirty-three? Or older? As a single woman? That sounds exhausting. You'd be far better served continuing to reap the benefits of the career you already have and finding a new husband if you want one, surely.'

'A new husband,' I repeated, unable to believe what I'd heard. I pressed my fingers against my eyes and shook my head, helplessly. 'Did you really just say that, Mom? You're aware that I'm still married to the old one, right?'

My mother sighed, as if I was being unnecessarily argumentative.

'There's no point clinging to something that's already gone,' she said, and the worst part, I knew, was that this was my mother's version of being gentle. Caring and thoughtful, even. It just happened to feel like a baseball bat to soft tissue. Surely she didn't *mean* it.

But I'd been telling myself that for a long, long time.

'I'm glad that you're over my marriage,' I said, when I could speak. Not that my voice was at all even. It was a mark of how upset I was that I was letting them see it. 'I'll let you know when and if I am, but I should warn you – it might not happen on your schedule.'

'I'm only trying to help you, Sarah,' Mom said, in that aggrieved way, as if *her* feelings were hurt, as they so often were. She put a hand to her temple as if she had a sudden headache – the implication being, of course, that I'd brought it on. 'You don't do yourself any favours by being so *intense* all the time, you know.'

This was not the first time my mother had told me I was too intense. Oh, no. *Intense*, as far as I could tell, was my mother's favourite code word for me. Sometimes it meant too loud, too passionate, too excited. Sometimes it meant pathetic and silly. Or just childish. Sometimes it was used as a pat on the head, something patronizing and dismissive. But one thing I knew: it was never, ever, a compliment.

I glared back at her, no doubt with all of that intensity she hated. And who knew what I might have said?

'I think this has gone off the rails a little bit,' Dad said then, forestalling whatever I was about to say. Saving me from a total meltdown, more like.

He smiled at me, but I couldn't quite bring myself to return it. 'I know you're upset, and I don't blame you. Who wouldn't be? And no one's saying you shouldn't be. You have the right to your feelings.' He leaned his elbows on the table, and angled himself toward me. His smile deepened. Every alarm inside me started ringing. Loudly and ominously. 'But what your mother and I really want to talk about tonight is what we can do to help patch things up between you and Carolyn. This family is our primary concern. Do you see that as any kind of possibility?'

It felt like a knife in the gut, a betrayal. He might as well have kicked me. Those internal alarms were never wrong – and still, I never listened to them. I might as well have kicked myself, really.

'There's no patching this up,' I said, my voice much calmer than it could have been, all things considered. 'I'm surprised you would think otherwise.'

'No one's asking you and Carolyn to suddenly be the best of friends after all of this,' Dad said, and the worst part was how kind he looked then, how compassionate. It made a part of me feel like some kind of monster for not being over the divorce that hadn't even happened yet. For not simply hand-waving away Carolyn's actions. Once again I saw that damned blue blouse, frozen in the air, stuck in the last moment my life had made any kind of sense to me.

Imagine, I thought now, if I'd been a little less reasonable and calm and easy about the whole thing from the start. If I'd taken Lianne's expletive-laden advice and burned all of Tim's belongings in a blazing pyre in the front lawn. If I'd punched Carolyn straight in her face, the way I still wanted to. The way Lianne still claimed she would. What would my parents have done then?

But I suspected I knew.

'You girls have never seen eye to eye, and this situation is only exacerbating that,' Dad continued in the same reasonable, rational, horrible way. 'No one says you have to transform yourselves into best buddies. But how about a little civility? Is that too much to ask?'

'Yes,' I said flatly. 'It is far too much to ask.'

'Oh, Sarah,' my mother said. So very sadly. As if I had reached across the table and plunged that fork of hers directly into her heart. 'This kind of thing will eat away at you and make you brittle if you don't find it in yourself to forgive and forget.'

'Then I guess I'm going to calcify right here,' I snapped, outrage and the deep hurt beneath it making me sound very nearly flippant. 'Because I'm not going to all of a sudden forgive Carolyn when she can't even bring herself to apologize for ruining my entire life, and none of us are likely to forget the fact that she's having my husband's child, are we?'

'And what about that child?' Mom pounced on that as if I'd walked into a carefully constructed trap. 'That poor little thing. It's not going to be the baby's fault that any of this happened, is it?'

I felt another surge of sympathy for that baby, who would be born through no fault of its own into this complicated mess. Of course it wasn't the baby's fault. But it also wasn't mine.

'Is it my fault?' I countered. 'Have you sat Carolyn down like this, to tell her what she needs to do to solve the situation?'

'This is not about Carolyn—' Mom began.

Which meant no, she hadn't sat Carolyn down anywhere, unless she was holding her hand in the ICU waiting room and offering her support she didn't deserve.

'It is entirely about Carolyn,' I said, cutting her off. 'And you know it.'

'Don't play the attorney with me, Sarah,' Mom snapped back at me. 'This is not a courtroom!'

'All right, that's enough,' Dad said then. He reached over and put his hand on mine, giving my fingers a quick squeeze. I wanted to yank my hand away, but restrained myself. 'No one is choosing sides, sweetheart. We're your parents and we're also Carolyn's parents. That makes us neutral parties in this.'

I looked at him for a moment, and then I looked at my mother. I thought about my sister. I thought about all the little things we'd all swept aside over the years, all the minor indications that Carolyn had no boundaries and no moral compass, and worst of all, no sense that she should ever restrain herself from going after what she wanted. So she never had. And look what had come of it.

In my bed.

With my husband.

Fucking doggy-style.

'If you're claiming that you're neutral,' I said quietly,

pulling on some inner strength I didn't know I had, when all I wanted to do was scream and sob and howl and break things, 'you're actually choosing sides.'

I moved my hand away from his. Pointedly, I admit.

'Sarah—' Dad started, frowning so hard that his regulation college professor beard bristled slightly.

'There aren't sides to take,' I continued, ignoring him. And then I started acting like the lawyer I was. Because this was a courtroom. Of course it was. This family had never been anything else. I held up my left hand, palm up. 'Here's Carolyn, who had an affair with my husband, who let me walk in on her in my bed with said husband, who broke up my marriage, and who then announced she was going to have my husband's baby.' I raised my right hand. 'And here's me.' I waited a beat, and then looked at each of my parents in turn. 'How are those two things the same? How do they even compare?'

For a moment, they were both quiet. I saw them exchange a look. A whole conversation in a single glance.

'Carolyn is our daughter too,' my father said eventually, with a ring of finality in his voice.

Because he had to sound that way, I understood. Because, of course, there wasn't any counter-argument to be made. There was no pretending that I had actually done anything to bring about this situation. There was no matching tally of my behaviour that could be trotted out to explain away what Carolyn had done. There was only my reaction to Carolyn's actions.

I wasn't being friendly enough. I wasn't pretending everything was okay. I was making a difficult situation worse. I wasn't *helping* anything.

They didn't like my *reactions*.

'The fact is, Sarah,' Mom said, in what was, for her, an attempt at a calm and reasonable tone, 'marriages end. Look at your father and me. We've certainly had our troubles. But we did what we had to do, quietly, and we moved on. What's the benefit of sharing your personal problems with the whole wide world?'

I could feel the curve of my lips, and I knew it was no smile.

'I haven't put up a billboard up in the middle of town saying *Tim is a cheating bastard and my sister is a whore*,' I pointed out acidly, ignoring the protesting noise Dad made at, I could only assume, my word choices. However appropriate they might have been, description-wise. 'Though the fact that the two of them have been shacked up in the B&B right smack in the middle of town kind of accomplishes the same thing, don't you think?'

My mother shifted in her chair. My father rubbed his hand over his beard as if it would tell him what to say.

'However unfortunate the situation might be, Carolyn is our daughter, and she's having our grandchild,' Dad said, with a tone in his voice that I didn't understand. Was that sorrow that it had come to this? Or was it some form of anger at me that I wasn't falling all over myself in understanding? And wasn't it sad that I couldn't tell the difference?

'I'm also your daughter,' I pointed out, as if it didn't hurt. As if I wasn't fairly certain I'd broken into ugly little pieces because I had to be the one to point that out.

'This can't go on forever,' Mom said after a moment. 'Tim will wake up, and when he does, I have to say, he's unlikely to be thrilled with how Carolyn's been treated. The angry looks, the threats, the silent treatment . . .' She let her words trail away and then shook her head. Sadly, of course. Always sadly.

'So, wait.' I sat back in my chair, ignoring the burning feeling behind my eyes that I would die before I'd let tip over into tears. Not here. Not now. 'You're telling me that my cheating husband might get mad at me for not being overly nice to his girlfriend? Do you think he'll do something *really* bad, Mom? Like maybe divorce me?'

'You already know how this is going to go,' my mother continued, her expression pinched. Mutinous. 'He and Carolyn will get married, and they'll have that baby. Are you planning to just avoid them for the rest of your life? What about family events? You already missed out on Thanksgiving, are you going to stay away for Christmas, too? What about next year? How long do you plan to make this stand of yours?'

Her words fell between us and sat there, nestled in with the salt and pepper and olive oil and vinegar in the centre of the table top. I stared at them as if they made sense.

As if it were really time, now, with Tim still in his coma and all of this so fresh and awful, to be debating family visitation rights.

'Please explain to me why I should be forced to spend Christmas or any other holiday with the two of them,' I said, fighting once again to stay calm. 'Really. Explain it to me. They get to act horribly, and do whatever terrible thing they like, but I'm the one who keeps being punished for it? Why is that okay?'

'No one is punishing you,' Dad said, his brow knitting in concern. 'Of course not. There's no debate here. What Carolyn and Tim did was inexcusable.'

'But life goes on,' Mom added. It was as if she couldn't help herself. She couldn't let a single statement roll by without slapping a qualifier on top of it. Not one.

'None of this is fair,' Dad said, as if he were supporting me, but he wasn't. I got that all too well, finally. He could talk a good game, but at the end of the day? He went for the path of least resistance every time. I knew that better than anyone – this was the first time I'd ever gone the other way myself, and look how everyone was reacting to it. 'We missed you at Thanksgiving,' he said, in that voice of his that I no longer found at all soothing. 'What do we have to do to make you comfortable about being here as we go forward?'

'You could not invite Carolyn,' I said bluntly. 'Problem solved.'

'We're not going to do that, sweetheart,' my father said

gently, even kindly, as if I was being wildly unreasonable and he hoped to tame me with his gentle voice. 'You can't ask us to choose between our daughters.'

'I'm not the one asking you to do that,' I pointed out, my jaw aching from the way I kept clenching it, keeping back all the things I'd *really* like to say. 'She is, since she's the one who did this.'

'You're welcome here anytime you like,' Mom said, stubbornly, clearly drawing her line in the sand. With both hands. 'As is Carolyn, of course.'

I pushed back my chair and got to my feet, only then realizing that I was shaking. I didn't bother to say anything else, I just grabbed my jacket and bag and headed for the door, praying that I would make it outside and into my car before I dissolved.

'This is a family,' Dad said from behind me. Piously. 'You don't just discard family members when they do things you don't like.'

I stopped in the doorway, and had a brief, vicious battle with myself. But I turned around anyway, and looked back at them. Hadn't I promised myself I wouldn't fight with them? Look how well that had worked out. And still there was that part of me that thought I could keep talking, keep explaining, and they would have to see the light. They'd smack themselves on the forehead in some cartoonish way, and wonder how they'd ever been so terribly wrong about things. About Carolyn. About me. But that was my biggest delusion yet.

At least the difference was that I knew it now. Hooray.

'Unless it's me, you mean,' I said softly. 'Then it's a whole lot easier, isn't it?'

If they called out after me as I left, then I didn't hear them.

Outside, the December night was darker and colder than it had been before; thicker around me, as if it might swallow me in one gulp. I wished for a moment it would. I let my parents' heavy front door slam shut behind me and discovered that I was panting. Clouds of breath hung there in front of me, sketched against the night for a moment. The cold wind rushed at me, claiming me, as I struggled to find the damned zipper on my jacket. As I tried to catch my breath.

What the hell was I doing here?

It seemed like a bigger question than one about my specific geographic location. I looked wildly around for a moment as if I were even more lost than I felt, then trudged over the frozen front garden toward the car I'd parked at the kerb. And when I got in, I cranked up the heat and sat there.

I wanted to go home. I wanted that more than anything, with a yearning that seemed to sear right through me. But I didn't want to maroon myself in that empty house of mine that sat up there on the top of the hill – that monument to my completely fake life. I didn't know what I wanted, but I knew it wasn't that.

Your parents have always been about the status quo, Lianne texted me from the middle of her late-night shift at the office, in reply to a few choice quotes from dinner I sent along to her. *None of this is surprising. It just sucks.*

That it does, I replied, feeling like a teenager again, adrift and angry, unmoored in my own home town and abandoned in every way that mattered by the people who should have been protecting me. I didn't know why I let them get to me like this. I didn't know why, if I knew they would make me feel like this, I'd set myself up for it by allowing the conversation in the first place.

This was exactly why I'd made rules before I'd gone over there. Why I'd been determined not to fight with them.

Come over later, Lianne texted back, just as she might have had there been text messaging when we were sixteen. *We'll watch something cute and eat something bad. And we'll psychoanalyse every terrible thing your parents have ever done. I remember them all.*

Thank God, I replied. *I think I blocked them out.*

But I couldn't bring myself to go home and sit in that house and wait for Lianne to get off work. I found myself driving in wide circles around Rivermark instead, hardly recognizing all the old, familiar landmarks through the tumult and chaos inside me. They all looked fake to me now. Like free-standing lies.

The old train station that had stood as an icon of the town, in brick and iron, since the late 1800s. The stately old library that commanded the whole north side of the manicured town green, buried though that picturesque lawn was now beneath the cover of snow. The village's self-consciously quaint main street preened against the night, all lit up with holiday lights that twinkled happily in the cold December dark. Even the bed and breakfast that I knew Tim and Carolyn had shacked up in was lovely tonight, with its white picket fence covered in ever-green garlands and wreaths in all the windows. I should have found it all pretty. I should have stopped to take it in, like all the tourists did. Hadn't I moved back here because I wanted to live like this? In a fucking postcard? But my head was pounding, my ears were alive with white noise, and I was breathing in loud little gulps that wouldn't take too much prodding before they tumbled into sobs.

I was completely alone.

I knew that wasn't true the moment I thought it. Not entirely, anyway. I had Lianne and her family, of course I did, but I didn't want to take advantage of them – any more than I already had. They couldn't be expected to make up for the various betrayals of my own family. I had a whole spread-out network of friends from college and life in New York with whom I kept in touch, some more closely than others, and I knew, intellectually, that there were any number of people I could call on if I needed them, in some capacity or another. But first I'd have to explain what had happened. And there was not a single part of me that felt as if that were something I was capable of doing. Not one single part.

And not one of the people who might be there for me was ever going to be my parents. That was a stark, simple fact. The little girl who still lived inside of me couldn't seem to get a handle on the harsh truth of that, but that didn't make it any less true, did it?

It felt as if there were a gaping hole punched right through my chest, and worse, like everything else this long, terrible fall, that it had always been there and I just hadn't noticed it until now. I clenched my hands hard against the steering wheel and felt the air blow hot at my face from the car's heater, much too hot, and knew that I had no idea how I was going to go about fixing this. Fixing *myself*. How could I, when I hadn't known everything was so wrong to begin with? When I'd actually been *happy* with what I'd imagined my life was?

Maybe my mother was right. Maybe the right thing to do was to rise above all this, to be the bigger person, to take the high ground – and whatever else people called it when you stopped fighting. When you surrendered. *Turn the other cheek*, and so on. Maybe I should give in and let Tim go without a fight, without even the passive, mostly well-behaved one I'd been waging since before the accident. Because what was the point of fighting to keep somebody if they wanted to leave? If they'd already left? How could that possibly end well?

There was probably something in that I should examine,

but I felt too beat up tonight to do it. Too outside myself. There had been too much revelation and not enough dinner, and I wasn't sure I'd survive a close and unflinching look into my own part in any of this tonight.

Tomorrow, I promised myself fiercely, as my phone vibrated in my pocket and I pointed the car toward Lianne's house, because I knew there would be no one else texting me. And I wanted to sit on her couch, eat something bad for me, and forget. I just wanted to forget. *I'll deal with that fresh hell tomorrow.*

6

But it was hard to get that dinner with my parents out of my head. It seemed to linger; to expand inside me until it took up far more space than it should. Even a night spent on Lianne's living-room sofa, acting as if we were sixteen again, failed to dispel the remnants of it.

'You can't let them get to you,' Lianne had said, passing me the giant family-sized bag of Cheetos while a classic John Cusack movie played on the impressive TV on the wall. 'They want you to give in and get over it because that would make things easier for them. Everything could just go back to normal.'

'They can't really believe that things will ever be normal again,' I'd argued, baffled and uneasy at the very suggestion, and what the possibility that my parents actually believed that might mean. 'Can they?'

'Here's what I know about parents,' Lianne had said with a long sigh, tacitly inviting us both to think about her own father, who had dealt with her mother's death by throwing himself into the dating world with unsavoury and unfortunate gusto – each new girlfriend shockingly and almost creepily younger than the last. The current one was barely of legal drinking age, we estimated. And we couldn't discuss the way he *dressed young* for these increasingly more vapid girlfriends – Lianne found it entirely too painful. 'There is no level of denial they won't cling to, as long as that means they don't have to face the truth about something they don't want to deal with. Believe me.'

I knew she was right. Of course she was. I just didn't want to believe it.

A few days later, exhausted from another long day in the hospital fending off well-meaning yet tiresome visitors like the difficult Annette, as well as an extensive and annoying conversation with the two local lawyers I'd handed off all the active Lowery & Lowery cases to while Tim's coma dragged on, I found myself on my hands and knees at the back of the huge walk-in closet off our master bedroom. I was digging through piles of Tim's and my detritus in search of those ratty shoeboxes filled with old photographs that I distinctly recalled stowing away in there years ago. The whim to do such a thing had overtaken me as I'd been haunting the upstairs hallway like something out of a Brontë novel, brooding over all the carefully displayed photographs laid out before me on the walls, which some part of me had wanted to take outside and set on fire in the frozen back garden.

A large part of me, actually, but I'd refrained. There was a far more insistent part of me that didn't want to do anything I couldn't take back, and yes, I was aware of the irony of that. My entire life was the irony of that.

I'd been staring at all the pictures I'd chosen to display along that hall, glaring balefully at the representations of a life that not only no longer existed but, I was forced to contemplate, had perhaps never existed at all, or not the way I'd imagined it had. I'd thought about how I'd always been the one to insist not just on taking all the photographs to document our life but to figure out how to display those pictures wherever we were.

Do you need proof? Tim had asked, his voice sleepy and indulgent, as I'd photographed him lying stretched out across the bed in our honeymoon suite in Nevis, so blonde and blue-eyed, staring out at the beautiful blue Caribbean sea.

Always, I'd replied, laughing. *Just in case you're tempted to forget – I'll have all these pictures to remind you!*

But this particular late afternoon, staring at the pictures, I'd wondered at my own compulsion to document my relationship with Tim so thoroughly – and at the selection process I'd used to decide which ones went on display.

What had made me choose these particular photos? What had made me put together this specific narrative in all these distressed frames? Because that was exactly what this was – what I'd done. This was a *story*. Looking at it from the critical distance these last few months had forced upon me, I hardly saw the pictures as just pictures any more – they seemed like some kind of pictorial fairy tale, with Tim and me no more than two-dimensional characters I'd slotted into predetermined roles. Look at the happy girlfriend, the delighted fiancée, the emotional bride! Look at the caring boyfriend, the charming engaged man, the loving husband!

Who were these people?

And that was when I remembered that when I'd moved in with Tim, I'd moved into his already-furnished apartment. It had been a gorgeous one bedroom on the Upper West Side, huge steps up from where I'd been living at the time. I'd been too much in awe to really put my stamp on the place. Instead, I'd fitted myself in around what was already there. His furniture. His art. His possessions. It wasn't until we'd moved out to Rivermark and into this house that I'd really been able to put my mark on things. I'd spent the most time on the pictures, as I recalled. And tonight, I found myself wondering about all the pictures I hadn't chosen three years ago. What story did *they* tell? Were they hiding all the things I'd managed to forget – like my own dreams? Had I banished them from view for precisely that reason?

What did that say about me?

That was how I found myself in the most crowded of the house's closets. That it was so spacious, with so many built-in shelves, had dazzled us when we'd moved here from the city. But we had soon packed it full to bursting.

I'd had to psych myself up considerably to dig around in there. Who knew what might be tucked away inside?

Not to mention, I hadn't been in the master bedroom much since That Day. I'd found myself unable to sleep in the bed they'd so defiled, even with a brand-spanking-new mattress, and so spent most of my nights pretending to sleep on the deep-cushioned sofa in the den – something I had started lying about to Lianne. She thought I needed to *reclaim* the king-sized platform bed in the master bedroom as my own. She insisted there should be a ritual to let me do so. Or a cleansing of some kind. I thought there was a long list of things I should probably try to reclaim from this situation, a much longer list than I really wanted to think about if I were honest, and the couch in the den was remarkably comfortable, really.

And anyway, it's not like I was sleeping very much these days. So who cared where all that insomnia happened?

I shoved aside some old golf clubs now, muttering to myself. This closet was like a temple to Tim, and it was giving me a headache. Here, surrounded by his clothes and accessories, it was as if everything that happened on the other side of the closet's pocket doors was a dream. In the cocoon of the closet, I could smell him, that mix of soap and the aftershave he only wore on important occasions, and that particular scent that was only his. It clung to his clothes, to the sweaters and shirts stacked so neatly on his side of the closet, like some kind of unwanted embrace. His dry-cleaned suits hung in neat rows in their plastic covers, and his dress shoes gleamed, reminding me that Tim hated it whenever any scuff marks appeared to mar those glossy surfaces and had spent many hours industriously polishing them away himself. I ran my fingers over a gleaming dark chocolate loafer near me and had to swallow hard on a sudden lump in my throat.

Annoyed at myself, I pushed into the deepest recesses of the closet with far too much force, upending the contents of the furthest shelf all over me. It was the damned shoeboxes, of course, and as they fell they spewed their contents everywhere, old photographs raining down on my head and shoulders, not gently, and one box actually glancing off my forehead.

Great, I thought. *Head injuries all around!*

But it was the piece of fabric that fluttered down after the avalanche of shoeboxes that caught my attention. I ignored the sting in my forehead and grabbed it, rolling it open in front of me like some kind of Dead Sea scroll, and laughed out loud, surprising myself with the sound.

I hadn't seen this in years. I'd forgotten it existed. I traced the nearest clump of words that had been painstakingly painted onto the large, once-white sheet in scarlet nail polish with my finger – I'd done it myself when I'd been all of eighteen years old, newly arrived at NYU and bursting with the sense of my own poetic melodrama. To say nothing of the illicit bottle of wine we'd smuggled into our dorm room. It was a few key lines from a Rainer

Maria Rilke poem I'd discovered that very same week, if I remembered it right.

For here there is no place that does not see you—
You must change your life.

Brooke and I had been thrown together into a tiny dorm room in Hayden Hall, one of NYU's residence halls located right on Washington Square Park. We'd both been suburban girls, Brooke from Main Line Pennsylvania and me from Rivermark, and we'd both been certain that New York was going to *change us forever*. And so it had. As if those Rilke lines had been prophecy, not poetry, after all.

We'd lived in that narrow little absurdity of a room, tucked up in our monastic single beds, the place more a bowling alley lane than anything else. The wonder was that we'd become such good friends so quickly and so seemingly permanently when, really, homicide might have been a more likely outcome from all that forced intimacy with a total stranger. But we'd bonded over silly things like this sheet, which we'd hung on the wall near the door and 'decorated' all throughout our years of living together. It had started as a freshman get-to-know-you exercise.

Years later, we called it the Sheet of Shame and joked that it was the roadmap to our secret histories, the ones only we knew. By that time we were living in that tiny little apartment in gritty Alphabet City that wasn't really all that much bigger than our initial dorm room, but which we'd loved anyway and lived in together, mostly harmoniously, until I'd moved in with Tim. We'd hung the sheet inside the hall closet door then, hiding it from public view as we grew older and pretended to be more mature, and we'd taken great pleasure in pulling it out on the odd wild evening in and updating it with cryptic snatches of songs or poems or deep thoughts, names and dates or bits of memories, creating a complicated and messy patchwork of our intertwined lives. We'd cut it in two the day I moved out, with great ceremony, promising that we would both continue the sheet's great work on our own.

I hadn't touched it since, except to roll it up and store it in the back of this closet.

I set my half of the sheet aside now, as if it were fragile, aware of a new wave of sadness moving through me, making my eyes start to blur. I blinked the blurriness away. I started to sort through all the fallen photos that lay around me, scattered over the shoes and all over the closet floor. There were so many of them.

There were stacks of me and Lianne back in high school, with Billy as often as not, the three of us musketeers rolling around Rivermark being bored together in the time-honoured teenage tradition. I'd thought we were all the same kind of bored, the kind that dreamed of nothing more than *escape* – and as I came across their wedding pictures in the backyard of that old house on Monroe Street where Lianne had grown up, I remembered how impossible it had been for me to get my head around the fact that they'd been getting married so young. Nineteen? And that they'd wanted a house in Rivermark and a few kids, not the escape I'd longed for.

I'd been obsessed with how different I'd felt then, how much I'd felt New York City had changed me in that single short first year of college. I'd felt so worldly and mature next to poor, suburban Lianne – something I'd thought I'd hidden at the time and yet was painfully obvious to me now as I looked at the pictures of myself, smirking through my overly red lips and lounging about in my inappropriate black dress like a wraith in the middle of Lianne's sweet summer wedding. What an asshole I'd been.

And now here we were almost fifteen years later. Lianne and Billy were still happily married and reasonably content, while smirky old me was crouched in the closet of her dream house, trying to figure out how her fabulous life had fallen into all these jagged pieces.

The rest of the pictures were all of Brooke and me. Brooke and me in a variety of NYU settings. Brooke and me living in that house on Nantucket with three other girls that one summer, all of us working random jobs waiting tables or serving ice cream, just for the pleasure of the odd days off spent sailing and at parties on the crisp, white sand beaches. Brooke and me dressed in corporate drag for our first summer internships. The two of us in graduation caps and gowns. The two of us on that never-to-be-discussed-aloud road trip to Savannah, Georgia, that one spring break. The parade of crushes and, more rarely, actual boyfriends. The other girls we'd known and spent time with in and around the coffee houses, bars and cheap restaurants of lower Manhattan. There were a few photos at the truly fancy restaurants we'd visited very occasionally in those years, to celebrate things like birthdays or law school acceptance letters, both of us feeling so *grown up*.

I stopped for a long time on a particular shot of us on our backpacking trip through Costa Rica. The two of us stood in front of a waterfall, our arms around each other, grins splitting open our faces. We looked a little bit grubby and darkly tanned, dressed exactly alike in faded jeans and black tank tops and hiking boots, though I thought now that that had probably been accidental – we'd dressed alike more often than not, yet it only seemed obvious later in the photos. We'd somehow been unaware of our similarities at the time. We'd been so young. We'd been all of twenty-three that summer, and we'd concentrated so fiercely on all the ways we were different. It seemed silly to me now, with clear evidence of the two of us dressed as twins.

I could remember that particular hike so vividly. We'd trekked for what seemed like miles up the side of that mountain, giggling the whole way over the Australian boys we'd met at the beach in Manuel Antonio the previous day who we were supposed to meet up with again that night. I remembered exactly how I'd felt right before we'd flagged down another hiker, one half of an intimidatingly fit German couple, to take that shot. I'd been looking at the blue sky, the precious few clouds, the bright green trees and the impossibly beautiful waterfall that sketched its way over the hard rocks to the gleaming pool beneath. I'd been awed by the *immensity* of what I felt, what I was doing, what my life – our life – would entail. It had been *right there, waiting*. I had been so sure that if I just stretched out my hands far enough, I'd be able to touch it. Hold it. Shape it.

And whatever that life might turn out to be, I'd known with a deep certainty that it would involve Brooke. I felt that sadness again now, a far richer strain. It worked through me as I set the photo aside and let out the breath I hadn't known I'd been holding. She had been, in so many ways, the first great love of my life. More intimate and important than any of those boyfriends either one of us had had in those years. Sometimes I'd suspected that I lived through the drama of whatever boy it was simply to get to the part where Brooke and I dissected it all on our crappy old couch in the living room, such as it was, in our Alphabet City apartment.

I picked up another handful of pictures and tossed them into the closest box, then another, and paused again. This time it was a picture of a tall, smoothly muscled and intense-looking man, his arms wrapped tight around me as we both looked into the camera, both of us in faded T-shirts, a picture-perfect Cape Cod beach arrayed behind us. He wasn't smiling, though his dark eyes were bright. His hair was a shaggy mix of copper, blonde and brown, and framed his lean, clever face in a way that suggested that, left to its own devices, it might look leonine. I was leaning back against his chest with an ease that spoke of deep physical comfort with this man, and I was laughing at something – at Brooke, I remembered, who had taken that particular picture on that particular morning, though I couldn't remember what she'd said to make me laugh like that, openmouthed and carefree.

Nor could I remember when I'd laughed like that recently. I threw the picture in the box with the rest. But I didn't pick up any more from the floor around me.

That Cape Cod shot was one of three existing photographs of Dr Alec Frasier and me from that long, momentous year we'd been together. I shook my head at my own silliness, because I still knew that number and worse, I knew exactly where the other two photos were. Or had been, anyway, way back when any of that had mattered. That was the kind of junk that I carried around in my head – the mess that filled the spaces where there could have been all kinds of other things. Things like some awareness of what had been going on in my marriage right under my nose, for example. If Brooke were here, she would have let out that cackle of hers and told me I was ridiculous, and I would have agreed. I sat back, leaning against the wall of cubbies that housed all of Tim's shoes and the shirts and sweaters he kept folded in neat rows. I felt almost lightheaded with loss.

What the hell had happened? How had I lost my best friend? When she'd been so much more than that term could encompass – when she'd been like another limb, or my heart and lungs, as integral to my ability to function as any of those things?

We hadn't had any fights that I could remember – and I felt sure I would remember. Wouldn't I? There hadn't been any big, traumatic scenes, any unforgivable words flung at each other. She'd been the maid of honour at my wedding – something that seemed odd to me, as I thought about it, given that I'd managed to put up pictures of our wedding all over this house yet not one of them with her in it. Things had become strained between us when I'd moved in with Tim, I knew, but I'd put that down to necessary growing pains.

Brooke and I had lived together for almost ten years at that point. We'd shared everything. Of course it was weird for her when I moved on. And then I'd really started focusing on my career, and she'd become busier and busier herself, juggling more book manuscripts per week than most people read in a year. We'd gone from talking all day every day to more and more infrequent phone calls, from living in each other's pockets to a dinner every month or so. We'd gone from knowing every detail of each other's lives and thoughts, so much so that we had our own language of private jokes and inferences and shared moments that we could communicate in a glance, to a few awkward hours of playing catch-up over sushi.

This was called growing up, I'd told myself then, as I'd prepared for my wedding and the life Tim and I so carefully plotted out together. This was what happened. All friendships had to change, because we weren't eighteen-year-old freshmen at NYU any more, and we wouldn't ever be again. Look at me and Lianne. We'd kept in touch throughout my Manhattan years, but had only really reconnected when I moved back to Rivermark. Which was right about when I'd last spoken to Brooke, now that I thought about it. We'd exchanged emails for a while – a few earnest lines here and there, promising to make plans that never materialized.

It was as if I'd discarded Brooke along with the rest of my twenties. I couldn't understand it. Just as I couldn't understand how I'd managed to block all of that out – my whole history – with such success that it now felt as if I didn't have access to my own life, my own memories. My mother had said I'd had *plights* I'd been so concerned with. Yet when I thought about it now, all I could remember about those years was Brooke. Brooke and me and all of that bright, gleaming future spread out before us, ripe for the taking.

How had I lost all of it? All of that brightness, and Brooke too?

My cell phone buzzed in my pocket then, though it took me a long moment to recognize the sound and vibration and haul myself out of the past long enough to dig it out. It was a text from Carolyn – who had finally accepted the fact that I wasn't going to answer her calls.

Come to the hospital right now!! 911!!!! it read.

I went completely cold.

This was it, I thought through the iciness that spread through me. It had finally happened. Tim must have taken a turn for the worse.

I held the phone in my hand and stared at it, realizing as I did that I was too much of a coward to text Carolyn back for clarification. I didn't want to know. I would find out soon enough whether I wanted to or not, wouldn't I?

I climbed to my feet and lurched for the door. As I staggered through the house, our house, I knew I should have been replaying all the scenes of Tim's and my time together, of this life of ours. I should have been telling myself something comforting – like that it didn't matter that parts of our life weren't what they should have been. That we'd built something good. That just because it had ended horribly and now tragically, that didn't erase all that had gone before.

But I didn't really feel any of that.

I just felt numb. All the way through.

I stood in the corridor outside the ICU waiting room and stared at my sister without comprehension, as if I could somehow make sense of what had just happened through the force of my glare alone.

'I don't understand,' I said again, hearing the strain in my own voice. 'Why did you text me at all? Why didn't you just talk to the doctor yourself?'

Carolyn actually rolled her eyes, as if this were a wholly unreasonable question. She leaned back against the wall in the hallway and wrapped her arms around her middle.

'I really can't,' she murmured, her voice hinting at a wealth of untold tragedies, so very much in the style of our mother. It made my shoulders creep up to a place right below my ears. 'I told you. It gives me horrible anxiety and it certainly can't be good for the baby.'

'I just want to make sure I'm fully understanding what happened here,' I said, aware that my tone was shifting into what my mother called my Lawyer Mode. I didn't try to modify it. Some things called for a little cross-examination, and this was one of them. 'You texted me, indicating it was an emergency, because you didn't feel like having a conversation with a doctor. That can't be what you're telling me, Carolyn. Can it?'

'I can do without the sarcastic tone, Sarah,' she replied, with another dramatic roll of her eyes.

'I thought Tim was dead,' I snapped back at her. 'Or dying. I drove down here preparing myself for impending widowhood. I was thinking about how to go about setting up his funeral service.' I forced myself to stop. To inhale. 'But he's actually fine. Better, the doctors wanted to tell you, even if he isn't awake yet – but you couldn't have that conversation.' I pressed my fingertips to my temples to keep my head from exploding. 'When did you become such a delicate, hothouse flower?'

Carolyn pushed herself away from the wall. 'I'm not

going to fight with you about this,' she muttered. She shoved her jet-black hair back from her face. 'And I'm not going to compete with you for terminology here. Is that why you're so angry? It's like you would take some kind of sick pleasure in getting to be Tim's widow because I'm not – and I get it. I really do.'

'What are you talking about?' My voice was absurdly, almost frighteningly calm. I shoved my hands deep in the pockets of the parka I hadn't had time to do more than unzip, and rocked back on the comfy heels of my winter boots. Anything to keep the drumbeat of potential violence at a low level I could control, rather than expressing it all over Carolyn's pretty face.

'I heard the way you said that,' she said, her voice shaking then, her eyes filling with tears. Crocodile tears, I was almost certain, although with her level of melodrama I could never be sure. 'Believe me, Sarah, I know you're still his wife. I know you're getting off on getting to play the role here. Still, despite everything. *I know.*'

The way she said that made my whole body fill with what felt like some kind of howling wind. Probably because there was that uncomfortable edge of truth to what she was saying, and I couldn't help but hate her more for it. For recognizing it and calling attention to it, so I couldn't pretend any more. I had to stand there for a moment until the tornado subsided to some kind of dull roar. Until I could be sure that I wouldn't unleash it if I opened up my mouth.

Carolyn, as ever, was completely blind to the danger. She pushed her hair back again and kept her hands there, on top of her head, making her face seem starker, somehow. The bones of it more delicate. For a moment she looked almost haunted, and I was struck by that. What ghosts made Carolyn's life a misery? What regrets? But maybe I was projecting. Maybe I wanted to imagine that she could feel those things. It made her less of a monster, didn't it? It made her my sister again. Maybe I wanted that more than I'd admitted to myself before.

'I know this hurts you to hear,' she said in that same wounded tone of voice, so much like our mother's it set my teeth on edge and made my heart pound in that familiar way I hated, 'but if he woke up, he'd want me. Not you. On some level you have to know that.'

So much for ghosts and regrets. And tornado control.

I let it rip.

'What do you think being a wife *is*?' I snapped at her, not even trying to modify my volume or my tone. 'You think it's all doggy-style in the afternoon and sneaking away to a bed and breakfast to play out some romantic fantasies? Dream on, Carolyn. Marriage is a lot more work than that.'

'I'm not going to compare relationships with you,' she said primly, as if from some high horse.

'You want to be his wife?' I threw at her. 'Then act like his wife. Feel free to take this over. I give you my blessing. I don't even know why I bothered. Other women in my position would have lit the both of you on fire weeks ago.'

'What?' She studied my face, blinking as if I'd surprised her, and as if she were not at all comfortable with putting that particular shoe on the other foot. 'What are you . . . ?'

'I'm sitting here keeping watch, keeping some insane vigil, and for what?' I realized at that point that I was talking to myself. That in no way slowed me down. 'Who am I proving myself to? You? Tim? What's the fucking point?'

'Are you okay?' she asked, and I thought it was cute, really, that she sounded like she cared. But I wouldn't make the mistake of believing those little flickers of humanity again. They were nothing more than shooting stars – rocks and debris combusting and pretending to be stars on the way down.

'As his wife, Carolyn, you don't get to have too much anxiety to deal with his medical care,' I told her matter-of-factly. 'You don't get to *opt out*. You have to sit by his bed and talk about it all, in detail, with every nurse and doctor who wanders by and glances at his chart. You don't get to lounge around in the waiting room like a pampered mistress. They put that shit right in the wedding vows, for exactly this kind of situation. *Sickness and health*.' I spread out my arms like I was taking in the whole hallway. Or about to take flight. 'And since you want all that so badly, have at it.'

She looked nervous. Or maybe that was just her version of confused.

'I didn't mean that I wanted you to—'

'Disappear?' I threw the word at her. 'Are you sure?'

'Look,' she said, frowning – and, I thought, uncertain for the first time in memory. 'I'm just really tired. And crazy emotional, okay?'

'I don't care,' I said, and it was delightfully, encompassingly true. It was like freedom, finally. 'That's his problem. And he's yours.' I even laughed. 'Text me if he wakes up.'

And just like that, I emancipated myself from what remained of my marriage. I didn't even think twice. If Carolyn wanted it that badly, she could have it. Him.

After all, I had other things to do. Like figure out what the hell had happened to me, and my life. And then work out how I was going to fix it.

And that, I told myself fiercely as I headed for the door and the me I'd left by the side of the road somewhere without even knowing it, had nothing to do with either one of them.

7

Of course, the reality of my supposedly epic journey into my own lost past started off somewhat more prosaically than I might have imagined when I threw those words at Carolyn and stormed off into the night, my righteousness all about me like a great cape.

As these things often did.

That didn't mean it wouldn't turn out to be appropriately epic *eventually*, I assured myself as some kind of pep talk the next morning, clutching a cardboard cup of coffee between my cold hands as I waited in the local train station. It just meant that like most things, this particular journey was starting off small, any epic qualities hidden under a barrage of tiny, insignificant and, frankly, irritating details. Like the annoyingly loud and boisterous conversation two splendidly suited young executive types were having in anticipation of the morning train, forcing the rest of us to listen to their breakdown of some sports event they'd both watched the night before whether we wanted to or not. Or the woman standing next to me on the freezing cold platform whose perfume, even under all of those winter layers, made me think I might either sneeze or vomit. Or both.

Life never allowed any graceful sinking into a convenient montage scene, did it?

I took the train into the city as I had a million times before, packed tightly and resentfully onto the Metro North commuter line all the way south through the pretty and not-so-pretty New York state Manhattan suburbs and then on into Grand Central station. All the black-clad, stone-faced commuters surged from the train the moment we pulled in, scattering into the frenetic December energy of mid-week Manhattan. They had jobs to go to, careers to tend, *very important things to do*. This was evident in every frown, every carefully blank expression, every impassive stare. I followed behind at a much slower pace, unwilling to admit to myself how hard it was to breathe through all the memories.

I stopped for a moment in the middle of the famous main concourse – taking my life in my hands by obstructing the flow of foot traffic, like all the tourists I'd once despised for getting in my way right here – and soaked it in. The morning light flowing in through the high windows. The restaurants, the famous stairs, the *magnitude* of it all. I wanted to go and sit in the Oyster Bar again or wander through the Market Hall for hours. I wanted to stand still until the terminal emptied out entirely, then filled up again, to experience the great tide of it. It was beautiful, crowded, wholly impersonal, and somehow welcoming all the same. It made something inside of me swell, then ache.

Tim and I had been commuters like the ones streaming all around me after we'd moved to Rivermark, for almost a whole year before we'd finally opened up our own practice. I'd rushed through this glorious, iconic space every morning, and had so rarely stopped to look around. I'd so rarely stopped at all. Sometimes I'd simply been focused on the day ahead of me. Other times I'd already been embroiled in some or other inevitably stressful conversation on my cell phone as I'd strode down the Lexington Passage and then outside for the quick, brisk walk to the firm over on Lexington Avenue. It seemed like a lifetime ago now. As if that had been someone else entirely.

Today, I had no particular agenda. No meetings to get to, no calls to return, no reason at all to join in with the rest as they charged toward the high-powered and hectic day ahead of them. I walked, slowly, through the passage, past the shops, and then out into the city.

Here I come, past, I thought as I pushed through the doors. *It's high time to fix what went wrong!*

But the first thing that hit me was the cold. It was *so cold*. Bitterly, viciously cold with that special, brutal wind that cut you in half whenever you turned a corner. Or stood still. Or did anything at all. Manhattan in December was an exercise in deep chill. And a blisteringly freezing wind chill, too. I wrapped my scarf more tightly around my neck and pulled the wool hat I was no longer too vain to wear down over my ears. I wiggled my fingers in my gloves and then shoved my hands deep into the pockets of my parka. The good news was I didn't have to appear in any sort of office today. No one would care if I looked windblown, or if the only shoes I planned to wear were my comfortable winter boots. I wouldn't have to worry about the effect of the salted sidewalks on a pair of prettier boots, or the necessity of carting around cute shoes to put on once I reached the safety of an office. I could simply walk the city I'd once loved so much it was like it was a person instead of a place, and try to remember why on earth I'd left it for the one town I'd always vowed I'd never live in. Voluntarily, anyway.

I kind of thought there should be something to mark this moment. Trumpets? A choir? Even a Salvation Army bell-ringer would have done the trick. But there was only the screech of brakes and the clatter of trucks, and another stream of invective behind me because I wasn't moving. I didn't know what I'd expected, but it was too cold to stand still on a busy sidewalk in Midtown and wait to figure out why I wasn't getting it. Also, someone might actually bodily remove me from their path if I didn't remove myself. So I started walking south, toward the part of my past I remembered best.

It was a long, slow walk, along the sometimes slippery and not always well-shovelled sidewalks, and around the piles of snow packed high at every kerb after the last big snowfall. I realized quickly that I'd lost that New York street rhythm that had used to come so naturally to me; that strong walking pace I'd automatically defaulted to whenever I found myself on a city street, charging toward the next WALK sign. I told myself this was different, that I was a tourist today like all the rest who clogged up Manhattan in the run-up to Christmas and that I had no need to fall into any old rhythms, but I felt the lack of that automatic, confident stride. Oh, how I felt it inside of me. It heated me up like shame.

My boots crunched against the salt and the still snow-covered patches where shovellers had clearly grown tired of dealing with the encroaching weather. I had to take care to navigate the deep slushy pits lying in wait at every kerb – the ones that always seemed to be that cruel inch higher than whatever boot I wore, that I'd inevitably sink into when I stepped into the crosswalk and would then have frozen slush and ice oozing all over my poor legs and feet as I stomped my way home. Or, worse, to class or to work, where I'd have to sit there, damply, for hours. I'd experienced that far too many times back in the day to take the possibility of accidental frostbite via slush puddle lightly.

I walked and walked. And as I did, I let my memories of my life here wash over me. I did not think about my sister. I did not think about Tim. I let go of hospital beds, ICU waiting rooms, pregnancies, my parents' limitations, and my own blue blouse, floating in the air. I did. Or anyway, I tried. And I walked.

I wandered down Lexington Avenue, all the way until it dead-ended at Gramercy Park, then I headed east. I took Second Avenue south for a while, then headed east again, making my way inexorably further south and east into the now remarkably spiffed-up reaches of Alphabet City, toward the red-brick-fronted walk-up near Avenue B and East 2nd Street that had been Brooke's and my home for so many years.

I still didn't know what I was looking for. There was still a decided lack of joyful music to announce my triumphant return, a notable absence of the Hallelujah Chorus. It was perfectly silent internally as well, if I was honest.

Outside my old building, I waited for some kind of epiphany, but there was nothing in the air but the plummeting temperature, the inevitable car horns, and salsa music from some out-of-sight radio. The place was still as gritty and relatively unwelcoming as I remembered it, with graffiti adorning the mailboxes on the kerb and visible on the edges of most of the nearby buildings, though I imagined the unscrupulous and possibly sociopathic landlord had jacked up the rent all these years later to something I would find laughable now. It had been highway robbery then, when this neighbourhood had been even scruffier and more marginal. There was a scrubby-looking bar at the ground level, a different establishment from the even seedier one that had been there when we'd first moved in. I didn't know why I found it all so charming, when it clearly wasn't. Nor had it been back then. It wasn't just the obvious attempts at urban revival and hipster gentrification, either, though I could see evidence of that everywhere, and had marvelled at how much more accessible and safe the area felt as I'd walked here. It was nostalgia, almost certainly – but it was more than that, too.

Maybe it was because I had to bob and weave to avoid walking smack into the ghosts of all my previous selves, all of whom littered the streets around me in this old neighbourhood I'd once known so well. A hundred different histories lurked on every corner, in every block, weaving around the occasional trees and unwelcoming stoops. I imagined for a moment I could see them all, all my former incarnations, superimposed over a map of lower Manhattan like flashes of light, and had to laugh at the notion. Would I trip over myself if I simply closed my eyes and let myself wander? I didn't see how I could do anything else. And maybe that would be a good thing – the epiphany I was looking for.

'It's here somewhere,' I assured myself, talking to myself at full volume without worrying if the delivery guy bustling past me on the sidewalk thought that was weird. The ability to treat public space as private space, thanks to the anonymity offered by the sea of people here, was just one more thing I missed. 'I have to keep going until I find it.'

With that in mind, I headed a little bit north and then west, across East 4th Street toward Washington Square and the heart of NYU, as I had done a million times before, both when I was an undergraduate at the College of Arts and Sciences and later, when I was at NYU Law. The city looked exactly the same all around me, and yet totally different, too. Strangers streamed past me, cars jostled for position as they manoeuvred down the choked-up little blocks in this part of the city, and life went on in its peculiarly New York way, just as it always had. Just as it always would. I didn't know whether that thought made me sad, or gave me some kind of solace. Both, maybe.

And neither was the answer I wanted.

I had a long lunch that bled into the afternoon in my favourite old café on the other side of Washington Square in Greenwich Village proper, where I had wiled away more afternoons and evenings than I could count. I sat on the gloriously baroque furniture, a bit grimier now from so many years of constant use than I remembered, and ate my way through my favourite obsessions on the menu: a thick French onion soup, a croissant, then, later, a *pain au chocolat* that I told myself tasted almost as good as one might in Paris, were I ever to make it there. I read my book, losing myself for long hours in the twists and turns of a star-crossed romance while remembering the boys I'd sighed and cried over here, so few of them worth the energy; the complicated nights that had seemed less painful after a few hours lounging on these solid, gilt-edged couches so far removed from their original splendour, which was how I'd always felt myself.

I did not think about Tim. I did not think about Carolyn. I did not let any of the things I'd left behind me in Rivermark infect me here. I told myself that none of them existed here, in fact. That none of them mattered. That this was all about me – the very first thing that had been about me in what felt like much too long.

I let the accommodating waiters bring me new steaming mugs of good, strong coffee as the place filled and then emptied, then filled again around me. If I closed my eyes, it could be any of those half-forgotten lost days of my own private history here, all of them bleeding into each other and around each other, painting the perfect picture of me seamlessly blending into MacDougal Street and Greenwich Village all around me. As if I was one more landmark, here, among so many.

God, I love it here, I thought when I finally wrapped myself up against the cold and headed back out into it. *How did I ever leave it?*

It was already the inky, full-bodied dark of near-winter on the street outside the heat-fogged café window. The streetlights above and car headlights inching by seemed rounder, brighter, surrounded by so much early nightfall. I stood in the overhang of a nearby bodega as I tugged on my gloves, and felt, suddenly, the full force of everything I'd lost when I'd left here. All the things I'd thought I'd known about myself. All the things I'd wanted. The comfort of so much familiarity, so much history, at every sticky café table. Even the way I'd walked down the damned street.

I shivered as the first flush of the frigid December evening really hit me, then I took a deep breath and finally headed for Brooke's place, where, deep down, I knew I'd been headed all along.

Brooke had sent me a change-of-address card when she'd finally moved out of our old place. It said something that she hadn't made a ceremony out of that – and that I hadn't been involved in her leaving, at last, the apartment that had been such a huge part of us, of our lives, for so long. Had I thought so then? When I'd received the card?

The card itself was one of those pretty, heavy and lushly embossed sorts, the kind that always made me feel that I was playing an eternal game of catch-up in the etiquette games, since I'd only sent out an email to my entire Outlook address book when we'd moved out of the city. She'd written an XO beneath the pertinent information, and then no more than her initial.

I couldn't remember how long ago she'd sent it. I couldn't remember what I'd felt when I'd read it. I couldn't remember if it had crossed my mind to question what had become of us, if that was all the notice and interest either one of us took in each other at that point in our lives. I only knew that I'd filed it away in the old school physical address book I kept tucked away in a drawer in the kitchen, which was where I'd found it last night. And then maybe I'd debated a yoga class, or a pastry, the way I always did. Because that was what my life had always been in Rivermark, before. Neat, orderly. Content. And for some reason, Brooke had had no place in that.

Today, I told myself as I shivered down her street, I wouldn't dwell on any of that. I wouldn't mourn. I would only marvel that Brooke had done what we'd always dreamed of doing when we were broke college students with more dreams than sense – she'd somehow moved to a very fancy address in the West Village. The block she lived on was a New York fantasy in every respect. A row of manicured brownstones lined the quiet street, some with wrought-iron railings that trumpeted the prosperity of their very stoops. It might even have been one of the blocks we'd liked to haunt way back when. We'd stuck a bottle of wine in a paper bag and had swigged from it as discreetly as possible on warm, pretty nights, sitting on the stoops of beautiful brownstones like these and telling ourselves wild stories about the kinds of lives we'd live that would lead to residence in one of these places.

I had given up. I'd left New York, the way so many did, and found other dreams. But Brooke had done it. She'd really, truly done it. I found myself smiling behind my scarf, and told myself that the sting in my eyes was the winter wind, nothing more.

I stared up at her building, and it was as if the moment I stopped moving the doubt rushed in with the swirl of icy cold. What was I doing here? What was my plan? And more to the point, just because I'd had a series of epiphanies on the floor of my closet, what made me think Brooke would be happy to see me? Friendships didn't just disappear, after all. Both parties had to work at it. What made me think this current state of affairs wasn't exactly the way she wanted it?

The fact was, I didn't know her any longer. I didn't know what the past few years had been like for her. I didn't even know how she'd managed to afford moving to such a tony address in the first place, a whole world and many tax brackets away from Alphabet City. Maybe she wasn't in publishing any more. Maybe she'd married an investment banker. Or a prince. What did I know about her now? *Nothing*. There was no reason at all to think I could just show up and demand access to her after so long, without even bothering to make an appointment. Without even reaching out in some more careful way, allowing her to react however she liked without me standing right there to witness it.

'Stupid,' I muttered to myself. Or *at* myself, I wasn't sure.

I didn't look at Brooke's building again. I turned and started trudging down the street, back toward the busier avenue up ahead. I hadn't really plotted out what I would do next, had I? I'd wandered around all day looking for something indefinable to rise from the streets and make sense of my life, but I couldn't keep doing that. I would find a hotel, first of all. I was tired of walking, and very, very cold. I wanted something hot to drink, and a warm place to sit and defrost as I thought through all the glimpses of my old lives I'd sensed around me today. I'd been so certain that I needed to come back to Manhattan, and I wanted to really explore that, if I could, even if I hadn't found what I'd imagined I would yet. Brooke might be a part of that, but then again, she might not. I'd send her an email, like a normal person. I wouldn't just show up at her door like some kind of stalker and—

'Sarah?'

I hadn't paid attention to the figure who moved past me on the dark street – I'd been far too busy scowling at the shovelled sidewalk in front of me – but I knew that voice. I would know that voice anywhere. I stopped in my tracks. It felt like it took a long time to turn, and then there she was.

We stared at each other.

I could hear horns in the distance, and the ubiquitous sounds of emergency vehicles racing somewhere in a hurry. But this little side street was quiet and still, and there was only this. Only the two of us, staring at each other across so many years, so many memories.

Her hair was longer, and spilled out from beneath the hat she wore to scrape below her shoulders. I thought she looked particularly stylish in a smart black peacoat and a bright patterned scarf. Almost French, which I knew she would take as the highest possible compliment. She had a couple of briefcase-like bags slung over her shoulder and a plastic Duane Reade bag dangling from one gloved hand. She looked elegant and accomplished, sure, but she also looked like Brooke. *Brooke*. Those impossible cheekbones. That wide mouth that I always thought of as laughing uproariously, never the way it was now, still and serious. Those dark, far too incisive eyes of hers that had always been able to read me much too easily.

Meanwhile, I felt like I was moulting. My hair was no longer in its professional bob, and so was sneaking down my cheeks toward my shoulders. I was unlikely to be confused for a French person in my puffy parka and snow-boots. I didn't look anything like the upmarket corporate lawyer I'd been when I lived here, or even the lawyer I played in Rivermark. Next to Brooke's gleaming perfection – and her address – I felt nothing but scruffy.

For a moment the gulf between us seemed so wide, so vast, that the fact she looked so familiar actually, physically, hurt me. I didn't know what to do. I didn't know what to say. I couldn't even imagine what look must have been on my face.

'Brooke,' I whispered.

Just her name, and it was so little. It was so much less than what I should have said, what was careening around inside of me, bursting to push free and light up the winter night all around us. Or maybe make it tremble.

But her eyes shone with something like the heat I felt in mine, and her mouth crooked into that familiar smile that I knew better than my own. And she threw out her arms as if she'd been waiting for me, for this, for a long time, and then she hugged me on that cold street as if we'd both come home at last.

'Jesus, Sarah,' she whispered into my ear, her voice thick with emotion and her free arm slung tight around me. 'It's been way too fucking long.'

8

'My grandmother died two years ago,' Brooke said by way of explanation as she led the way into the brownstone, up the stairs, and to the door of her converted two-bedroom apartment on the second floor. 'Let's be clear that working in the publishing industry does not lead to buying a condo in a Greenwich Village brownstone. Not at my level, anyway. That was all Granny Chersky.' She fiddled with the locks and then tossed the front door open, ushering me inside with a wave of her hand. 'She was mean as a snake there at the end, but she was also very rich, apparently. May she rest in peace.'

'Holy crap,' I said as I walked inside, because there was no other possible response, and then I just ... gaped.

Hardwood floors stretched before me toward a whole wall of windows overlooking the street. There was a kitchen and a bathroom off the small hallway near the entrance, and then a two-storey sweep of glory, the likes of which I'd seen on television shows but had certainly never seen in real life. Not belonging to a person I actually knew. I felt a physical pang – like a sharp cramp – and knew it was simple jealousy. I couldn't even beat myself up for it. The place took my breath away.

Once inside the great main room, with the wall of windows two storeys high and another wall of books – miles and miles of books spread across acres of shelves that stretched the length of the apartment and had a rolling ladder propped up against them like a real library, making that cramp turn vicious and nearly take my feet out from under me – I stared around at what looked like a real fireplace on the third wall, in the centre of a cosy seating area. And then I turned back toward the interior and saw the staircase that led up to the second level, where there was a space lined with windows that looked like some kind of indoor sun porch or something equally lovely and unheard of, opening over the room beneath.

I liked my house in Rivermark. But the whole reason people left the city and moved to places like Rivermark was because it was impossible to find – much less afford – places like this in Manhattan. I wasn't just jealous that Brooke got to live here. I was jealous of the entire life she must have now to go along with living here. So jealous I wasn't sure I could speak through it, so I didn't try.

This is the life you gave up, I told myself, even though there had been no rich grannies lurking around in my family tree, waiting to bestow New York City real estate upon me. *This is what you turned your back on.*

It didn't matter if that was unreasonable. That was what it felt like.

'There are two bedrooms up there,' Brooke said, coming to stand next to me and looking towards the upstairs, too. 'I use the front one as a kind of den and office.'

She didn't pretend that it wasn't perfectly normal for me to stand and stare, speechless, in an apartment this beautiful. This was a city filled with people living on top of each other, but in vastly different circumstances. I'd known people who'd gone to insane lengths to get a glimpse of new apartments in desirable buildings the moment it was hinted they might be up for rent again. *This* place was like the ultimate Manhattan fantasy apartment. Of course we had to put our troubled history on hold so I could properly stare at it all.

I thought maybe my mouth was hanging open, and I was too awed to care.

'Wow . . .' I said. Maybe not for the first time. 'I think I actually hate you.'

'I know,' she replied. 'You're not alone.'

When I looked at her again, she was shrugging off her coat and tossing it over the nearby armchair. I sank down onto one of the sofas when she indicated that I should, feeling as if I'd accidentally discovered that someone I'd thought I'd known everything about was, in fact, the lost Anastasia or something equally far-fetched and improbable. A secret princess. The hidden heiress to some robber baron fortune. Yet I remembered grumpy, beady-eyed old

Granny Chersky and her modest house in Gladwyne, Pennsylvania, that she steadfastly refused to light or heat adequately. She had been anything but glamorous. She was the last person in the world I would have thought might be sitting like a magpie on a secret stash of wealth.

The old radiator in the corner clanked to life, the noise making everything seem normal again, suddenly. Even paradise had old pipes and cranky heating, apparently. It let me breathe. It made the cramps subside. I peeled off my own parka, and took entirely too long to pull off my scarf and gloves. Wasting time in the sudden stretch of silence and I knew it.

Brooke only waited, sitting down on the couch opposite me, across the expanse of a glass coffee table piled high with magazines and interesting little objects, including the tiny ceramic turtle we'd each bought in Costa Rica. It made a deep swell of something like gladness move in me to see it, green and happy-looking and hanging out with her here even if I wasn't. It made me hope.

And then we . . . looked at each other.

'This is weird,' she said after a long moment of that. She shook her head. 'You look so much the same, and so different. I'm having trouble reconciling the two.'

I felt exactly the same. I'd just been looking at all those old pictures, after all. Brooke at eighteen, twenty-three, twenty-five. This was Brooke at thirty-three, and while it was still Brooke, she was definitely changed from the last time I'd seen her, and certainly from my memories of her.

She wore jeans tucked into stylish boots, and her dark hair hung down past her shoulders looking sleek instead of tousled. She wore a simple black sweater that seemed to scream effortless chic, and she looked like what she was: a senior editor at one of the major New York publishing houses. Not an easy job to get or keep, and yet here she was. I would have told her I was proud of her, but was afraid that would sound patronizing.

'You look like a grown up,' I admitted, and she laughed. The familiar sound made me laugh, too.

'Exactly,' she said, her dark eyes warm on mine. 'And if *you* look like a grown up, I can't imagine what *I* must look like. Yikes.'

I knew what I looked like, sadly. I'd seen my reflection in the mirror she had on the wall as I'd come in, and it was as I'd feared. Dark blonde hair completely frizzed out from being shoved under a hat all day, face reddened from the cold. And there was no getting away from the look of too many recent and unpleasant life changes stamped on my face, like an advertisement for insanity. Or a quiet little breakdown. Having not had to dress for any office today, my jeans were faded and old and the winter boots I wore were better suited for navigating snowdrifts than important meetings. And I wished I'd thought to wear something other than that same old blue hooded sweatshirt that I was beginning to worry I would wake one morning to find welded to my body. As much a part of me as my pain.

Had there been a competition as to who had thrived without our friendship, it was clear that I would not be winning it. I raked my fingers through my hair as if that might help. I doubted it. Then I wondered what I would have thought if I'd come to see her *before* – if I'd found a way back to her while I was still proud of the life I'd been living. What would that have looked like? How would I have felt?

But I knew that I wouldn't have come here, before. I wouldn't have looked her up at all if my life had been what I'd thought it was. A complicated mixture of guilt, shame and something far too prickly to call hope sloshed around inside me as I recognized the truth of that. And the realization that she probably knew that too, that she knew me well enough to guess that my being here wasn't spurred by simple nostalgia. For a moment that made me feel almost naked . . . But then, I reminded myself sharply, this was why I'd come here, wasn't it? Because she did know me. Because she'd known me inside and out for years. Just not my most recent years.

'I guess you're wondering why I'm here,' I said, when I realized the silence had gone on too long. I gave up on my appearance and my might-have-beens. It was what it was, and fingers through the hair and a parcel of regrets certainly weren't likely to solve the problem at this point. I picked at one of the cuffs of my sweatshirt.

'A little bit,' she agreed. She shrugged, and smiled again. 'But it's so good to see you that I can live with the suspense.'

'Are you good?' I asked instead of explaining myself. I was stalling. 'Your life, I mean?'

'I think so.' She looked around, as if seeing the apartment for the first time. Taking pride in it, maybe. I knew I would, if it were mine. It was the kind of place that *made statements* about how fantastic the life lived in it must be. Though that could be me projecting. 'I have a great life. I love my job. I have good friends when I want to go out and I have a terrific place to relax when I want to stay in. It's pretty much the exact life I wanted when I dreamed of these things way back when. That's pretty cool.'

'It's very cool.' I was afraid, I realized then, a little bit surprised at myself. Or if that were too strong a word – anxious. I was anxious. There was a ball of tension in the pit of my stomach and I could feel it grow heavier with every kick of my heart.

Brooke smiled wider, and settled back against the couch. She didn't look anxious at all. Or she'd become far more difficult to read since I'd seen her last.

'That's the press release I trot out for my parents, especially around the holidays,' she confided dryly. Her brows rose. 'The truth? My job can be unbelievably frustrating, the hours are crappy, and I sometimes wonder why I'm killing myself to do it well when it would be much easier to give in and do something else entirely. I haven't had a serious relationship in years and the dating pool in this city is pathetic if you happen to be a smart, educated, straight woman with standards.' She waved a hand in the air. 'My standards come and go depending on my level of desperation, which at this time of year is pretty high, I can admit. I refuse to get a fucking cat to complete the picture, and I'm starting to think about the very real possibility that if I want kids the way I always thought I did, I'll have to do that on my own.' That crooked, self-deprecating smile again. God, how I'd missed her. 'But this apartment rocks. That part is true.'

I blinked. Then I let out a breath, feeling that heavy knot inside of me dissolve. Or ease, anyway.

And then, as if it were any given night from all our years together, as if no time had passed at all and it were just another random Tuesday on our beat-up old couch, I knew I was going to tell her everything. Every last sordid, humiliating detail. And the first words were the hardest, so there was no point waiting for them simply to happen organically. They wouldn't.

'Tim cheated on me.' I just blurted it out. 'I walked in on him in bed.' I sighed – or maybe choked – 'With Carolyn.'

For a moment, Brooke seemed to turn to stone. I wasn't sure she so much as breathed.

'Carolyn?' she echoed. Horrified understanding flashed across her face. 'Not . . . ?'

'Yes.'

'But . . . But she . . . *Carolyn*?'

'Carolyn.' I nodded again, as if that confirmed it. I blew

out a breath that had been too shallow, anyway. 'Doggy style.'

She put up a hand as if to stop me. As if she needed a moment to process that mental picture. Which, naturally, I fully understood.

'*Doggy style?*' she asked in a hushed, deeply appalled tone, when she could speak.

'Doggy style.'

'Like . . . full on?' She put her hands out as if to brace herself against the coffee table. I could see – and appreciated – how she suggested the position yet refrained from fully acting it out. 'One hundred per cent?'

'More like 150 per cent,' I said, considering. Remembering, despite myself. Beyond the blue, for once. 'They were really, really into it. Complete with red faces and *expressions*.'

I couldn't help myself. I made the face. Carolyn's face, Tim's face – it was kind of a composite of everything I hadn't wanted to see behind my blue blouse, hanging there between us. I hadn't even known I had it lurking inside of me, waiting to be shown. To be acted out like this, making it all real. And that much more awful, if shared. But here it was.

Brooke sucked in a breath and closed her eyes as if in pain. 'Oh. *God*. Wow. This is the worst story I've ever heard.'

And for some reason, that seemed to warm me up from the inside. It made it all slightly less awful, somehow. I kept right on talking, bringing her all the way up through the accident and the coma and the pictures in the closet with the Sheet of Shame falling on top of me.

'Like a sign,' she said. Her dark eyes glowed. 'I always told you that thing was magical.'

'So you did.'

'Maybe the next time I tell you to write down every guy you ever kissed on a sheet we hung in the middle of our dorm room, for all to see, there will be a little less push back,' she said in that amused way of hers that I remembered so well it made me want to cry out in recognition, even if she was bringing up what we'd always referred to as our Very First Fight.

'Maybe I will,' I agreed, unable to bite back my grin.

The story all told, even including today's tour of our history here in New York in search of some kind of explanation, I felt lighter than I had since sometime back in August. I leaned back against the couch and waited for Brooke to pass judgement, as she always had, somehow making everything better as she did it. Or at least making it all make sense, in her inimitable way. Separating my life into easily digested sound bites, making it all part of a better, broader Story of Me, of which Brooke had always been the best and most faithful narrator.

Tonight she only studied me for a long moment, and then got to her feet.

'I think this calls for wine,' she said, heading toward the kitchen, which was, I was happy to see now that the first wave of jealousy had passed, small and cramped as

Manhattan kitchens often were, rendering this absurdly lavish apartment something less than perfect. A needed dose of reality, I thought. *Thank God.* If it had been something out of *Architectural Digest* like everything else, I suspected I might have tossed myself out of the wall of windows.

Because it wasn't just that her apartment was pretty, I understood even then. It was that this was her dream. That she'd achieved it. And for the most part, she was *happy*. Not perfectly happy, but happy nonetheless. I'd thought I was there too, not so long ago, and I'd been horribly, humiliatingly wrong. Yet I had the sense that Brooke's happiness was the real deal.

She came back in with a bottle and two glasses, and set about pouring. When we each had a glass, she lifted hers and tapped it to mine, then took a sip. I followed suit, not surprised to find it was a much more sophisticated vintage than one we might have sucked down while lurking out on stoops in this same neighbourhood all those years ago.

'I feel as if you're deliberately restraining yourself from saying something,' I said after a moment. Carefully. Very, very carefully. 'Which makes me think you're even more grown up than you appear to be.'

'I have learned tact and manners, it's true,' she said, her lips curving. 'Though I generally try to keep such things in my professional sphere and let it all hang out at home. What am I, a saint?'

'Clearly not.'

'Clearly.' She took another sip and sat back again, crossing one leg over the other and looking at me. 'I guess I don't know what to say that won't sound patronizing, which I don't want to be, especially because I haven't seen you in so long and I'm afraid that if I take my eyes off you you'll disappear again in a puff of smoke. Like you did last time.'

'Was there smoke?' I asked idly, running my finger around the rim of my glass. 'I thought we moved to Rivermark.'

'You disappeared a long time before you moved, Sarah,' she said gently. But her eyes held mine, and didn't soften as she said it. 'Rivermark was the last nail in that particular coffin.'

Some part of me bristled at that, immediately. I hadn't been the one who grew jealous – who had been so nasty and unsupportive of mine and Tim's relationship. But I tamped it down. This was a fact-finding mission. A deposition, even. I hadn't come all this way to argue with Brooke's take on things. Quite the opposite. I was hoping she could offer some clues as to how I'd ended up where I was. That meant I had to listen, however much I might have wanted to argue instead.

'The funny thing is that I don't really remember any of this the way I should,' I told her. I set the wine glass down on the table before me with great care, all too able to envision myself accidentally slinging the whole of it across the room, destroying the lovely oriental carpets that stretched over gleaming expanses of polished hardwood. And I'd never know if it was nerves, clumsiness, or pure jealousy. Better to be safe. 'It's like so much of the past five years or so is a big blank. I mean, I remember what happened. What I did. But it's like there are these huge holes in it that I didn't even notice were there until a few days ago. I feel like Sydney on *Alias*.'

'In the third season when she lost her memory of the previous two years,' Brooke said at once, nodding, as I knew she would. She sighed, obviously lost in her memories of what had once been a favourite show of ours. Then she blinked. 'But I don't think there's anything particularly nefarious going on here, if that's what you're worried about. I think you made certain choices, and you got rid of the things that didn't support those choices. Simple, really.'

'Including you?' I asked. I shook my head. 'How did I do that?'

She smiled again, and this time it hurt. 'I wish I knew.'

'I don't understand—' I began again, but she sat forward then, cutting me off. She put her own glass of wine down, with a loud *clink* when glass met glass.

'He made you a Stepford wife,' she said, her voice tight, as if she'd waited years to tell me this. As if she were thrilled that I'd finally asked. 'He was everything you hated and you fell for him anyway, because you thought that would keep you safe, or something. And in order to believe that – to really suck down all of his bullshit – you had to get rid of anything that reminded you that once upon a time you'd been somebody else entirely.'

That wasn't really how I remembered it, and I had to fight to keep my expression neutral. I remembered flirting with Tim in the office, our secret late-night billable dinners, the first time Tim had kissed me on the street near Columbus Circle. I remembered thinking that finally, *finally*, I'd found someone I could trust. Someone who could be depended upon completely.

'I'm sorry if that sounds harsh,' she said stiffly. 'I don't mean it to be. If anything, that's the watered-down, time-heals-all-wounds version of how I feel about Tim Lowery.'

'It's not that I don't believe you,' I said after a moment, still fighting to fit her words into what I knew, to make space for them in the things I thought were true about me and the choices I'd made. To keep myself from snapping back at her, from accusing her of very old transgressions I hadn't known I was still holding on to. *This is a deposition, nothing more*, I told myself. *You want to know what she thinks, even if you don't like it.* 'It's just that I don't remember it quite like that. I don't remember having big fights with you over Tim.' Because she'd been so snide and snippy every time the subject came up. But I shook that off. 'Did I really block that out?'

'We didn't fight about him.'

'Good,' I said. I even smiled, though it felt a bit wan. 'I was beginning to think I'd gone completely crazy.'

Brooke shrugged, and her eyes flashed with something I might have called hurt, long ago when I'd been able to read her so well.

'There was no argument to be had on the subject,' she told me. 'You made up your mind about him and that was that. If anyone – if *I* – even hinted that maybe it was moving too fast, you just . . . disappeared. You stopped returning calls. You stopped talking about it. You made it very clear that I could get on the Tim bandwagon or get lost.'

I shook my head, trying to take that in. Trying to see what she'd seen. But what I remembered was her rolled eyes, her pointed sighs whenever I mentioned him. I remembered the unpleasant night she'd tried to set me up with someone else, completely ignoring the fact that I'd told her things were serious with Tim, and she and I had ended up in a slightly tipsy screaming match on Avenue A at three in the morning. So maybe we had fought about Tim at least once. I remembered lying in my bed in the tiny walk-up after another tense evening with Brooke, shaking with fury as I turned over the latest batch of snide remarks or flippant asides she'd thrown at me. It was the first time we'd ever been so far apart on anything, and it had scared me to death.

But I'd been so sure she was wrong. That she was being a baby. That she needed to grow up and realize that we weren't going to spend our whole lives there, in that crappy old apartment that I hated more and more every time I stayed over at Tim's sleek and beautiful place. That we were going to move on and this was me doing it, and her unable to handle that fact. I'd been positive that she would come round, and equally certain that she was, at the heart of all of it, incredibly jealous that I'd found someone I would think about leaving her for.

Our relationship had been that tight, that suffocating. That all-consuming. I remembered thinking that back then. I remembered feeling that realization go off in me like a light bulb. I remembered that I'd thought very seriously about the possibility that I was never going to be capable of having a real relationship with a man if I was *this* embroiled with my best friend, this woven together with her. I remembered Tim agreeing with me, but not in the divisive way I knew Brooke thought he operated. And I had never told Brooke that theory; I'd thought it would be too cruel.

I had to bite down on my lip to keep from saying it now. *A fact-finding mission does not involve restarting fights from seven years ago*, I snapped at myself. *This is about listening, not defending.*

And anyway, there were so many things that weren't at all true about my marriage, like that it was happy and good and filled with trust, that I hadn't seen until it was too late. Why shouldn't my memories of how it all started be more of the same? What did it hurt me to consider that possibility?

'This is a few years of therapy talking, by the way,' she

said, smiling blandly at me when I concentrated on her again. 'I used to be much, much angrier about all of this.'

I couldn't tell if she was kidding or not. That was the first time it really dawned on me; how far apart we'd grown. There was a time when she wouldn't have had a single expression I couldn't read from across a room. Oddly, realizing this made me feel something more like calm. We weren't those angry girls in our mid twenties any longer. We could be much more serene adults, looking back at things we didn't need to feel so acutely if we didn't want to.

'The way I remember it,' I said in that spirit, telling myself I felt nothing at all but *serene*, 'is that things changed when I got serious with Tim. When we got engaged.'

'You mean five minutes after you started dating him?' she asked, a definite edge in her tone. She smiled ruefully, as if she'd surprised herself. 'I'm still pretty angry, I guess. It's still in there.'

'I remember that you were very – that you didn't like it,' I said, determined to ignore my own anger and the fear that I would offend her. Determined to just get it out. It's not like I could create *more* distance between us than there had been, could I? 'I remember that it was hard for you.'

'Oh, right,' she said, with a different sort of edge in her voice this time. 'Because I was jealous or something, right? Because I either wanted what you had, or because I had an unhealthy and adolescent attachment to my best friend. That was your take on it, I know. See?' Her smile then was strained. 'You do remember, after all.'

'Just tell me how it all happened, from your perspective,' I said, feeling significantly less serene, but determined to push through it. 'You're not going to hurt my feelings. I came here, didn't I? I want to know what you think.' She looked uncertain, so I leaned forward, propping my elbows on my knees. 'I promise I can take it,' I told her, though I wasn't in the least bit sure of that. I wanted to hear it anyway, and that was what mattered, wasn't it? 'I really can.'

She sighed, and shifted in her seat, and something old and sad seemed to move over her then, making a slight chill snake through me in response. *Maybe*, a little voice piped up then, *there's a good reason you have completely different memories of all of this* . . . But I shook it off, impatient with myself.

'What I remember?' she asked. 'Even if I know you don't agree with what I think about all of it? Or you didn't back then, anyway?'

'Especially if you know I don't agree,' I assured her. 'That most of all.'

She raised one shoulder, a slightly jerky movement that looked like the physical embodiment of the same *what do I have to lose* thought I'd had a few moments before.

'Tim was after you from the start,' she said in a quiet, sure voice. The tone she'd always used to tell me my own story, to make it real, to remind me. It was both comforting and dislocating to hear it again. 'From the first second of your summer associate programme, despite the fact it was inappropriate. That was Tim. Mr Inappropriate. When you first described him to me, you laughed at him. You thought he was so full of himself – the stereotypical corporate lawyer.' She shook her head. 'When you started dating him, you kept it a secret for almost two months. You said that you thought I would hate you for sleeping with the enemy, but I really thought that the truth was, you hated yourself.'

I let out a breath, and wasn't surprised that it was shaky. But when Brooke looked at me, eyebrows high like she expected me to explode, I waved for her to continue. I even sketched some version of a smile. *Just finding out a few facts here*, I told myself, addressing what felt like a possible panic attack, or a white hot fury, brewing deep inside. *Doesn't mean they're true . . .*

'You were so depressed,' she continued in that far-away voice, like she was consulting her own memories. She rubbed her hands along the tops of her legs, which I knew meant she was anxious too. 'So broken. But you refused to admit it. You . . . changed. When I'd try to remind you that this was never who you wanted to be before, you acted like *I* was crazy. Like *I* was the one having a break-down. That was the major theme – I was a lunatic who couldn't cope with your new, great love and brand-new life goals. You hammered that point home. It didn't occur to me for years that you actually believed it yourself. That you probably had to if you wanted to go through with it. Which you did.'

It was almost funny that she could tell me a story that was so much like the one I remembered, but which ultimately wasn't the same at all. Almost.

'Why did I have to do something like that?' I asked her in a small voice. 'Why did I want to?'

'Because you had to make sense of this big new story you were telling yourself, I guess,' Brooke said, with a helpless sort of shrug. 'I don't know.' She paused for a moment. 'Maybe a lot of people do this. Maybe this is just what settling looks like. I really don't know. But you were the kind of person who always said she would rather die than settle. And I always thought you meant it.'

I found that I was wringing my hands together and forced myself to stop. To listen. To let this penetrate, even if none of it sounded real to me. Even if, despite that, it was dripping into me like some kind of poison. I could feel it moving through me, burning through my veins, making me entirely too afraid that she was telling the truth.

But that was crazy. There was no one truth here. There was no wrong or right. The fact that she remembered it all so differently didn't invalidate what I remembered. It didn't make her *correct*. Just because she thought I'd settled didn't mean I had.

It was really important, suddenly, that I held on to that.

'And so you married him,' Brooke said after a moment,

in that same too calm, matter-of-fact way, like these were facts instead of opinions based on perceptions. 'I had to stand up in a preppy dress that the old you would have mocked and wax rhapsodic about the beauty of your love and I'll tell you, Sarah, I hope that one day you recognize that as the act of love and sacrifice it was.' She let out a little laugh. 'But then it all became about this fantasy you claimed you'd always had to move back to your home town and live there. And there was no telling you that this wasn't a fantasy you'd ever had in all the years I'd known you. You said that things changed when a person got married – that I would understand it some day when I got married myself.' Brooke spread her hands out in front of her, as if staring at her ringless fingers the way we'd done when we were girls fantasizing about our future husbands. Our Prince Charmings, who were never hanging around the East Village bars with the rest of the NYU students like we did, chugging down cheap pitchers of beer. 'So I guess you could argue that I still don't understand, that this is nothing more than the rantings of an embittered single lady that you and Tim can chuckle over when you get back together.'

'That was when you and I stopped seeing much of each other,' I said, hearing far too much in the rasp of my voice in the quiet room. Not at all sure what was happening inside me. 'After the wedding.'

'You didn't want to see me, Sarah,' Brooke said gently, with a wealth of old pain beneath it. At least seven years' worth of pain, and I could feel every one of those years hanging on me like a weight. 'You didn't want any part of me. I was nothing but a bad memory of a life you wanted nothing to do with any more. I wasn't surprised that I didn't hear from you once you left New York. To be honest, I never thought I'd hear from you again. When I first saw you tonight, I thought I was seeing a ghost. I really did.'

That sat there between us, all of it, ugly and misshapen in the centre of the glass coffee table, plunked down on top of the latest issue of *The New Yorker* and several *New York* magazines. I stared at it, as if I could make sense of it that way. But I couldn't. I knew she wasn't lying, necessarily. She believed the story she was telling me. I just knew the other side of it. The real truth about Tim and me in those days, long before Carolyn had delivered that killing blow to what we'd been. It was like Brooke and I had seen the same movie, but she was now offering a different interpretation of it, and only I had read the script.

It was very hard not to say that.

'I don't understand why I would do any of those things,' I said eventually. I thought back through all the things she'd said, and blinked back the dizziness and chaos that threatened to blind me – that were far too close to a full-blown panic attack for comfort. Or maybe that was just the tears I was trying not to shed. 'Did you say I was depressed? Why was I so depressed that I would date some guy I hated? And then go over all Stepford? Why would anyone do something like that?'

She really did laugh then, but stopped when she saw my face.

'Oh my God,' she said, sounding somewhere between astonished and scandalized. 'You're serious.'

She picked up her wine glass then and took a long, hard pull. Then she let out another laugh, but it was a shocked sort of sound. Like some kind of stark disbelief.

'I'm serious,' I agreed, feeling tentative, suddenly. Or *more* tentative. And definitely afraid this time – in addition to panicked, and a little too close to a fit of hyperventilation that would definitely not end well. 'I honestly don't know what you're talking about.'

She shook her head, and then she put her wine down again, with another audible click, and smoothed her hands over her hair. She dropped them eventually, and then she sighed.

'I'm talking about Alec Frasier,' she said, and I could *see* him the moment she said it, like a storm roaring in, elemental and destructive. Unstoppable. 'Dr Alec Frasier, whose name I promised I would never speak in your hearing again, but I'm going to go out on a limb and assume we're past that.'

I could see that Cape Cod picture I'd found in my closet and more than that, I could see his clever gaze on mine and that lean, fascinating face of his I could have stared at for days. And had. His thoughtful hands and that easy, masculine grace he wore so carelessly. His rare smile, his surly impatience. His infectious laugh, his lone wolf tendency towards brooding. That impressive, formidable intellect of his that had often left me breathless with yearning. How had I ever forgotten him?

Because you had to, some tiny, hidden voice whispered. *You had to forget about him or die. You had no choice.*

'When he left it broke you,' Brooke said softly. Kindly, as if she thought the words might break me. As if she knew they already had. 'Wrecked you. I get why you refused to go with him and I think you were right, but you never, ever forgave yourself for it.'

I stared back at her, stricken, as memories I hadn't allowed myself to touch in more than seven years poured back into me like a river. Like a flood. Making a mockery of my plans to conduct an emotionless deposition of my own life. Making me question why I'd thought any of this was a good idea in the first place.

'You never forgave yourself,' Brooke said again, a matching sort of misery in her own eyes as she looked back at me, as if, even now, after all this time, she still loved me enough that she would spare me this if she could, 'and so I guess you decided it was easier to become somebody else. So you could stop trying.'

9

Later on, when we'd given up on restaurant ideas and had ordered a pizza instead, like one of our run-of-the-mill evenings in our tiny walk-up in Alphabet City, we tucked into the bottle of wine and pretended that all of that emotion, all of it repressed yet simmeringly obvious, hadn't happened. Or hadn't mattered.

Then again, maybe that was just me. The list of things I didn't particularly want to think about seemed to grow longer by the day.

The familiar debate over whether to go out or order in, and then where to order from, seemed to take away the heaviness of our initial conversation. Or ease it, anyway. That was either a great relief or a terrible mistake, and I wasn't at all sure which.

'Tim did not make me a Stepford wife,' I informed Brooke after the initial pizza frenzy had subsided and we'd shoved half the pie in our faces. I was half-lying on her couch, no longer all too terribly concerned about the wine glass in my hand. I felt too full and slightly blurry, and I was sure that was what made me sound so much less defensive than I did in my head. 'I'm the one who decided that he was the right guy for me, not the other way around. Just to be clear.'

Brooke cackled, that wicked little sound I hadn't heard in too many years to count, and it made me inordinately happy – even if she was aiming it at me in this instance. She scraped her long hair back with one hand while she took a bite of her slice of now-cold pizza from the other.

'Okay,' she said. Ever so slightly patronizingly, I felt, though I was aware that I could easily be projecting all my left-over, repressed emotions into this moment. 'If you say so.'

'I really appreciate you telling me how you think all of that went down,' I continued, choosing to ignore her tone. 'How you saw it. And I appreciate you wearing that bridesmaid's dress at my wedding. I do. But Tim is not some bastion of evil. You can't hate him because he used to be a corporate lawyer and we used to be significantly more bohemian. Or whatever you want to call those years.'

'Are you sure?' Her tone was richly amused then. Her dark brows arched skyward. 'I'm sure I remember that we made specific rules. There were to be no stuffy lawyers when you took that job. It was supposed to be about your student loans, not hooking up with The Man.'

'The truth is that I totally misjudged Tim when I first met him, and so did you.' I sat up a little bit, the better to frown at her. 'And weren't you dating that tragic musician right around then? What was his name? Lloyd?'

'Boyd, actually,' she corrected me, with an air of great dignity somewhat marred by her smirk. She waved her half-eaten pizza slice in the air as punctuation. 'And he was not a *musician*, Sarah. He was a *conceptual artist* whose *medium* happened to be *the architecture of sound*. God.'

'If you want to talk about sleeping with the enemy, I think it all starts there,' I argued, unable to wholly contain what I suspected was a matching smirk. 'We made vows, Brooke. There were to be no more musicians past the quarter century mark and you were twenty-six. Twenty-seven? Whatever. You broke the rules before I did.'

'These would all be fair and interesting points if this discussion was about the inevitable decline of my relationship with Boyd the so-called musician and his lame bicep tattoo of Joe Camel.' She shuddered theatrically. 'Thank God, it's not.'

'Maybe it should be,' I said stubbornly. 'I think it's relevant.'

'Boyd was irrelevant even as he happened, and completely forgettable almost before he disappeared into the mists of Bowery Bar, never to be heard from again,' she said, still waving her slice of pizza around over the white box splayed open on the glass table in front of her. 'He probably sells car insurance in some place like Poughkeepsie. No one's cared about Boyd in years. Why don't you tell me how we misjudged Tim?'

She took another huge bite of her pizza, and I paused to think again how great it felt to be with someone I had been so comfortable with for so long, so that it was so easy simply to snap back into the habit. Even with all the things I didn't want to think or feel swirling around underneath. How good it felt to be with someone who could say *we* and make me wish there had never been such a big gap between us. There had been no debate over our pizza order, no polite compromising over toppings neither one of us loved but thought we could live with for the sake of harmony. There was no need.

Brooke had ordered the same pepperoni, garlic and black olive pizza we'd lived on way back when. Extra large. She didn't even ask. And I loved every bite of it, no compromise necessary. Tim tended to be a little bit of a health nut who saved the pizza ordering for extremely special occasions, like maybe twice a year, and preferred a vegetable-heavy pizza that he could pick from and thereby pretend he was eating a salad. I'd missed the full assault of grease and garlic. I'd missed the tang of good New York City pepperoni and that perfect thin crust, crunchy and chewy at the same time, which was impossible to get quite right anywhere else. The fact that I was so full I wanted to die didn't in any way prevent me from scooping up another slice.

'He's not the guy you thought he was,' I told her. My tone was light, but I hadn't forgotten our previous conversation. Much less the way it had hit me. But we'd moved out of that particular space, and I wasn't sure I wanted to go back there. Too much lurked there, just out of sight, which was right where I liked it. Even so, I felt sure I could clear up a few misconceptions without treading too far into that territory. 'He's really not.'

'Then who is he?' Brooke asked in that very nearly plummy voice that made me want to spill everything, even things I hadn't told myself. I had a sudden vision of her in some leather editorial chair in her office, dispensing serenity to packs of excitable writer types in exactly the same tone of voice. She'd always had a version of it at her disposal, but I could recognize that the passing years had honed it, perfected it. Made it into something very much like a weapon. 'You refused to talk about it back then. It was like you'd decided he was it and that was the end of it, no discussion allowed.'

She didn't say that one of the reasons that had struck her so hard was because our lives until then had been one great shared discussion, with no end in sight. There was no detail too small or seemingly meaningless to keep to ourselves – no minor moment that we couldn't obsess over and tear apart and dissect for days. It was our currency. More than that, it was how we talked our world into being around us as we moved through it. It was how we decided who we were. I understood exactly what I'd done by cutting that off. By amputating what we'd been – and I hadn't asked Brooke or warned her that I wanted to do it, needed to do it; I'd just gone ahead and done it. There was a part of me that still felt guilty about that, no matter how necessary I'd long since convinced myself it was.

'He had a plan,' I said at last, almost helplessly, trying to fit all of the things that I knew about Tim into a simple description that might help her see him, too. The way I had, even if that had gone bad all these years later. That didn't change what he'd been to me then. I wouldn't let it. I shrugged. 'I wanted a plan.'

'Oh, come on.' She rolled her eyes, and God knew, she was good at rolling her eyes. She could say more with an artful eye roll than some people could say in whole, dense lectures. This particular one said a great deal, none of it complimentary about Tim. 'I have a plan right now. I want to eat the rest of this pizza and then figure out the chocolate situation, and I will execute that plan. That doesn't make me anything but a little obsessive and overinvolved with my food.'

'I thought he was cute,' I said then, around another huge bite of pizza. 'I still think he's cute. Yes, even now. I liked how he could make everyone in any room stop and listen to him, simply by talking about whatever he happened to be talking about. It's like he was a little *more* than everybody around him. He had a spark, or something.' I anticipated her expression more than saw it. 'His eyes were *so blue* and when he looked at me, I really believed that he would love me forever. I really, truly believed it. And that, because he was Tim, and the particular kind of guy he was, he would take care of me forever, too.'

There were so many parts of him that I'd loved. That if I was honest, I still loved. It hadn't all been turned off because I'd discovered the affair. It would be so much easier if it had been. And I missed those things, even now. Even here. His endearing meticulousness. His sense of order and how it should be imposed on the chaotic world around him. How strict he was with himself and his routines. What he ate, when he worked out. And the way that he could laugh at all those things, and admit that he was a little bit crazy, and he liked himself that way. *It's what makes me a good lawyer*, he'd told me once. *I've never met a client as crazy as I think I am, which means I'm always three steps ahead.*

I'd always kind of loved how delighted by that he was. And I'd really loved that I wasn't the crazy one, for once. It was amazing how much I'd loved that – and how different that dynamic had been from that of any other relationship I'd ever had.

'I guess I never saw that part of him,' Brooke was saying – carefully, I thought, but more or less sincerely. 'I only saw that Wall Street wannabe thing and it didn't make sense to me that you would choose that kind of guy. Not to *marry*.'

'I was tired of playing games,' I said, lifting my shoulders and then dropping them again. I thought of Alec and shoved that aside. Hard. There was no point dredging all of that up now, not when it was so far away, so beyond my reach. When he had been nothing but a lost cause from the start. There was no point and never had been, and I'd accepted that a long time ago, hadn't I? Brooke had seen that as depression. I remembered it as *realism*. 'I was tired of the same old guys with the same old stale promises. All those marginal, *maybe* sort of lives. Tim was a grown up. He knew exactly what he wanted and he wasn't afraid to ask for it. He had a great job that he liked and was good at, and he wasn't embarrassed to say so. He told me he wanted to marry me on our third date.'

I smiled slightly, remembering that night vividly. He'd made me dinner at his place – an impressive gourmet meal in his beautiful, undeniably adult Upper West Side building complete with doormen, an elevator, and a kitchen that was not, in fact, a galley slapped on the wall of the living room. He'd kissed me and told me he thought he could marry me. When I'd only stared at him in response, he'd said that the truth was he *wanted* to marry me, and who cared if that might be rushing things because that was how he felt.

There had been a time in my life when the fact that a man indicated interest in me would have been all the information I needed to do whatever he asked – but I'd never felt that kind of edgy desperation around Tim. Not once. I'd never felt wild and out of control with him – I'd felt calm. Like I didn't have to make any decisions with him from a place of fear. That had felt revolutionary. I'd told him that marriage wasn't something I could think about at that point in my life, that it was much too soon even to think about the conversation, and he'd smiled.

I can wait, he'd said, his blue eyes clear. *I'm in absolutely no rush, Sarah. I'm not going anywhere.*

There was no part of me that hadn't loved that.

'I liked it,' I told Brooke now. 'I liked knowing exactly where I stood with him – exactly how important I was to him.' I caught her gaze then. 'And I really, really liked being that important to somebody. Being a priority. So much so that he was perfectly happy to wait until I was ready to take our relationship to the next level. And he did.'

Brooke pressed her lips together, and I knew we were both thinking the same thing. Of course we were. Dr Alec Frasier. He had been noble and good. He saved lives. With his own hands. He was everything a hero should be – so handsome, so smart, so capable. God knew, I'd thought he was a hero come to life, even if he was markedly more gruff and irritable than heroes usually were in my fantasies.

But heroes didn't make particularly good boyfriends. Or at least, not for me. I had never felt *in control* with Alec. Not ever. He loved me, he'd said, but he wasn't the marrying kind and anyway, there were worlds to save. He would love it if I came with him, he'd said, in his brusque, take-no-prisoners way – but that had to be my choice and yes, he'd be fine on his own. And no, he hadn't been willing to wait.

There had never been any solid ground to steady myself

upon. Never any way to trust that I wasn't the only reason we were together – that he would care or even notice if I stopped trying so hard. And after a while, life without a base, and without any kind of quantifiable future, became increasingly difficult to manage. Too difficult for me, anyway. Alec never made promises, he'd only offered me choices, and he'd demanded I make those choices alone.

And more than all that, there would never, ever, be anything as important to him as his job. His beeper. Any woman who stayed with him would have had to accept that she would always come a distant second to his calling. A far distant second, if she even made the list when there was a crisis he had to handle. And the truth was, I couldn't begrudge that. I didn't. Every patient wanted her doctor to have the same work ethic as Alec had, the same level of total commitment. Especially a doctor like him, who'd had every intention of saving the world one third world country at a time. One epidemic at a time. With the force of his formidable will alone, if necessary.

But I had been equally, heartbreakingly, sure that I was not that woman.

And Tim had been a deep, beautiful breath of fresh air next to that goddam beeper.

'I don't get it,' Brooke said then, studying my face. She tucked her legs up beneath her on the couch. 'You don't seem angry at him. Shouldn't you be?'

'Alec?' I hadn't said his name out loud in such a long time, it felt like an incantation. As if I'd kicked up magic all around us, just by invoking him, and there would be a price for that kind of carelessness. There always was. I repressed a shiver. Brooke finished chewing her piece of pizza and eyed me as she licked her fingers.

'Not Alec,' she said gently. 'Tim. That story you told me was all about Carolyn. How furious you are with her and all the crap she pulled at the hospital. Not that she's not guilty here. You know I've never particularly loved her whole thing or the way she treats you. But he's your *husband*. Isn't his the greater betrayal?'

I shifted against the couch, suddenly far more uncomfortable than the question probably warranted. How was I supposed to answer that? The truth was, I wasn't sure I'd even thought about it in those terms. Lianne had, I knew. She held the two of them to be equally guilty. Any bonfires she built or face punches she dispensed were, she'd made it clear, to be shared between them.

But I was less certain.

'Carolyn's known me since I was born,' I pointed out, possibly hedging. 'Tim's only known me for the past seven years. I actually lived with Carolyn longer than I did with Tim, you know. If we're counting things like that.'

Brooke leaned forward and topped up her wine glass. She didn't speak until she settled back against the couch again, and when she did, I got the sense that she had very carefully chosen not to say any number of things. It was as if those unspoken words hummed in the air between us.

'Do you actually believe that?' she asked.

I opened my mouth to answer her and then shut it again. What did I believe? Shouldn't I know? All I felt inside of me was the wine, the pizza and that great rage at Carolyn that nothing seemed to ease. Not even a little bit. And I didn't feel that way about Tim.

It wasn't that I wasn't angry at him – of course I was. Deeply, wildly angry. But it seemed that every time I started to fume, I fumed over her. Every time I thought about it, I thought about her. *He* was almost incidental to the situation. Was there something wrong with me for thinking that? He was the one who had made vows to me. He was the one who had broken them. Brooke was absolutely right.

Why didn't I focus on Tim instead? I realized as I asked myself this that I'd gone to great lengths to erase his part in all of this – even the scene I'd walked in on. I'd made this all about Carolyn's *evil clutches* and had created some fantasy Tim, who'd blown into her talons like an easy summer breeze.

But that wasn't the Tim I knew. He was a planner. He plotted for years, he didn't succumb to passion. He was tenacious and he *waited*. He had never toppled over weakly to anything in all the years I'd known him.

It was possible that the sudden punch of nausea that made my stomach buckle was one reason why I'd avoided thinking about that.

'I guess I don't care that much about what happens to my relationship with Carolyn,' I admitted after a while had passed and I was sure I'd keep my pizza down. Though it was a close call. 'She's always been so challenging. While some part of me really thought, for a long time after I walked in on them, that things would work out with Tim. I thought that right up until she told me she was pregnant and honestly? On some level I still thought it until I walked out of the hospital yesterday.'

Brooke said nothing, and it felt like more of an indictment than if she'd unleashed the entire argument I was sure she was very carefully keeping to herself behind her calm exterior. Which was why I didn't tell her that if I was completely honest, I still hadn't given up on him. Not all the way. Not yet. It was that coma, I thought now. Again. I still believed that he could wake up a changed, penitent man. I still wanted him to do that, no matter that there was a baby now. I still wanted him to make this right.

'Look,' I said, restlessly fidgeting forward and up until I was on my feet. Then I had to face the fact that I didn't have any idea what to do once I was standing. 'We had a whole marriage. It wasn't a lie. It wasn't something I just made up in my head. It wasn't *settling*, not the way you mean it when you say it.'

'I'm not judging you for that, or at least, not really,' Brooke said with a sigh. 'I mean, what do you think my life is really like, Sarah? I'd kill to find love, and some days I think any reasonable facsimile will do. I'm not even that fussy. I just want someone who likes me a lot, who won't become one more task I have to manage.'

I didn't want to talk about Tim any more, and I wanted to talk about Carolyn even less, suddenly. Even though I knew that Tim was no facsimile. I'd wanted him. I'd wanted every part of him. I hadn't thought I'd *settled* on our wedding day – I thought I'd won a great prize. I hadn't been pretending. I'd been thrilled. And I'd thought Brooke's dress was pretty.

But I understood that she wouldn't believe me, even if I could bring myself to admit that now, knowing where it all had ended up. What he'd done with all those things I'd believed. Did the way things ended change the way they'd been before? Did what had happened now retroactively make everything that had gone before invalid? I didn't think so. I didn't *want* to think so.

I walked toward her stunning array of books instead, sighing in pleasure as I reached over and traced the raised lettering on the spine of something very old and not in English.

'I can't believe that you're single for any reason but your own personal choice to be single,' I said after a proper moment of reverence. 'Not you, Brooke. You always had packs of them fighting over you in the street.'

'Fighting in the street, yes,' she said dryly. 'Over me, not so much.'

'That's revisionist history if ever I've heard it.' I picked up a framed photo of some black-and-white street scene. Somewhere stark. Bold and a little bit sad. Berlin, maybe.

I imagined she'd taken her own trips in these years. The way I'd wanted to do and yet had never found the time. 'You've never walked into a bar in New York City without coming out with three men begging you for your number. It's never happened.'

That had never been my experience in the desperate wilderness that was the Manhattan bar scene. I had never exactly shone brightly under those circumstances. I had comforted myself with the knowledge that I wasn't one for the first impression, but the long, slow build. It hadn't really been comforting at all.

'And yet somehow that has not led to lasting romantic bliss,' she said, and when I glanced back at her she was making a wry sort of face. She caught my eye and grimaced. 'Don't,' she said, holding up her free hand to stop me. 'Don't do the thing where you talk about how they're all so intimidated by my poise or beauty or intellect or whatever else. That's just not true. In the whole history of the world, that has never been true, and only women think otherwise. Men never sit around and tell each other that the hot chick at the bar failed to approach them because she was intimidated by their charm, wealth, and good looks. It would never occur to them to say something so ridiculous.'

'You're thirty-three years old,' I pointed out. 'It's hardly time to decree yourself a lifelong spinster and find yourself a Boston marriage to while away your latter years, is it?'

'Don't think I haven't thought about it,' she said, sounding particularly aggrieved. 'My problem is that I'm just not gay, no matter how much I'd like to be, intellectually. Which is really too bad, because all the really interesting people I know are women. And mostly single, as a matter of fact.'

'New York City is really hard for single women,' I said helpfully. Or maybe not so helpfully, now that I heard myself say it. 'Everybody says so.'

'I don't even think I really want to get married,' Brooke said with a sigh. 'But I'd like the option to mull it over at some point. To consider it carefully and come to the appropriate conclusion. You know?'

I did know. That was exactly what Tim had given me. The option. I decided not to share that with her, either.

I walked down the length of the shelves, amazed anew at the sheer quantity of all her books. All shapes and sizes. Paperbacks stacked on top of hardcovers. Squat, fat ones and lean, glossy ones. Art books and coffee table books next to true crime stories and the odd sculpture or photograph. So many books I'd already read, and a hundred books I wanted to sit down and read right this minute, now that I'd seen them here. She'd always had entirely too many books. They'd spilled out all over the floors and onto the windowsills and radiators in that tiny Alphabet City apartment and in the bowling alley dorm room before it. We'd lived in a precarious hazard of words.

'Did you miss me?' she asked in a small voice.

I could hear how much that cost her – and I could feel it ricochet in me, like a bullet. And I understood, then, exactly what had happened – what I'd done. I even knew why. I'd had to step away from Brooke to figure out who I could be without her. But I hadn't done that, had I? I'd jumped right into Tim's world instead. I'd become Tim's perfect wife. Tim's partner. Lived in Tim's dream life. Who was I, after all of that? Just some kind of demented Goldilocks creature who went around trying on whole lives as it suited me, leaving nothing but wreckage in my wake? I didn't much like that image. But that didn't make it any less true.

'Oh, Brooke,' I whispered, not able to look at her, too afraid I would collapse into sobs on her floor. 'I missed you so much I had to lie to myself about it for years.'

She was quiet for a very long time, and it took me that long to blink away the hot rush of heat that obscured my eyes and made it impossible to read the spines of the books in front of me. She cleared her throat.

'Well,' she said. 'Don't do it again.'

I smiled, and something hard seemed to melt away inside me, some wall I hadn't realized was there until it was gone. And then, towards the end of the shelves closest to the windows, I saw them. One more thing I'd forgotten about that I knew again at a glance. The too-tall, too-thick row of them, familiar and beloved and a bit battered over the years.

'Holy crap,' I murmured in awe. In delight and disbelief. 'Your photo albums.'

Brooke grinned, wide.

'Oh yes,' she said. 'Bring them over here. It's definitely time for an extended trip down our own memory lane, don't you think?'

'Do you still have that horrible series of sophomore-year Halloween pictures?' I asked. Brooke smiled serenely, which was all the confirmation I needed. 'Because I only recently managed to get over *that* horror.'

'You have to think of these pictures as a time capsule,' Brooke said soothingly. 'Nothing more.'

I lugged an armful of the heavy albums over to the coffee table, and sat down next to her as she flipped open the first one. It was the end of our freshman year. We were dressed in men's boxers and giant sweatshirts, with our faces covered in some kind of blue-tinted mud, standing on our narrow cots and brandishing cleaning implements as if they were swords.

'Lovely,' I said, and heard myself giggle as if I were still eighteen.

Brooke only smiled, and turned the page, and led us back down those bright hallways into our memories, picture by picture, until it was as if there had never been any separation between us at all.

10

'Stay,' Brooke had said later that night, when we were both becoming too sleepy to concentrate fully on the abiding horror of ourselves dressed up and out on the town as scantily clad twenty-four-year-olds. 'As long as you want. Until you figure things out.'

'You could be biting off more than you want to chew here,' I'd replied, as cautious as I was thrilled at the invitation. At the fact that we had made it here, to this place where the invitation could be given and considered at all. 'I'm on a mission to *find myself* here in the big, bad city, and as you know, that could take a while. The length of a whole sitcom series, for example, if you're not careful.'

I had been trying to make her laugh, but she didn't.

'Stay,' she'd said again instead, her voice lower that time, and for a moment something had shimmered between us, fragile and good and threaded through with the reasons I had loved her so much for so long, and I stayed. Of course I stayed.

I never wanted to leave.

Staying with Brooke – *living* with Brooke – was like slipping into an old pair of jeans that I'd been sure I'd completely outgrown, only to find they fitted me as beautifully as I remembered they had in their heyday, however worn and patched they might be now. I thought there might be some awkwardness between us – some build-up of all that tension we'd managed to accrue before we'd lost track of each other years before. I thought that maybe that first night was a fluke – that when we strayed back on to heavy topics, as we were more likely to do than not, we might stay there and I'd remember all the reasons I'd torn myself away from her before.

But that didn't happen.

And we talked. We talked about everything. What we'd been doing with ourselves. What we wanted to do with ourselves. Old dreams and new ones and *if I had a zillion dollars and no responsibilities* ones. We both wanted to move to a Hawaiian island, for example, despite the fact that neither us had ever set foot on one. We agreed that that was irrelevant. We talked through all our old escapades, careening around lower Manhattan like fools, and too many silly evenings to count. We levied very old accusations and retold very old, still only funny to us, jokes. We relearned our old language of stories and signs, glances and innate understandings. Within a few days, it felt as if we were close enough to fluent again.

Brooke went to work each day and I continued

exploring the city neighbourhoods I thought were most likely to lead me somewhere, that loomed largest in my memories. Anywhere that I thought resonated inside of me. I looked for that *click* I'd felt in my freshman year when my parents had dropped me off in front of Washington Square Park. That instant, irrevocable understanding that I'd finally come home. I looked for it everywhere, up and down the avenues, in and out of the side streets. I spent a lot of time traipsing around in the cold, in the snow, in the freezing rain. I took to the streets of Manhattan like some kind of possessed creature, so sure I would run myself down on some corner somewhere if I could only find the right one. And I was determined to find it.

I met up with all the New York friends I'd lost touch with after I'd moved off to the suburbs. It was as if I'd raced out of the city like a refugee when I'd left, and had never bothered to look back over my shoulder to see what was behind me. I shouldn't have been so surprised to discover that what was behind me was perfectly fine. Nice, even. Making me wonder what, exactly, I'd been so afraid of. I made my lawyer friends weep with laughter over my tales of Benjy Stratton and other such luminaries of the Rivermark drunken-driving scene. I knew they didn't envy the tedium of my cases, but by the same token I didn't envy them their institutionalized panic over things like their billable hours, much less the leashes their firms kept them on. I caught up with so many of my old college friends that it started to feel like an extended reunion. And the best part was, while I did all of this, I got to live with Brooke again. It was almost as if we were ten years in the past, with a much fancier apartment and Brooke's lovely, desperately fashionable wardrobe shared between us this time.

So ten years ago, but better.

'You can buy clothes if you want,' she'd said that first morning, when I'd pointed out that I hadn't really planned any of this too well and had only brought a *just in case* change of underwear and a toothbrush with me, stashed away in my purse. 'Or you can help yourself to my closet.' She'd smiled. 'Just like you used to. And the same rules apply. If you stretch out anything with those boobs of yours, I'll kill you.'

'Noted,' I'd said dryly, eyeing her perky little A cups as she crooked a brow at my far more unmanageable Cs. And in her clothes, somehow, I felt more like myself and less like whatever I'd been before – frumpy, scruffy, significantly less *contortiony* than Carolyn.

We laughed so much we convulsed. So much it actually hurt. We watched all the old movies we could remember loving so much in college and those mad twenties years afterwards, and found we could still quote them all almost verbatim. We sat in her beautiful living room in front of the fire and read books, as snow drifted down outside the windows.

Brooke was so refreshingly the same, I thought one

afternoon as she worked from home. So far, working from home for her meant settling in with a virtual stack of manuscripts to edit on her e-reader while fielding several calls from the office. I lay on the floor near the fire and paged through her beat-up copy of *The Unbearable Lightness of Being*, which we'd both loved beyond reason in our junior year of college. But I wasn't concentrating on the words in front of me, I was listening to Brooke. I heard my old friend in the way she laughed, or the lightness in her tone here and there, but there was so much more to her now. I could hear the authority in her voice now, the easy confidence that rolled off of her in waves. She was in control. In charge. She had come into her own, clearly. I had no doubt at all that she was good at what she did and more than that, loved doing it, and I knew without having to indulge in any desultory self-examination that the same was not true of me. I did not have that particular air. I was not as firmly set into the choices I'd made, so much so that I now bloomed from within them. I didn't have that kind of confidence, and I wondered, more pointedly than before, if I ever would.

One day, she decided it was time to deck the halls in deference to the fact that it was her year to host her family's Christmas morning get-together the following week. We acted out the stereotypical New York City Christmas scene, slipping down the icy sidewalks with a pine tree between us, then wrestling it up the stairs and into her apartment. It lacked only the Harry Connick Jr soundtrack, which we quickly remedied inside as we hauled out the decorations and got to work. Later, Brooke insisted that we hit up the famous tree at Rockefeller Center, hot chocolate in hand, and I belatedly realized what she was up to.

'You are trying to seduce me into moving back here,' I accused her in a mild tone, as we gazed at the skaters packed into the ice rink. I took a sip of my hot chocolate and wished for marshmallows *as well as* whipped cream the way I always did. 'You are taking me on the glossy picture-postcard tour of the city.'

'I don't know what you're talking about,' Brooke replied blandly, rolling her own cardboard grande hot chocolate between her palms. 'My entire life here revolves around tourist attractions these days. I meant to mention that before.'

I didn't have to look at her to know we were both grinning.

This is perfect, I told myself as I battled my insomnia on the pull-out couch in Brooke's den. *We're making up for lost time and it couldn't be more beautiful. More right.*

And that was true. Of course it was.

Did you disappear into the city again? Lianne texted. *I hate it when that happens. Like that entire decade.*

Just visiting, I assured her.

I told myself I didn't actually know if that were true. That I didn't know what I wanted.

But the greater truth was that I wanted to disappear. I

wanted this New York City life back – all the different parts of it. I wanted Brooke back, and the rest of my friends, and I wanted to be a part of the magic of the city again, the way I had been before. I wanted late nights at the gay bars and long mornings at the charming cafes, surrounded by so many like-minded strangers. I wanted the dirt, the struggle, the thrusting majesty of the skyscrapers. I wanted to be carried away in the pace of it, the energy. I wanted the city to define me, so I wouldn't have to worry so hard about doing that for myself. I wanted the person I'd been when I'd lived here before to come back, to take me over with her drive and energy and endless access to all those wild and impossible dreams.

I wanted to be myself again. I wanted that more than anything.

And I wanted to feel more at home here in New York than I ever had anywhere else. I wanted to feel it in my bones, a deep knowing stamped in the marrow. I wanted to feel *sure* again. Ready to move in and get back down to the business of living life the way I'd always planned I would. At peace again. *Home*.

And I refused to admit to myself that I didn't.

'When are you coming back to Rivermark?' my mother asked one morning when I'd been back in the city for going on five days, in that brisk tone of hers that *suggested* annoyance without actually *sounding* annoyed. It made me regret picking up the phone at all. Dealing with anything and everything back in Rivermark made my attempts to sink back into this New York life all the more difficult, and it was easier to resent her for that than question it. So I went with it.

'I don't know that I am,' I told her, fighting to maintain the calm and reasonable tone I knew she preferred. 'There's nothing for me there, is there? Why would I rush back to participate in that awful little triangle, arranged around Tim's bedside like a bad reality show? Maybe I'll just stay here instead. Everybody wins.'

I assumed that she would tell me if anything new, or bad, had happened in my absence. I refused to ask. I would not ask about Tim's health. His current prognosis. I would not ask about Carolyn's attempt to play the good wife. *I would not ask.*

But it surprised me how much I wanted to know.

I stood by Brooke's wall of windows and let the sharp winter sun fall over me, lighting me up. I pretended it could reach inside and wash me clean. I pretended it could make me over into nothing but sunshine. I pretended I could feel that way, right now, right here, my mother and the things she stirred in me be damned, simply by wishing it.

'It's not like you to stick your head in the sand, Sarah,' Mom said, in a strange moment of unexpected incisiveness. As if she could actually see me or sense, somehow, what I was doing – what kinds of things I was telling myself. In fairness, her tone was not particularly nasty. But I bristled anyway.

'What would you like me to do, Mom?' I asked, perhaps more icily than was entirely fair. 'You're the one who told me to be *realistic*. To look for a new husband, even. Shouldn't you be happy I finally took your advice and left Carolyn and Tim to their great love?'

There was a strained sort of silence. I couldn't bear it. I leaned my head forward, letting my forehead touch the glass. It was shockingly cold. I shivered immediately, jerked back, and pulled Brooke's flowing dark-grey sweater tighter around myself. Why did my mother make me feel so much more lost than I already was? Did she mean to do it? Or was this a product of our dynamic – did we simply ... bring out the worst in each other? All I knew was that we always had. I assumed we always would.

'Christmas is next week,' she said eventually, her voice stiff. Awkward, maybe, though it was something new to think of my mother that way. I wasn't sure I welcomed that insight.

'I know that.'

'We would love it if you'd come home,' she continued. Her voice started to sound excessively deliberate then, as if she'd practised this particular speech. 'We're not going to go all out, of course, with so much going on, but we'll celebrate all the same. A bit more subdued than usual, that's all.'

'Mom.' I sighed, and turned my back on the window. I frowned at the wall of books instead. Brooke was at work, editing masterpieces in a lauded publishing house, and I was freeloading in her house, having quietly heart-rending conversations with my mother on the phone. If this was my life, I wanted no part of it. *Come on Manhattan*, I thought fervently, *hurry up and take me back!* 'I'm not coming home for Christmas. You know that.'

'You're always welcome—'

'So you've said,' I interrupted her. 'But that doesn't mean much when you refuse to entertain what I'd need for that to happen, does it?'

She made a noise that I interpreted as somehow connected to that way she liked to rub at her temples, as if conversations with me caused her pain. Maybe that wasn't an act.

'I only want to invite you home for Christmas, Sarah,' she said in a wounded tone. Always so wounded. And my response was always so *annoyed*. I wondered why, thirty-three years into this dynamic, neither one of us had ever come up with an alternative. A middle road. 'I don't appreciate being belittled for the sentiment. I don't think that's fair.'

'I don't think any of this is fair,' I bit out. The silence hummed between us, and it hurt me. It always hurt me. But this felt different, somehow. I pressed my own free hand against my temple, just to see what it was like. 'But thank you for asking,' I heard myself say. 'I know you mean well.'

I disconnected the call and wondered if I should take myself over to the hall mirror to check for demon possession, or whatever else might have caused me to take leave of my senses and talk to my mother like that. She meant well? Had I really said that? When on earth had my mother ever actually *meant well*? At least, to me? It had to be Brooke's infectious Christmas spirit, I thought then, glaring balefully at the plump, bright tree that stood near the fireplace; one more perfect New York postcard to reel me in against my will. It encouraged me to work on that *peace on earth* nonsense where it was least deserved. The tree sparkled invitingly, I could smell the clean, crisp scent of cut pine and resin in the air, and there was something about an evergreen tree in the dark of winter, even if your feelings on Christmas were dubious at best. It made my heart feel glad, somehow, despite everything. And when I knew it should have been far too cold and bitter to feel anything of the kind.

And so I told myself that it was time, finally, that I let go. That it was past time. One finger at a time from the stranglehold I'd held on my marriage, and each one harder to release than the last. The truth was I didn't want to do it. I only knew I had to. I might not have liked the things Brooke had said to me. Her perspective. Her opinions. I might not have agreed with her take on Tim, or on me. But I couldn't deny the fact that by any rationale, I should have been angrier. With Tim himself and really, just overall. I'd had *pathetic* covered from the start, hadn't I? I'd waited. I'd loomed around town like some kind of Ghost of Wives Past. I'd told myself I was waiting for Tim to change his mind, but why had I imagined he might? He hadn't wavered at all. He hadn't shown the slightest hesitation in asking for a divorce.

And could I blame him if what Brooke said were true? What had become of me? I might have had good solid reasons to choose the things I did when I met Tim. There were a lot of great things about the life we'd planned, and I wasn't going to pretend otherwise now. But what had happened to *me*? How had I gone from the girl who wanted to save the world, who wanted to dedicate her life to helping others, to someone who defended drunks from their rightful punishment? It was as if I'd abdicated any claim to anything that might require some personality. It was as if I'd forgotten all about the huge, overarching dreams that had once defined me and had become instead the sort of person who revelled in her own minutiae. There was nothing wrong with that, necessarily, I thought now, still staring at Brooke's Christmas tree as if I could see what I was looking for nestled in its branches, in between silver balls and dangling reindeer. But it wasn't me. It wasn't anything like me.

And say what I might about Carolyn – I could think of many things to say, as it happened – but she had always known exactly who she was. As a girl. As a teenager. As a twenty-five-year-old, when she'd packed up everything she owned, thrown it in the back of a car, and announced that she was moving to the other side of the country. Just because she'd felt like it. I hadn't ever had any particular desire to move to Portland myself, but I'd understood even back then that Carolyn's sense of herself was something awesome – something monolithic. She'd even moved back home earlier this year without a shred of self-consciousness, taking up residence in my parents' house as if it were a grand hotel.

It's not that I'm opposed to looking for a job, she'd told me over the summer, by which time, for all I knew, she had already started sleeping with Tim, *but after being made redundant, I'm in no hurry to get back out there and experience the economy again. I think I'll wait a while, and see what happens.*

Even if she'd been talking about Tim then, even if he was what she'd been waiting to see about, what I admired was her *certainty*. Her sense of purpose even in her lack of purpose. I would have been in an extended panic attack if I'd lost my job, determined to *figure something out*, for fear that others – my parents, friends, gossipy Mrs Duckworth in the supermarket, for God's sake – would judge me.

Who could really blame her for trying on my life for size? Wasn't that what I'd been doing myself? It was as if I'd been marking time in my marriage, pretending I was the kind of person whose goal in life was to argue with Annette the office manager over who should do which duties. Maybe I'd even become that person without noticing. I'd cut my hair off into that bob I'd believed made me look professional. I'd dressed in lawyerly drag.

But none of that was who I'd wanted to be. It wasn't at all who I'd *meant* to be.

And I had the strangest, not at all pleasant, notion that this was why I wasn't as angry at Tim as I should have been. Because deep down, I worried that he knew this already. That he'd known I was doing nothing more than treading water and he'd decided simply to get out of that pool. I might not particularly support his methods, but I couldn't deny that he was right.

I wished I knew what that meant.

'Would you do it again?' Brooke asked a couple of nights later. I had been in New York for just over a week. We were picking our way down a treacherous stretch of pavement outside the restaurant where we'd just finished a long, giggly dinner with a pair of our old college friends. I hadn't thought about Tim or Carolyn or my own revelations in at least two hours. Maybe even three. I was feeling full of myself, and even more full of Thai food.

'Eat that fried banana fritter thing?' I considered. 'No. I should have gone for something chocolatey. I don't know what I was thinking.'

'Not your dessert,' she said, laughter in her voice. 'Your marriage. Would you marry Tim again, knowing what you know now? Would you leave New York the way you did?'

Would you leave me, she did not ask directly, but I heard her.

We separated to walk around a slow-moving pedestrian

in front of us, then came together again on the other side to slow at the intersection as the light changed and traffic surged.

'I don't know,' I said, the question taking me more by surprise than perhaps it should have done.

I knew what she wanted me to say. What I wanted to say. That those years had been a mistake. That I'd been sleep-walking, maybe, or taken advantage of, somehow. That I regretted it all. That I wished I could simply rewind and act as if none of it ever happened.

And I wanted to feel that way. I wanted it so much it felt like a new hunger. But I didn't.

I didn't want the life I'd left behind to marry Tim. I would never have found Tim in the first place, would never have dated him or married him, if I hadn't felt that it was too . . . much. Too close. Too confining. Maybe Tim wasn't the best choice, in retrospect, but he'd been the best choice then. Or the right choice, anyway. For me. Even if I'd gone ahead and lost myself shortly thereafter. That didn't negate the choice itself.

This life didn't fit me any more. I wasn't that girl. I knew that with the kind of deep, abiding certainty I'd wanted to feel about coming back here but hadn't. It clicked, and even as that made me unutterably sad, I knew it was right. My marriage might not have been what I thought it was, but then, neither was I. I didn't regret it. I couldn't.

Brooke looked at me, and her mouth curved into something that wasn't quite a smile. She looked away again, out into the pulse of traffic that raced past us and down Seventh Avenue, deeper into the Village. I'd forgotten that we were open books to each other again. I'd forgotten how naked that made us both, how vulnerable. There were reasons friendships like this, so terribly close, were so hard to maintain sometimes. They took *so much*. They took everything. I'd left it – her – before because, after Alec left the country and more to the point left me, I'd had nothing left to give. On some level I'd known I couldn't turn myself inside out like that again, and I'd known Brooke could see much too far inside me, into all the dark little corners I'd wanted to pretend weren't there. I'd wanted to be new. Clean. I'd wanted to throw away the past as easily as I'd been thrown away, and staying close to Brooke had meant I could never, ever, do that.

One more thing I hadn't known until this very moment. One more thing I wasn't sure I *wanted* to know.

'That's okay,' Brooke said softly then. 'I get it.'

'This isn't my life.' I didn't know what I meant to say until it burst forth, and then lay there between us, as cold as the concrete sidewalk. The light changed again, but we didn't move. 'I want it to be. So badly. I love everything about it. You. Being here. It's like a dream come true in so many ways, Brooke. It is. I wish I could just come back. I wish I could erase everything.' I shrugged, feeling helpless. 'But this isn't my life any more.'

I braced myself. Seven years ago, admitting something like that would have caused a terrible scene. We weren't necessarily yellers, Brooke and me, bar one or two memorable occasions, but that wasn't to say we couldn't land the verbal blows when we felt called to it. She could be breathtakingly snide. And I could be shamefully mean in return. I didn't want that.

But tonight she only looked sad for a moment, and then reached over to loop her arm through mine. She pulled in close, so our shoulders bumped, then leaned away again.

'I wish it could be,' she said. 'I wish you could move right into that second bedroom and it could be ten years ago all over again.'

'I think this has been such a great week,' I said, and I could hear all the emotion of it bubbling inside me, catching in my throat, 'but you have a whole life, Brooke. A great life. I'd love to be a part of it – but neither one of us has room to go back to the way things were before. Neither one of us wants to strangle on our own closeness again.'

Her mouth crooked up higher, and there was a flash of something like wariness on her face. She glanced at me, then back at the street.

'After you moved,' she said, her voice as careful-sounding as I realized mine must have been, 'I spent all this time being *so* angry. How could you leave me like that? How could you actually leave *New York*? Getting married was bad enough.' She laughed slightly. 'It took me a long time to realize that what I really was, down beneath all of that, was a little bit relieved.' Her eyes searched mine. 'I missed you so much. Every day. But maybe we needed a break.'

'I think we did,' I agreed, my voice much too rough, and I refused to cry on a street corner. For one thing, I was no longer twenty-two. And for another, my cheeks were already frozen solid against the night without the addition of tears.

'What are you going to do?' she asked after a moment, and maybe that was a hint of some kind of resignation in her voice, but maybe that was just the relentless cold. 'Go back to Rivermark? To the hospital?'

'I guess so,' I said. 'I mean, I'm still married to him, whatever else happens. Whatever that means.' I shook my head, feeling something a little too close to dizzy for comfort. 'I don't really know what to do, to be honest.'

I was still processing what I hadn't known, not entirely anyway, not with any real clarity, until I'd said it just now. Until I'd admitted it out loud. That this wasn't going to work for me, this attempt to slip back into my old life here – *our* old life here – as if the intervening years had never happened. That there was no pretending, after all, that all these things could be erased, just like that. No pretending that I hadn't changed too much – and whether that was a good thing or a bad thing was irrelevant. I couldn't go back. I couldn't pretend to be in my twenties any more. I didn't know what that left me, or where. All this, I realized then, and I still didn't know what I wanted. What if I never did?

But Brooke nodded, and set her jaw in that obstinate

way that spelled either trouble or genius, sometimes both. And I loved her for it. As I had always loved her. Once even enough to leave her.

'We'll figure it out,' she said, a little bit fiercely. 'I promise.'

'We will,' I agreed.

And I knew that this time, we both meant that *we* in exactly the same way. We started down the street again, arms still linked, and even though I had no idea what came next, even though that scared me, I felt okay. Better than okay. I wasn't going to lose Brooke again. I couldn't hide here, with her, the way I wanted to do. But leaving New York this time didn't mean leaving Brooke, too. I wouldn't let it.

We wouldn't let it.

11

I got Brooke's text on the train ride back north to Rivermark, as the train was in its final early-morning approach into the village through the frozen winter fields and barren trees that made up the Hudson Valley landscape at this time of year.

I wanted our time to be about us, she wrote, *and maybe that was selfish. And maybe you don't want this information anyway. I honestly don't know. But . . .*

It took so long for the second text to come in that I considered calling her and demanding she stop the torture – but then my phone buzzed in my hand again, and there it was.

A certain doctor emails me every once in a while, just to say hello, the second text read. *So I happen to know that Alec is home for the holidays, up in Vermont. Just in case you find that relevant to anything you might be doing. Love you, B.*

I read the text once. Twice. Then I shoved my phone in my pocket and looked back out of the window at the painfully bright morning rushing alongside the train. The sun bounced off of the snow, so brilliant it hurt. It made my eyes water and made me glad I had a pair of sunglasses in my purse that I could shove on my face. It was entirely too bright, I told myself. Today was the third day of actual winter, after all, and it showed. It glittered hard all around.

I'd left the city under cover of darkness, the better to force myself to really, truly do it. I knew that I would take any excuse to stay, because what was there to go home to but more uncertainty? I knew a leisurely morning wallowing further in Brooke's life with all of its echoes of our old one would lead to another whole day spent there, and while that wasn't the end of the world, I knew it was time to move on. I tilted my head back against my seat, and told myself that this was the right thing to do. *It was.* I didn't move again until the train pulled into Rivermark's pretty little train station, and I was forced to disembark and face my life. Or what was left of it that early in a brand-new, post-Manhattan morning.

I didn't have time to think about Brooke's text. I didn't have time to think through the possible implications. I had too many other things to do. I'd just spent a week excavating the past and that was enough, wasn't it? Even Goldilocks's attempts to find the right fit had been finite. How many more possible, discarded lives did I think I had to try on before I grew the hell up and lived the one I had?

I took a taxi back up to the house, and felt like a ghost

the moment I walked inside. It moved over me like a shiver, like ice down my back. I'd just had a whole week in New York slowly coming to terms with the fact it wasn't home to me any longer. I recognized the sensation when I felt it again, and I felt it now.

This was nothing more than a house. It wasn't my dream any longer. Had it ever been *mine* or had it only ever been *ours*? Today, it didn't feel like my home at all. I made my way through the chilly, empty rooms, then up the stairs to the master bedroom to change my clothes. None of it felt like mine, I realized, as I walked along the hall and into the bedroom. None of it felt the way I thought it should, if it was something worth fighting so hard to keep.

I tried to shake the feeling off – maybe it was some kind of intimacy hangover from all those days with Brooke, I thought, which was only to be expected, really – and stripped out of my travel clothes. I did this in the bathroom, not the bedroom, as I still couldn't shake the creepy feeling I got showing any kind of skin near that poor, abused bed. I ignored the unpleasant sensation this morning, and turned on the heated tiles in the bathroom floor to combat the chill as I pulled off my clothes. I wanted to wear something else, something new. Something that wasn't that blue hoodie that I'd been forced to don again for the trip back to Rivermark and which, after a week of wearing Brooke's lovely and stylish clothes instead, made me feel disgusting. I threw it in the corner of the bathroom, watching it land between the hamper and the wastebasket, as if it were an emblem of my indecision. As if it were taunting me. Toss it or clean it? I told myself I would decide its fate later.

And, of course, mine.

Then I walked into the closet, and scowled at my clothes. Nothing appealed to me. It all seemed like so many *costumes*, suddenly. Brooke's clothes had felt that way too, but the difference was, there was a large part of me that *wanted* to play the role of fabulous New York editor, complete with family money and an addiction to truly delectable boots. There was a whole lot less of me that was interested in reprising the role of Rivermark DWI lawyer and oblivious wife to a cheating husband. I flicked through the racks of my workday suits and the shelves of upscale yoga wear I usually wore for Saturday errands and the occasional class. It was all fine. It was all nice enough. But it didn't feel like *me*, suddenly, and I thought I should pay attention to that feeling. It wasn't the worst thing in the world to start a voyage of discovery with the knowledge only of who I *wasn't*. It was a start.

I ended up making do with a pair of jeans I'd bought a very long time ago because I'd seen them in a store window and had then never felt they were entirely *appropriate*, because they were more rocker than respectable, and then I dug out a very old pair of Frye motorcycle boots that I'd bought in a vintage store in Brooklyn back in college. After that, the long-sleeved T-shirt and sleek v-neck sweater I pulled on seemed that much more cool.

Or maybe not cool at all, but a lot less *that person who hijacked my life* and a little more *the person I was supposed to be*. It was the little things, I told myself with more pride than the situation warranted, and then I marched back downstairs and drove to the hospital. It might be barely nine in the morning, but I felt more in control than I had since I'd walked in on the two of them months before.

Because I was still Tim's wife. And so these were still my responsibilities. I figured that should matter to someone.

And that someone might as well be me.

No one I recognized was in the waiting room, and the nurses were all distracted when I walked toward the ICU desk, so I kept right on walking toward Tim's little cubicle. I tiptoed in and peeked around the curtain, and then froze in my tracks right there.

Carolyn was slumped in the visitor's chair next to Tim's bed, her head tipped back to rest against the back of it. Her eyes were closed, as if she might have slept like that. She looked drawn and exhausted even so, her dyed ink-black hair making her seem washed out without the make-up she usually wore to go with it. She'd pulled Tim's hand over from his bed and had rested it against her belly, palm down, and then covered it with both of her hands.

It was a striking family tableau. It was incredibly inti-mate. Unsettling. It was the sort of moment that should have been private. That should have been something only they knew had ever happened. A secret smile that was only theirs. It was that poignant. And Tim's machines sang a little song all around them, as if in accompaniment.

I had never felt more discarded. More alone.

I backed out of the room and then made my way out into the main corridor. I didn't know why my head was spinning. Why I felt charred through, down to bone and ash. Why it *hurt*—

But of course I did. I knew exactly why.

It was one thing to think of them having sex – to have seen them having sex – all passion and physicality and that animalistic *grunting*. A quiet moment was much worse. A soft sort of moment that said all kinds of things I didn't care to know about them. About their feelings for each other. Or about Carolyn's feelings for Tim, anyway. And her feelings about her baby.

For a terrifying moment, I thought I might be sick, right there on the squeaky hospital floor. But I breathed through it. Again and again, until the spinning faded and I could start walking.

Right, I thought, trying to sound brisk even inside my own head. *Perhaps you can check in on your responsibilities later, when there's less chance of heaving all over the floor.*

If I could, I would have reached in and scrubbed that image out of my head. With my very own hands. I noted the *swish* of the ICU doors behind me, but I didn't stop walking until I heard my name.

She said it again and I turned, determined to smile as if I hadn't seen anything and if I had, that it hadn't shaken me so profoundly. It occurred to me that I had had entirely too many conversations with Carolyn in this same goddam hallway. I would be thrilled when this strange interlude in all of our lives was over. When we could have whatever interactions were left us once the dust of all this settled somewhere – anywhere – but here.

'What are you doing here?' Carolyn asked. If I'd been asked, I would have described her tone and expression as suspicious. Unduly suspicious, in fact. I blinked.

'What do you think I'm doing here?' I asked. More curiously than aggressively. Because surely there could only be one reason for my presence. The same old reason there'd always been.

'I can't imagine.' She sniffed. 'You told me to text you if he woke up, and he hasn't, so . . . ?'

I fought to keep myself from rolling my eyes, from playing further into this, from contributing to this mess in all the ways I could see, now, that I'd been doing from the start. The facts were very clear here. There was no getting around what Carolyn had done. If she felt guilty about it, well, she would have indicated that in some way by now. She hadn't. Ergo, my attempts to play the martyr so that *she* would be forced to feel bad were, at best, a whole lot of misplaced energy on my part.

'Mom said you were in New York with that Brooke person,' Carolyn continued, apparently totally unaware that I was having a breakthrough adult moment mere feet from her. 'No one expected you back for months. I thought the two of you would disappear into that little fantasy world of yours and stay there.'

I blinked again. 'There's a whole lot to unpack there,' I said slowly. 'And I'm not really up to the challenge. I think I'll just point out that you don't really know Brooke—'

'Are you checking up on me?' Carolyn demanded, cutting me off and taking a step closer. I saw that her hands were clenched into fists at her sides. 'Are you here to confirm all your worst impressions about me? Or is it that you honestly can't believe that I could ever do something that you did? That's it, isn't it?'

'I just got back into town, Carolyn.' I kept my voice low. I felt as if I'd accidentally ripped the lid off of some intense internal battle of hers, and the last thing I wanted was for it to bubble over and drown us both where we stood. 'I have no particular agenda here.'

'Bullshit.' If anything, her fists seemed to clench harder. Tighter. 'You wouldn't know how to take your next breath without an agenda!'

I raised my hands in the air. I also might have smirked, which definitely didn't help the situation. But I stepped away from her, which I thought made up for it.

'Okay,' I said in a soothing tone – a smirky soothing tone, I could admit. 'I think maybe you're having a blood sugar moment. You need to consider the possibility that I don't care about you or what you're doing at all. And that I came here purely to see how Tim is doing. That's my entire agenda, if I have one at all.'

'What the hell do you care?' she threw at me, her voice shaking, making me wonder how many imaginary fights she'd been having with me in my absence. 'You're the one who stormed out of here over a week ago. What? Did all that time in Manhattan reliving your glory days remind you that you had some unfinished business to take care of?'

I rocked back on my heels. I felt like her anger was some kind of hot wind, swirling over me and around me, but I didn't have to stand there and take it. I really didn't. I could ... step away from the weather. I didn't have to be the sort of person who scrapped with her sister in a hallway over the same man. I didn't have to live this trashy, skanky reality-show life, no matter if it happened to be mine. I could remove myself from this situation. Because who in their right mind would put up with this? I'd just seen what she was fighting for, very much against my will. But what was I doing here?

Besides, she had a point. If not the one she thought she had.

'As a matter of fact,' I said then, ignoring the mounting colour on her face and the murderous way she was looking at me – not even really caring about either, if I were honest – 'I do have some unfinished business. Thank you, Carolyn, for reminding me.'

And then I walked out of the hospital, climbed into the car, pointed it toward Vermont, and drove.

*

It was a remarkably easy, pretty drive.

After a quick stop at the house, I headed out of Rivermark, taking the back roads through old Dutch farmlands toward the famously tight curves of the Taconic Parkway. Eventually I headed east, leaving New York state behind and crossing over into Massachusetts. Once I hit Route 91 a little bit north of Springfield, I started the drive toward the great frozen north that was Vermont.

Goldilocks was going to check out one other life before she made her final decision about what to do about the one she had. One other discarded possibility. I owed it to myself, didn't I?

All around me stretched fields and farms, woods and hills, framed by pines and birches and open, empty branches on trees that looked cold and bare. The drive up was like a tour through my favourite Edith Wharton novel: stark farmhouses silhouetted against the winter, the frozen earth forbidding yet picturesque, and chimneys sketching faint hints of warmth and cheer against the sky. It was beautiful, of course, in that solitary way of winter, but it was also somehow exhilarating. As I raced along the ever lonelier stretch of highway, cutting through the heart of New England, I found myself singing along with the satellite radio. The day wore on and the light began to get thinner, colder even as it bounced back at me as bright as ever from the piles of snow at the sides of the road.

I knew the route by heart. I told myself that was because

it was simple, and because I'd always had a head for directions. Both of those things were true. Also true was the fact I hadn't been up here in a long time, but there was no forgetting the way, for some reason, as if the map were burned into my brain. Once I crossed the state border into Vermont I was about halfway there. I couldn't quite sit still.

I hadn't thought about Alec in so long. Brooke had indicated that she thought I wasn't being entirely honest about that, but I really hadn't. No idle imaginings. No late nights on the computer, innocently typing his name into Google. No random daydreams while I was going about my day-to-day life. I'd had strange phases where I'd thought about other old boyfriends – a rather overly optimistic term to use to describe some of the situations I'd subjected myself to in my college days and shortly thereafter, when I'd often mistaken smirks for signs of intelligent life where, sadly, none could hope to grow – but I hadn't thought about Alec. I hadn't *not* thought about him either – there wasn't some big blank spot in my memory that I tiptoed around or anything. I knew perfectly well that he was the doctor I'd dated as he'd finished his fellowship in New York, and before he'd left to work at a clinic in a war-torn African nation. But that was pretty much all I ever thought, on the few occasions I thought about him at all.

Yet here I was. Following a third-party text into the winter wonderland of Vermont, to drop in unexpectedly on a man who could, for all I knew, have a wife and six kids by now. In fact, it would be highly unlikely that he didn't.

I remembered, then, all those snooty Ivy League girls who'd crowded around him when I'd first met him, competing with each other over their impressive vocabularies and stylish glasses, with names like *Madeline* and *Elise*, who'd raised their eyebrows at me over their very intellectual black turtlenecks and murmured to Alec about the latest opera, the newest art exhibit, the exciting new literary *tome*. He had been like catnip for brainy girls back then, and I'd certainly had my share of insecurities about it, especially centred around his most significant ex-girlfriend, a nightmare made all of gazelle-like limbs and self-possession coupled with an array of degrees and complementary languages. And possibly a Fulbright thrown in there too, for good measure. *Audrey*, her name had been. Of course. Slightly off-beat, supernaturally confident and entirely too erudite by all accounts.

I'd never met her but God, I'd hated her.

I forced my attention back to the present and reminded myself that it didn't matter if Alec had in fact married the loathsome Audrey and if together they'd created a veritable Jolie–Pitt-like menagerie of international tots to call their very own. I was only conducting another deposition here. I was only looking for the significant facts of my own life. Not because I doubted my own memory, but because I didn't entirely trust it. And because I thought that having a different perspective on how I'd gotten here would make the fact that my life really *was* a bad afternoon talk show better somehow. Or different.

Anyway, it couldn't make it worse.

I pulled the car off the smooth expanse of 91 at the familiar exit. I followed the pretty little road into the tiny town, which consisted of no more than a gas station, a general store, a drugstore that was also a restaurant, and a grocery. Nothing had changed since the last time I'd been here, almost ten years ago. It was like driving into a painting. The winter shadows were starting to pull long, and the December sun seemed bigger and more golden as it made its way toward the trees. I turned off the main street and headed up into the rolling slope of hills. There were famous ski slopes not far in all directions, I knew, but this little town's only claim to fame was its picturesque New England charm. Which was considerable, to be sure.

I saw the farmhouse first. It sprawled across the hillside, the main building bright white even against the surrounding snow. There were two outbuildings: one which had once been a working barn and one which might still be working stables, for all I knew. I pulled the car into the cleared area in front of the house, sucked in a breath, and then climbed out.

It was impossibly quiet. And stunningly cold. I stood for a moment processing that, glad I'd changed into my winter boots again before leaving Rivermark earlier. I could hear the shiver of wind high in the branches of the trees all around me and in the darkening woods behind the house, and the faint melody of wind chimes, though I couldn't see the source. There was no traffic, no sound of any trains in the distance, nothing at all but snow and silence and what was left of the sun. I took a breath so deep it made my lungs hurt. Cold and sweet and clean straight down to the bone.

I climbed up the steps to the door and rang the bell. As I waited, I noted the beat-up old truck near the barn with snow piled up all over it and a dark-coloured Grand Cherokee closer to the farmhouse itself, that one scraped clean. But there were no sounds from inside. I shoved my hands in my pockets and rethought my plan, such as it was. As I stepped back off the porch, I couldn't help but take a moment to look at the view spread out before me: smudges of blue and green and a sea of sparkling frozen white in all directions. From halfway up the hillside there was nothing to see but the far hills and the woods all around, and the cosy town snuggled up on both sides of the river that cut along the valley floor. It was gorgeous. And down below the house there was a figure shovelling snow from the surface of what was, if memory served, a small pond in summertime. I must have driven right past it on my way to the house.

Past him.

I set off down the lane rather than take my chances on the field and in untouched snow that could, for all I knew, come up to my waist if I tried to walk on it. As I drew closer to the pond, the figure stopped shovelling, and waited. Watched me approach.

It occurred to me that what I was doing was actually, certifiably insane. Who dropped by unexpectedly to see an ex-boyfriend seven years later? No one who didn't also boil a bunny or two in her spare time. I knew better than this kind of behaviour. Every woman who'd survived her twenties knew better than this.

But it was too late.

I could see him now, and I was certain he could see me, too. I could feel it, like a kind of electric charge in the frigid air.

He rested his hands on the handle of the shovel as he watched me come closer. He wore his jacket open over an untucked flannel shirt, and his gloves were cocked back to show slivers of tanned skin at his strong wrists. His jeans looked a thousand years old, and were tucked carelessly into the tops of his boots. He was still that same rangy kind of lean. His mouth was still serious in a way that made me want to lick it, though I hated myself for the thought, and his dark eyes were still so clever, so fascinating, as they took me in. His hair was on the shaggy side today, a riot of colours like an experiment in shades of *tawny*, and disarmingly haphazard. Pay too much attention to his often-silly hair, I knew, and you might find yourself blindsided by the thrust of his intellect. It was one among his many weapons.

I stepped onto the cleared ice of the pond. At the other

end, he tossed down his shovel, and started toward me. As he moved, he pulled off his gloves, one and then the other, and then shoved them both in the pockets of his open parka.

It was still so quiet. It felt something like ominous, so at odds was it with the tumult inside me and the alarms that blared there, the riot of sound and fury I wanted to pretend wasn't happening.

Off in the distance, a dog barked enthusiastically, and it sounded far too intrusive against the blanket of noise-lessness: almost shocking. I wanted to look and see what it was barking at – to look away, at anything else, at anything at all but him – but I couldn't seem to move so much as a muscle. There was only Alec, all these years later, walking towards me in that way of his, so distract-ingly loose-limbed with that suggestion of athletic ease in every step. There was only that same impossibly intel-ligent face of his, older now, more weathered, but still entirely too compelling.

I fought to speak. To explain my presence somehow, in a way that played down the obvious crazy and possibly made some kind of sense out of it. But my mind was a blank.

He stopped right in front of me, and I had to tilt my head back to look at him. He was still tall enough to make my heart beat a little faster, and he looked down at me as if I was a ghost. But not the kind of ghost I'd thought I was before, in Rivermark. Not like that at all. He looked at me as if I were something he'd gone to the trouble to conjure up himself, just him and perhaps his Ouija board, and now here I was, like a spell that had finally worked the way it was supposed to.

Hours could have passed. Ages. I was aware only of him, and my pulse racketing through my body, and the way his dark eyes seemed to kick up fires inside me that I didn't want to admit could still burn at all, much less so hot. So high and bright.

Say something! I ordered myself desperately. *Anything!*

But his serious mouth crooked up in the corner, and his dark eyes gleamed. And I could no more have spoken then than I could have leapt straight into the air and flown around the moon that was visible despite the daylight, high up over the nearest tree. I didn't even want to speak, suddenly. I didn't want to do anything but this, this drinking him in as if I were so terribly thirsty, unaware that there was a world around us.

'Took you long enough,' Alec said, in the voice I remembered, rough and soft all at once, that always hit me in places that made me blush.

Which I did. I couldn't seem to help it. Or, to be honest, care too much that I was turning red beneath his scrutiny.

And then he reached over, slid his hand over my jaw and into my hair with a gentle intent, tugged me closer, and kissed me.

12

It was as if no time had passed at all.

He kissed me as if we were both drowning and he was air, and I fell into him, against him, and didn't even try to swim.

I just fell.

He tasted the way he always had, so male and right and *Alec*. My hands looped around his neck, skin touching skin, and it was a revelation. I moved closer to him without knowing I meant to do it. But I couldn't help myself. I couldn't stop. He angled his mouth against mine, making it all that much hotter. Deeper.

And I felt it again. The way the world rocked and tilted, knocking me off-balance. Right off my feet, even as he held me against him with such ease. As if I belonged there.

It had always been like this. Heat. Fire. All that impossible light. And no hope at all of balance.

Finally, I pulled away, appalled at myself. I couldn't lie to myself, either, though I wanted to – I hadn't stood there passively, allowing him to kiss me. Nor had I pushed him away. I'd been in it. Too in it, really. I'd kissed him back as if I wasn't, in fact, married to someone else. Who cared what the extenuating circumstances were? I'd ceded the moral high ground, and I hadn't even paused for the scantest second to consider the ramifications of that.

Even so, it was harder than it should have been to pull my hands away from the heat of his skin. He didn't pretend it was easy either; his thumb traced a pattern across my cheek, then grazed along the curve of my lip, before he dropped his hand to his side.

'Well,' I said. My voice sounded absurd against the quiet, in the wake of all that wild, roaring passion that still hummed through me. Too high. Too foolish. 'Um. Hi.'

He let out a breath that became a kind of laugh, and his eyes crinkled up in the corners, though he didn't quite smile. Not serious, dedicated Alec. Not even now. He scraped his mess of hair back from his face with one hand, and *looked* at me from those clever eyes of his that saw far more than their share. I felt my face redden. Again. Still. I felt my whole body react to him, so predictably, as if that damned gaze of his was hotwired directly into my flesh and could turn me on like a gas fire. I could feel it in my breasts. My sex. My heart as it knocked hard against my chest.

'Come on,' he said, indicating the farmhouse on the rise above us with a tilt of his head, with no hint that he was as affected as I was. And with that familiar air of command and the expectation of obedience that was so much a part of the big, bad, Dr Frasier I remembered. 'It's cold.'

I stared at him, nonplussed. And off-balance, again. As usual. *As ever.* I'd always told myself that if I kept being knocked off-balance like this, that eventually he'd knock me back *into* balance, surely. But it had never happened.

'Aren't you going to ask me why I'm here?' I demanded. 'Aren't you going to point out that it's bat-shit crazy to show up at your parents' house, a couple of days before Christmas, after more than seven years of radio silence?'

'I could,' he said, his voice that lazy, amused drawl that had always had this same effect on me – that had always made my limbs a bit too heavy and my breath a bit too shallow. 'But you just did it for me.'

It should have felt like a slap. But instead, I smiled. Almost in spite of myself.

We walked back up the road together. I felt . . . too big. As if my clothes didn't fit. As if I was bloated up, expanded, and everything might just burst from the pressure. It was uncomfortable. It made me feel panicky. It made me want to forget about all of this. It made me want to climb back in the car and run away from here, from him, before I *really* made a mistake. A bigger one.

But the only thing crazier than driving for five hours on the twenty-third of December to see an ex-boyfriend you hadn't so much as spoken to in over seven years was, I was all too aware, seeing that ex-boyfriend, kissing him like he was my long-lost love, and then leaping back in my car and driving off like a madwoman ten minutes later.

So I followed him into the house instead. He pulled off his boots and coat in the little entryway, and I followed suit. Then, our feet clad only in socks, we made our way across the honey-coloured wooden floors in the friendly family room to the huge kitchen. Something about being in my socks made me feel vulnerable, somehow. As if my shoes were defensive weapons I'd handed over without adequately considering the ways in which I might need them. As if my toes being visible in the middle of winter would tell him things I didn't want him to know.

He moved around the kitchen with that efficiency and grace that I discovered I still found entirely too attractive. I settled myself gingerly on one of the stools next to the granite counter at the kitchen island. He poured me a big mug of coffee and then slapped down a carton of hazelnut creamer beside it, without asking or even really looking at me. When he brought over his own mug and leaned against the counter across from me, he also slid a packet of sweetener and a spoon over my way.

I stared at all this evidence that he remembered exactly how I liked my coffee, and that he was as sure of himself as ever, and I wanted nothing to do with the strange set of internal explosions that detonated in response. I pressed my lips together, as if I were bracing myself, or afraid of what I might say without meaning to speak, and then went about adding the creamer and sweetener.

'Where are your parents?' I asked. There was so much of a ruckus inside me that I'd forgotten it was completely silent in the house, and my voice sounded much too loud. Almost brash. I let my spoon clank against the side of my mug as if that could divert attention from the echo of my question.

'Florida.' He cupped his own mug in his hands, but he still looked at me with those dark, knowing eyes. He'd never been much for small talk, as I recalled. Too busy being brilliant and focused and completely impossible. I should have hated that. I never had.

'And what about your sister?' I realized as I asked it that I probably shouldn't have. The last thing in the world I wanted to do was open the conversation with sisters. It could only lead to Carolyn and her numerous trespasses against me, which was not a subject I wanted to dive right into with anyone. Much less Alec.

'Still lives here in the village. Happily, as far as I can tell.'

He looked at me. He waited. He was, I could see, not at all fooled by this little sidebar into the pleasantries. I told myself I found that irritating.

'And saving the world?' I asked, aware that my voice was a little strained, then. 'How's that going?'

He smirked then, in his smart-assed way. It was an edgy sort of curve of his mouth that did things to my equilibrium. Dangerous things.

'Brooke told me you were married a few years back,' he said, instead of answering my question. Cutting to the chase, I supposed, and who could blame him? 'I guess I forgot that when I saw you. I'm sorry if I overstepped any boundaries.'

He couldn't have sounded less sorry if he'd tried. Or more arrogant. Two things which should have made me find him wholly unattractive, yet did not. And I was fairly sure he knew it.

'Don't be silly,' I said dryly. 'I assumed you greet everyone that way these days, since you're so warm and fuzzy. The postman, the guy who bags your groceries . . .'

'I'm a popular guy,' he agreed, his eyes gleaming, his tone sardonic.

The moment pulled taut between us. I could feel the tension of it, shimmering between us and resonating deep within me. I didn't want to feel this. This wasn't why I'd come here. I'd wanted to talk to him, remember him. Not relive him. Didn't I?

'My marriage is in a tricky place,' I blurted out, succumbing to Alec's kind of kamikaze truth-telling within minutes, like an amateur. 'I'm kind of investigating how I made the choices I did, how I came to this particular point in my life, and how it all ended up this way. Where it is now, I mean.'

'Is that like following breadcrumbs through the woods?' he asked in a mild tone that didn't fool me at all. 'Doesn't that usually end up with someone's head in the oven?'

'Happily, you're a doctor,' I said, smiling thinly at him. 'I'm sure we'll both be safe.'

'Depends on your definition of safe,' he replied. But I must have given him a look, because he shifted, his dark eyes flashing and his mouth taking on that sardonic cast. 'What clues did you follow to my particular gingerbread house? Or is this a different fairy tale altogether?'

'I'm trying to answer a few questions for myself, that's all,' I assured him. 'Like, why did I choose the kind of law I practise? Why did I choose to live in one place rather than another? No trolls under the bridge to worry about.'

'Not for me, anyway.'

The way he looked at me then made me wish there was more space between us – more room to breathe. I tried to keep my expression smooth, but it wasn't easy when he looked at me like that, so darkly arrogant and amused in some way I imagined I wouldn't like.

'Why did you choose to work in a corporate law firm rather than come with me to Africa?' he asked. I stared at him. He stared back, giving no quarter, his dark gaze like a weapon, and then his brows arched. 'For example.'

'For example,' I agreed. My throat felt scraped dry.

I took a sip of the perfect coffee, exactly how I loved it, and wondered if he could see how hard my pulse was pounding, how close to dizzy I felt, that I was simply throwing all these things on the table in front of him as if they didn't mean anything to me. As if it didn't mortally wound me, on some level, to admit to Alec of all people that the man who I'd decided was much better for me than he was maybe wasn't so great after all. As if this really were a deposition and I the cool, calm, collected lawyer I wished I'd ever been around him.

'I think if I could answer that question in particular,' he said, his eyes never leaving mine, daring me to look away from him, a note of steel in his voice, 'if I'd ever been able to answer it, you wouldn't have to be asking it now.'

That went through me hard, leaving marks. I sat back on the stool, as far back as I could without falling off onto the floor, and wondered what the hell I'd been smoking when I'd decided this was a good idea. But I hadn't decided so much as reacted, had I? Carolyn had made me angry again – the scene I'd inadvertently interrupted had simply hurt more than I'd been able to handle – and I'd leapt headlong into this. Maybe someday I would learn the value of calm, cool reflection before action where this man was concerned. I could only dream.

'It's good to see you,' he said instead of elaborating on anything. Instead of following any of the unspoken pieces of our old relationship that hovered around us now down into their various dark places. Another man might have sounded sweetly nostalgic when he said something like that. But not Alec. He sounded entirely too sure of himself, as ever. And with that crack of temper beneath it. His eyes gleamed, as if he could read my mind. 'I mean that.'

The chaos inside me reached some kind of boiling point

then, and I couldn't take it. I slid off the stool and onto my feet, wincing slightly when they slapped against the floor with far more force than I'd intended.

'This is so crazy,' I said, shaking my head as if I could shrug this all off. Or rewind, somehow, until I was sitting quietly in my house and had never leapt in the car to come here. 'I've gone completely nuts, haven't I?' As if this was some silly whim, some funny story I could tell my friends later while howling with laughter about the wackiness of the adventure, the madcap hilarity. Instead of what it really was, which was a colossal and potentially very painful mistake. 'I think maybe I need to seek out some psychiatric help, not an ex-boyfriend. Wrong kind of doctor, ha ha ... I am so sorry. I should never have come up here and tried to force you into this—'

'Sarah.'

And I stopped talking.

Because oh, the way he said my name. The way it sounded in his mouth.

It had always been like this. He had always managed to make such a simple, ordinary name sound like some kind of complicated melody, even when he said it like he did then. Like an order he expected me to obey.

'You didn't drive all the way up here to run out the door the moment things get a little tense.' He shrugged in that supremely unconcerned, masculine way of his that simultaneously annoyed me and made me wish ... all kinds of things I refused to acknowledge. 'Did you?'

So challenging. With a hint of impatience, too. Like he was a little bit bored and had to be in surgery five minutes ago and how dare I hold him up with my waffling? There was clearly something wrong with me that I found that kind of endearing.

'Maybe I did,' I said.

'Then you should have done it years ago,' he said in that same offhand, just this side of openly mocking way, 'so we could be past this shit by now.'

Because Alec never cared if things got too intense, too dark, too anything. In fact, he encouraged it. He only insisted that it all be *honest*. If that sounded easy, it wasn't. It was *easy* to be honest about whether or not you liked white chocolate – that was a yes or no question. It was more complicated when the kind of honesty he wanted was the kind you hid from inside yourself. But I'd known that, hadn't I?

I breathed in. Out. I let the riot inside settle. I blinked back the heat threatening to spill from the backs of my eyes.

'I couldn't have come years ago, unfortunately,' I heard myself say, in such a matter-of-fact, scarily *precise* sort of way. 'Years ago, I thought I was happily married. Years ago, I had yet to walk in on my husband having sex with my sister. So.'

Alec looked at me for what felt like a long time. I stared back, not at all comfortable with the things I worried he could see, but what was the point of hiding them? I'd already showed my hand. There was no appearing out of nowhere all these years later and then trying to be cagey.

He straightened from the counter eventually, and wordlessly motioned for me to precede him into the big family room. I did, happy to have a little break from all of that intense scrutiny. I took in the high, exposed beams and the large fireplace dominating the far wall. The happy art, the warm colours. I set my coffee on the nearest table and sat down in one of the comfortable-looking armchairs, curling my legs up beneath me. I watched as he threw some logs into the fire and quickly, competently, got a blaze going. The man was still so very good with his hands. When he was done, he dusted those capable hands of his off on his jeans and threw himself down on the couch near my chair.

'Are you going to stop staring at me in all this ponderous silence?' I asked. His mouth didn't move, but those dark eyes filled with laughter.

'I'm adjusting my ego,' he said, in a tone that suggested he was doing nothing of the kind. And besides, I knew his ego all too well. It was far too impressive and extensive to suffer any minor dents. 'My fantasies tended to feature you appearing before me because you'd seen the error of your ways, not because you'd seen the error of someone else's and thought I'd make a good consolation prize.'

'I take it back.' I met his gaze and managed to keep from rolling my eyes. 'I think I prefer the ponderous silence, thank you.'

'I'm glad you felt you could come here,' he said after a moment, and it was the kindness threaded into his usually darker tone that killed me.

I knew he meant it. I knew that even if he was taking some measure of satisfaction in the state of my marriage, as anyone would, he also meant what he said or he wouldn't have said it at all. That was Alec in a nutshell. I'd never known him to lie. About anything. Not to be polite and not even when it might have helped him out of a tough spot. Not ever.

And for some reason, the fact that he was still so completely and unassailably *him*, so ornery and beautiful and arrogant and kind, just as he'd been all those years ago, when I wasn't at all sure what was left of me, made that great sadness I'd been so determined to deny well up inside of me. It was like a flash flood of sensation, washing through me and over me until, to my absolute horror, I started to cry. And cry.

And *cry*.

I tried to hide my face in my hands, but I was still entirely too aware of him – entirely too aware that I had just tipped over the edge from maybe kind of amusingly crazy to full-on psycho. And there was nothing I could do to stop it. I sobbed and sobbed, crying out all those pieces of my broken heart, Tim and Carolyn, my parents, those lost years without Brooke and yes, Alec. Too many pieces to name or even appropriately categorize, such a mess of them there were, and I couldn't do anything about it but ride it out.

I sensed more than saw him move, and then those capable hands of his were on me, and before I could react, he lifted me up, turned around, then sat down and settled me on his lap. I should have leaped off of him as if I were electrocuted. I should have dived for safety. I should have immediately pulled myself together and removed myself from this kind of close contact with him, draped across his lap like some kind of small, broken thing that only he could fix.

But instead, I leaned into him as if he really was as safe as he felt, let him hold me close like he still cared, and even though I knew I shouldn't, I just . . . let go.

When I finally stopped crying all over him, when I was wrung out entirely and my face felt like very old parchment or some kind of recently unearthed archaeological artifact, I finally gained the presence of mind to understand how awkward and foolish it was to be tucked up in my ex-boyfriend's lap. I was no better than Tim. Who'd had, at one point, a very serious sensitivity to Brooke's deliberate and consistent mentions of *Saint Alec, the fucking healer*. Tim's phrase, not mine.

I peeled myself off his chest and carted myself away to the downstairs bathroom with a haste that I might have called undignified, had my previous behaviour not already made a mockery of the very word. I was thankful he miraculously managed to keep himself from saying something cutting and/or mocking as I went. I stared in the tiny little mirror over the sink and quickly understood that no amount of cold water in the world, not even cold water in December in *Vermont*, was going to repair the damage this crying jag had done to my face. And there was no point cataloguing the mess inside, thank you. I was going to have to live with the swollen, watery eyes and the stuffed-up head, to say nothing of the great swathe of broken-ness within, and I accepted that inevitability as one more hit in a long tragic line of them.

Of course I had just treated Dr Alec Frasier like my personal wailing wall. *Of course* I had chosen to do this after all this time, after he'd kissed me, after I'd taken it upon myself to descend upon him like his very own Dickens-worthy Ghost of Christmas Past.

Of course.

I felt almost philosophical about it. I'd been doing so well, all things considered. There'd been the insomnia and the blue hoodie from hell, and certainly there'd been the unpleasant tension and fighting with Carolyn and my parents, but the truth was, I was long overdue for a good and ugly breakdown. It was a rite of passage for any soon-to-be-divorced woman, surely. I was actually kind of impressed with myself for making sure my version of a breakdown involved collateral damage – and not just any collateral damage. Oh no. I'd chosen to drive five hours out of my way to lose my shit in front of the only person on earth who I really, *really* wanted to go on thinking my life was a beautiful and perfect dream without him.

Well done, Sarah, I thought, too disgusted with myself to even really take the appropriately scathing tone in my own head. But it was implied. The whole situation implied it.

There wasn't even any point hiding in the bathroom. There was no containing this disaster. It had already happened. The mushroom cloud hung directly over me and there was no disguising it.

'I kind of want to kill myself,' I announced as I walked back into the living room. I stood near the stairs that wound up to the second floor, as if too little distance too late would help somehow. Alec still sat in the chair where I'd left him, propping up his chin with one hand, his long legs stretched out in front of him, and no doubt very, very soggy.

'Please don't,' he replied idly, his gaze flicking over me. 'The ground outside is too frozen. I'd have to either cremate you in the fireplace or put you on ice in the barn and wait for spring. Neither of which feels particularly Christmassy to me.' He considered. 'And anyway, I'll be in Africa by the time it thaws around here, so it could all get very smelly.'

I would have said that I would never smile again, but I smiled then, however anaemically.

'You're still as creepy as you ever were,' I pointed out. 'I really appreciate the unsavoury little details, Alec. The *smelly* part, particularly.'

He stood up then, and I found that unduly alarming.

Like it meant he was about to *do* something. I didn't even know what that might have been, but it hit that panic button in me anyway.

'I have to go,' I said, the smile toppling from my face. 'Right now.'

'You can't,' he replied, his tone perfectly mild. As *mild* was not a word I would ever choose to describe this man, I paused.

'That was less of an invitation to debate, and more of a statement of intent,' I said. But I didn't move towards the door.

'I get that.' He shrugged, with far too much easy confidence. 'But you can't go now. Obviously.'

'Why not?' I sighed. 'If you have some expectation of further dramatic displays from the crazy person in your house, I think that I'm all tapped out. It's time to take the three-ring circus back home where it belongs.'

'You appeared out of nowhere and cried all over me,' Alec pointed out, that glint in his dark eyes that had never boded well for my self-control, and why should this be any exception? 'I think that at the very least, you owe me dinner.'

We looked at each other for a moment. Behind him, the fire crackled and popped. I felt a sense of lightness that made no sense, given the circumstances. Maybe I really was as crazy as I was acting.

'You feel like you already put out, and you want a little payback?' I asked. 'Is that it?'

'Exactly.' His mouth crooked slightly. 'I'm a whore like that.'

Which was how I ended up pushing a trolley around the adorable little grocery store in the pretty clapboard and Christmas-lighted downtown, Alec roaming along beside me, in a painful enactment of domesticity that, on some level, I thought was a greater betrayal of my marriage vows than that earlier kiss had been. Men liked to concentrate on physical betrayals, which I hadn't really understood until now, with blue blouses and doggy-style porno on an endless loop in my head, but women knew how treacherous non-physical things could be. Like the intimacy inherent in arguing over brands of tomato paste, in gathering ingredients together for a meal we planned to make and share, or in choosing the perfect loaf of crusty French bread to complement it. I was too aware of Alec's every movement, his every breath. I could anticipate exactly where he would be when he was next to me, how he would shift down an aisle or reach for something on a shelf. We walked through the store together, making the idlest of conversation, simply *fitting*, and I understood that I had been lying to myself about my marriage for a very long time.

Like so many truly shattering things, this realization only swelled in me, making room for itself, and then stayed there, like a bell that couldn't be un-rung. I didn't want any part of it. I didn't even want to think it, but there it was.

'Who's that?' I asked to distract myself from what was happening inside me, nodding toward a bundled-up woman near the canned vegetables, who was waving. Not at me, clearly. Alec scowled in her direction, reminding me how difficult he was and always had been. As a matter of course.

'How should I know?'

'Because you were born here?' I raised my eyebrows at him. 'Because you lived here your entire life?' A suspicion dawned. 'Alec, is that one of your relatives?'

He actually grinned then, however fleetingly.

'I'm not an animal, Sarah,' he said with a hint of offended dignity that the way he was looking down at me contradicted.

'Are you sure?' I asked. 'Because you're a little bit feral. I say that as a friend.'

'I greet my family members,' he said. 'That's not a family member.' But he eyed the woman again as he strode towards the cash register, and his mouth curved. 'I think.'

Later, I sat on a stool again as Alec moved around the kitchen, putting together the meal with that same masculine grace that made me feel so embarrassingly weak. Not that there was much further to go where embarrassment was concerned. I found that truth oddly liberating.

'I thought I was supposed to cook,' I said, as he poured a glass of red wine and handed it to me. 'Doesn't you doing the cooking defeat the whole purpose?'

'Symbolically, maybe,' he said. 'But I'm a much better cook than you are.'

I sniffed. 'You don't actually have enough information to make that assessment. You've missed years in which, for all you know, I could have become a stunning gourmet, capable of anything.'

He took a swig of wine from his glass. He eyed me.

'Did you?'

'No.'

'Then drink your wine and shut up,' he suggested.

So that's what I did.

And then, when whatever ridiculously savoury stew he'd thrown together was bubbling away in the oven, making culinary magic that I could already smell, rosemary and garlic and all things mouthwatering, he pulled up the stool next to me and focused all that attention and intensity of his on me again. Dark eyes and that serious mouth, too close and too knowing. I repressed a shiver.

'So,' I said nervously. 'Dating anyone?'

'Cute diversionary tactic.' That mouth of his didn't so much as crook toward a smile this time. 'Think it will work?'

'Are we pretending that you're some kind of monk?' I asked, blustering along as if we could sidestep our entire history and relationship and act like beer buddies propping up some sports bar somewhere. Well, I could, certainly. I waved my hand at all of his glory. 'Please. As if.'

'I'm not a monk.'

I didn't love the way he said that, with all of that carnal

knowledge lurking there in that low tone and that look in his eyes.

'Of course you're not.'

Why had I started this conversation again? Maybe he could whip out his phone next and show me pictures of all his many conquests over the past seven-plus years. Naked, one could only hope. Maybe there was even an old Audrey series, featuring her in fetching poses with her towering intellect on display!

Maybe I really should have killed myself when I'd had the chance.

'It's going to be a while until dinner's ready,' Alec said. He shifted on his stool, and I had the sense that he got bigger somehow. That he took up more space. I swallowed, too hard.

'I thought maybe you could tell me why you were so determined not to go to Africa with me.' He reached over and tapped my hand with his, as if to underscore his point. As if it needed underscoring. 'I was in love with you,' he said, the way I imagined he might inform a patient they had something infectious: matter-of-fact yet vaguely compassionate. 'I thought you were in love with me. Was I wrong about that?'

That was Alec. I should have remembered that there was no escaping the brutal truth with him. Not for long.

'There's a lot of water under the bridge,' I began, because I had to try to avoid it, futile as that might have been. My heart wasn't really in the attempt.

'Which you drove right over when you pulled into my driveway,' he said, as I supposed I knew he would. 'This isn't a fight, Sarah. It was a long time ago.'

'It was a big fight then, though.' I wrinkled up my nose at the memory. 'A giant, no-holds-barred, scorched-earth fight, in fact.'

'Because you left me.' His dark eyes flashed, and I felt it. I felt it like a punch in the gut. Long time ago or not. 'Which was not what I wanted, in case you've forgotten.'

I looked away, back at my wine glass, and wondered why I'd thought I would ever want to do something like this. A years-later postmortem that felt far more like an exhumation. What was left of who we'd been but skeletal remains? We weren't even those same people any more. We would never be those people again.

Even if he could still kiss me like that. Like nothing else in the world, before or since, could ever matter.

I shoved that aside and ordered myself to *think*.

'Our entire relationship had an expiration date, from our very first date,' I said slowly, trying to think back, trying to separate out all the things I'd decided were true about that searing year with him after it was over, and what I'd actually, honestly believed while it was happening. It was all a jumble inside me, though, with that realization from earlier hanging over all of it like a dark, brooding cloud. 'I remember being so aware of that. I always knew you were going to leave. You never made any secret of it.'

'Then it shouldn't have been so traumatic when it was

time for me to go.' His voice was still so matter-of-fact. His gaze very nearly cold, as if discussing this didn't bother him at all. I almost believed it. 'It shouldn't have been like a bomb going off.'

'You could have stayed,' I pointed out, so very evenly. So calmly. The way I imagined someone should talk about a very painful thing that had happened so long ago it had long since ceased to matter. It was purely academic, this discussion. Another deposition that didn't – shouldn't – involve my feelings. That hardly involved *me*. 'But you never considered it.'

'You could have come with me,' he replied, his gaze intense. Or maybe I was the one who simply *felt* intense. 'But *you* never considered it.'

'And look at that.' I shook my head slightly to ward off the strange feelings I kept telling myself I wasn't feeling, the pull and push of memories and never-quite-forgotten agonies. 'It's like déjà vu.' He looked down at the counter top and I could *feel* the same old argument in him, rolling out of him, thundering right beneath the surface. 'What would I have done in Africa, Alec?' I asked, rather than waiting for him to erupt. 'Hold your scalpel? Carry your backpack as I trotted along beside you? That wasn't what I wanted from my life. You know it.'

'And what you have now,' he asked softly, still not looking at me, and neither of those things disguised the way the words cut into me, 'is that what you wanted? Was it worth it?'

'Fuck you.' I didn't say it particularly strongly or loudly, but it hurt anyway. I might as well have screamed it. I jumped off of the stool and put the kitchen island between us, but it wasn't enough. Almost eight years hadn't been enough, I thought then, wildly; what hope was there for some granite and a few cabinets? 'You don't know anything about my life.'

'That wasn't a judgement.' He crossed his arms over his chest and watched me, dark eyes glittering, so dangerous and male and *focused*. 'It was a question.'

'You wanted me to move across the world with you,' I said, very distinctly, as if there were a bullet-pointed list inside me that had been there in some hidden compartment all this time, and here it was, ready to go on cue, 'but you refused to make any kind of commitment. I would have had to have been an idiot to do something like that, and I considered it anyway. I really did. But come on.'

'I was in love with you,' he said, incredulously. With that bite beneath. 'What more of a commitment did you want than that?'

'Really?' I couldn't help the sarcastic tone. I didn't even try to help it.

'I don't believe in marriage.' That was even more like déjà vu. That same old sentence. It echoed in me like a very familiar, profoundly shitty gong, and made me feel just as horrible as I could remember feeling back then. Again, that temper crackled in his dark gaze. 'You know that. You even know why.'

'Well, now you know why I didn't go to Africa,' I said, perhaps too flippantly. I didn't want to think about his parents' disastrous yet continuing marriage, the one that had messed him up about the institution forever. I didn't want to feel sympathetic. I didn't want to care. I shrugged. 'I'm sorry if that's as unintelligible to you as your marriage aversion is to me. I didn't tell you not to feel that way, you know. I just didn't want to spend my life banging my head against that particular wall, battling malaria and political unrest for the rest of *your* career, exactly as you wanted it. And who cares what I might have wanted?'

He looked at me for a long moment, and if possible, his gaze got even darker, even harder. I pretended it didn't bother me. I pretended I couldn't feel it, tying my stomach into knots.

I pretended I just wanted to keep talking, that I wasn't a little bit afraid of what he might say next.

'You don't make promises,' I said, gentling my voice. Finding that reasonable tone inside of me and grabbing onto it. Trying to pull it around me like a cloak. 'I needed them. In the end, I think it was just that simple.'

'I don't make promises I can't keep,' he corrected me, his voice rougher then. Deeper. Hinting at a world of pain, of emotion, that I didn't want to acknowledge. Temper was almost easier. 'I never have. And you knew that.'

Whatever moved in me then was spiked and remarkably painful, and it made it hard to breathe. God, the things I didn't want to know. Or feel. But right behind it came a great rush of my own temper, galloping through me, sweeping everything else away. And for a moment, it felt a lot like *clean*.

'Have you been sitting around mourning me all this time, Alec?' I laughed as I said it. I wanted to fight, I didn't want to feel. I didn't even know why. 'Rending a garment or two? Weeping all over your patients? I find that hard to believe. When I met you there was a sea of women around you, and it wasn't like they went away when we started dating, either. Do you really want to act like you've spent all this time racked with agony over something that ended—'

'Says the woman who showed up on my doorstep and then sobbed in my arms for an hour,' he interjected, cutting me off that easily. He might as well have picked up one of his knives from the block in front of him and chopped me off at the knees. 'I'm not going to forget reality because you poke at me, Sarah. Though you're welcome to try, if that's what gets you off.'

I definitely didn't want to stand in front of Alec thinking about what *got me off*. There was nowhere that could go that wouldn't make everything that much more complicated. *That much worse*, I corrected myself sharply.

'I didn't come here to fight with you,' I said then, but it felt like a concession, and I wasn't sure why. Or even why that mattered.

'Okay.' He eyed me in that infuriating way of his, all dark intent and ingrained male confidence. 'We don't have to talk about ancient history.' I didn't trust the way he looked at me then, as if he were reading all kinds of things in me I wouldn't want to share with him or anyone if I could help it. 'Why exactly did you come here today, with all of your fucking breadcrumbs? What did you think I could tell you? Why don't we start with that.'

13

We stared at each other.

I hated the fact that he'd read my desire to fight with him so easily. And then undercut it. I hated that a lot. I hated that it made me face that unpleasant urge inside me, rather than prodding him into some show of temper that I could use to make myself feel better. *At least I'm not so* angry *all the time*, I'd used to think smugly when I'd managed to provoke him. As if that were a badge of honour. Or even true.

The kitchen seemed darker, closer, and I realized that whenever the sun had gone down outside, I'd missed it, too busy overturning rocks I probably should have left untouched in our shared history. But now it was already night, I was trapped in this house with Alec, and there was no one to blame for any of this but me.

He watched me as I stood there across from him, resting my hands on the countertop. There was something simmering in him, something darker and thicker than the tone of voice he'd just used suggested . . .

And then I understood.

'You're angry with me,' I said after a moment. 'You're actually *pissed* at me. That's what that look is.'

He didn't deny that he had *that look*, whatever that was. 'You say that like you're surprised.'

'Of course I am.'

'Are you really?' He shook his head, impatience exuding from him. 'I don't believe you've suddenly become so naïve in the past few years, Sarah. Of course I'm pissed. Not actively. It doesn't keep me up at night these days. But you broke up with me.' His mouth curved slightly, but it wasn't a smile. It was too sharp for that. 'I was in love with you. You broke my heart and it took me a long time to get over that.'

I blinked. Then again. 'Oh.'

Of all the lame things to say. But I didn't know how to process that. I knew he'd been unhappy when we'd broken up – we'd both been unhappy. I'd been so unhappy, according to Brooke, that I'd changed my entire life to be sure I never felt that way again. Yet even so, I wouldn't have said he'd been *that* miserable. I wouldn't have even said that he'd been broken-hearted by the decision I'd made. Nor would I ever have imagined that he would tell me so, all these years later.

Alec was the kind of man that women lined up to ruin themselves over. He was the ultimate unattainable, *not the marrying kind, flight already booked to far-off Africa* kind of guy. He was difficult and sardonic and entirely too serious for his own good; he had no time for games or subtleties, and that obviously meant that the ladies prostrated themselves in front of him in the hope they could be the one to change him. That we'd been together a whole year had seemed impossible at the time. It had certainly never seemed remotely likely that someone like me, in the wake of a series of Audrey-like creatures, every one of them ethereal and as unreachable as he was, could possibly affect *him*.

'Yeah,' he said softly now, with that undercurrent of steel beneath that made me shift from one foot to the other. 'Oh.'

I didn't seem to have anything to say to that. My ears felt as if they were buzzing slightly, or maybe I was seeking distraction from the way he was looking at me. I swallowed, and looked down at my hands instead. My wedding rings were still there: the diamond solitaire Tim had given me in those snowy woods so many Christmases ago now and the platinum band that matched it. It hadn't occurred to me to take them off in all this time. I'd assumed Tim was coming back. Despite all evidence to the contrary, I'd been so sure of it. Until today. Staring at my rings, I realized that what I'd seen in that hospital room this morning changed everything. That was why I was here, wasn't it? That was why I'd let Alec kiss me like that. That was why I was standing here still, talking about our long-dead relationship again, as if it still mattered.

That was why I'd finally understood the truth about Tim and me in that tiny little grocery store, as little as I wanted to admit that to myself.

'And now here you are, marriage on the rocks, showing up on my doorstep like my very own Christmas present, wanting to know what happened back then to lead you down the path you took. The path you didn't want to take with me.' Alec's mouth crooked up in the corner, and once again, I was aware it was no smile.

'That's me,' I said, deciding to go with bravado, because what else did I have tonight? I'd clearly left grace and dignity by the side of the highway. 'I'm like your personal Santa Claus. Ho ho ho.'

'But what do you *want*?' His clever face hardened then, and his voice did too. 'I know you don't want me, because you already left me once and let's face it, my life isn't any different now. I didn't start hungering for a wedding ring while battling AIDS, poverty and the effects of a hundred endless wars over there. I didn't decide that what I really wanted from life was a Norman Rockwell practice in some sweet little town like this one, dispensing lollipops and tugging on pigtails. I'm the same man you walked away from eight years ago.'

'Exactly the same?' I asked, keeping my voice cool, telling myself I'd pick through all those landmines later, when it was safe. When he wasn't watching me and cataloguing my reaction. 'No change at all in almost a decade? That's a little scary, isn't it? Maybe you need some psychological help.'

'The general package is the same,' he amended, a grudging sort of amusement in his gaze. 'Same career. Same philosophy on life that you didn't really love. Otherwise, I guess I've mellowed.'

'You? Mellow?' I laughed. 'That's exactly how I'd describe you, Alec. Completely relaxed and at ease. Lazy, even.'

'Did you drive all the way up here to avoid the question?' His voice was like a whip and I felt the lash of it on my skin. 'To pretend? That seems like a waste of everyone's time. And by that I mean mine.'

I blew out a breath, not feeling entirely steady. I glared at him, mostly because I knew he was right. If I'd wanted shallow, social conversation, there were any number of people in Rivermark who could accommodate me. I had no shortage of acquaintances. Great for parties and a coffee out, but certainly not worth a long drive and all of this soul-searching.

Stop being such a coward, I ordered myself.

'I loved Tim because he was the antithesis of you,' I said after a moment. If he wanted cards on the table, I could do that. God help us both. 'He made plans. He wanted a future. He asked me to marry him on the third date.'

'A paragon of virtue, indeed.' Alec made a noise I couldn't quite categorize, and those dark eyes were narrow on mine. 'Tim? That's his name?'

'I get that you think that marriage is juvenile. That it's unnecessary.' I shrugged, a sharp sort of jerk of my shoulder, as if I were warding him off. 'But it was necessary to *me*. I needed it. And you knew that, and you not only refused to accept that it was perfectly reasonable to want that kind of thing, you refused to even think about any kind of compromise.'

'What compromise was there?' he asked, his gaze hot though his tone stayed almost smooth. Almost. 'I couldn't marry you. And not because it was you – I can't marry. Or I guess I won't. But you insisted it was that or nothing. I begged you to reconsider and come with me—'

'I wanted to save the world myself, Alec,' I interrupted him. 'I didn't want to be your sidekick while you did it.'

He made an abortive gesture with one hand. 'Why couldn't we have done it together?'

'You always could have stayed,' I said, already sick, again, of the endless cycle this conversation looped into. It was just like way back when. There was no winning it and no ending it. There was only how much it hurt, and the scars it left in its wake. No wonder I'd gone out of my way to forget all of these details. 'For some reason, that was never a reasonable option.'

'Because I'd already made a commitment to the clinic,' he said impatiently, temper in his voice, gleaming like heat in his eyes. He shook his head. 'You came out of nowhere, Sarah. I never expected to meet someone like you while I was doing my fellowship. I'd been planning to work in Africa since halfway through medical school. I applied for the job before I even met you!'

'I know all of this,' I said, exhausted. It was a very old

exhaustion mixed with the new, and it made me want to crawl back into my car, drive anywhere, and try to sleep it away. Hibernate until it disappeared, maybe. 'I get it. Your commitment to a clinic was more important than your commitment to me. On some level I honestly admire that, Alec. I do. But I didn't want to spend my entire life being an afterthought.'

He didn't like that. His whole body tensed, though he didn't otherwise move.

'I keep my promises,' he gritted out. 'Always. I thought you understood that. If you'd just trusted me enough to come with me—'

'Trust had nothing to do with it!' I exclaimed.

'It had everything to do with it.' There was an odd, final note in his voice then, as if this were something he'd given a great deal of thought to over the years: 'I was the one who fell in love, who owned that, who tried to figure out a solution. You were the one who threw down ultimatums and walked away.'

'You told me from the beginning that anything that happened between us was temporary,' I retorted, fighting to keep my voice even. Why was I getting upset now? This was a different life we were talking about. This was an academic exercise. A deposition, nothing more. There was no need to *feel* it like this. 'You'd already walked away, before we even started. What was there to trust or not trust? I simply took you at your word.'

'Bullshit.' His gaze was hard on mine. 'That's a convenient story to tell yourself, isn't it? But it's not what actually happened.'

I was considering throwing something at his head when the oven timer buzzed. I'd forgotten all about the meal we'd planned to eat. It took me a moment to remember where we were. Not in that tiny studio of his in Chelsea all those years ago, but in his lovely country kitchen, the one his parents had renovated into gleaming, cosy perfection years before. Not in those painful final days of our relationship, but all these years later, with whole other lives under our belts.

It made me feel slightly better that Alec looked as thrown out of time and place as I felt.

'Dinner's ready,' he said unnecessarily. He smiled then, a bit ruefully. 'Go sit at the table.' His voice was gruff. 'I'll bring it.'

I walked over to the rough-hewn wooden table and the great window that dominated the wall of the kitchen. It looked out over the frozen pond and the rest of the valley, reduced to only a distant twinkle of lights against the dark now, with the blaze of the moon already sinking below the far swell of hills. It would be much too easy to pretend this was a life I could sink into, I thought as I heard Alec clanking around behind me, setting out the dinner he'd cooked and the utensils to go with it. Much too easy to tell myself that this pretty little country life was what we were arguing about. Or for.

But I remembered what he'd said earlier, when he'd urged me not to kill myself in a fit of humiliation after weeping all over him. That he'd be back in Africa before the spring thaw. And he'd made sure to reiterate that just now, lest there be any misconceptions: he was the same man, with the same career and the same life that entailed, and I'd already proved I couldn't handle it once before. I already knew I didn't want that, didn't I? I'd wanted what Tim had given me. What he'd promised me. I'd wanted that kind of security, that kind of safety.

Alec was temporary. He was always and ever on loan. He wasn't something anyone could keep, not for long. Lots of things might change, but never that.

I accepted the part of me that wanted to fit myself into his life, the way I'd tried to reinsert myself into Brooke's. I was trying so hard to Goldilocks my way into a solution. I was trying to see if some external force could save me from the sad fact that whatever else had happened, whatever Tim and Carolyn had done, I'd already given up on myself in a hundred ways. I'd walked away from Alec. And then from Brooke. I'd let myself become a DWI lawyer when it was the last thing I'd ever wanted to do with my law degree. I'd thrown out all the dreams I'd had in my youth and pretended they'd meant nothing to me. I'd lost myself. Alec couldn't find me. Only I could. All these trips through the past, and all the way to Vermont, were making that abundantly clear.

I didn't want to fight Carolyn for Tim. Nor did I want

to sit around, frozen in my inaction and martyrdom, like some tossed-aside puppet waiting for the puppeteer to come to his senses and bring me to life again. If Carolyn was what Tim wanted, she could have him. I'd have to investigate the legalities involved in divorcing someone who was incapacitated, but I was sure I could do it. After Christmas, I thought. It would be my New Year's present to myself. I would stop holding onto things I'd already lost. And I would stop looking for myself in other people's lives. I would make my own. And whatever else it was, it would be mine.

The truth was, I wanted it all. I wanted all the things I'd always wanted, and all the things I'd set aside. I wanted to keep my memories of Tim, of all the reasons I'd married him and loved him. It didn't matter what had happened afterwards. It didn't matter how it had ended. I could hold on to the beginning, to the life we'd planned and shared, however briefly. I could hold on to my newly resuscitated friendship with Brooke. I didn't need to live with her, or even in New York, but we could still be as close as it felt like we should be now. I wanted that back. I wanted her in my life, where she belonged.

And I could let myself remember Alec the way it had been, not the sanitized version I'd allowed myself these past years. I could let myself really remember all of his dangerous passion, his challenging forthrightness, and how much I'd loved him before I'd lost him to his own dreams. I didn't have to hide that away just because he was the man I could only have in tiny snippets here and there. The man I could never really have the way I wanted him. That didn't invalidate how I felt when I was with him. Or it shouldn't.

I didn't want to give parts of myself away any more. To anyone. No matter what. I didn't want to choose between diminishing options, the lesser of two evils. I had to figure out how to go about holding onto what mattered to me. And I figured that like most things, that meant letting go of the rest. Of the things that didn't fit, and maybe never had. I stared down at my left hand, at those rings that symbolized something I understood, finally, was irreparably damaged. There was no putting it back together. These trips through my old lives, these Goldilocks attempts, had taught me that, if nothing else. I swallowed, and then I tugged both of the rings off my hand and slipped them into my pocket.

There was no going back. And that was okay.

I really believed that, for the first time.

'Let's eat,' Alec said from behind me, and when I turned to face him, I felt entirely new. At last.

And so we ate. The night seemed to ease out around us, holding us, smoothing all our history away and making it into magic. The tension from before changed into something brighter, warmer. Familiar. It didn't so much disappear as grow into something else, something with roots and different possibilities. I decided to stop thinking about it. I let myself fall instead.

'I can't help but think that wild, detailed fantasies about being tapped to join some secret occult sect can't lead anywhere good,' Alec argued at one point. 'What kind of person will that make you? Why not learn about the real world? About responsibilities and consequences?'

'Because, first of all, that's boring,' I retorted. We'd long since finished our meal and were still sitting at the comfortable kitchen table, our chairs pushed back, debating our way through a bottle of wine. Thus far we had covered the Kardashians (Alec believed they were a harbinger of the End Times; I agreed but had argued otherwise for the pleasure of watching his disbelief) and what he called the tattered remains of the American education system. 'No one would want to read that book. You sound like a pompous after-school special.'

'I think life is complicated enough without resorting to flying around on broomsticks in your head,' he said. As usual, his face was so very serious while his dark eyes laughed.

I laughed back at him. 'I think you're jealous because Harry Potter has a magic wand and you don't.'

He actually smiled then, and it didn't fade away immediately.

'Probably true,' he conceded. 'I could do a lot of good with a wand.'

'So does Harry Potter.' I raised my eyebrows at him. 'This argument might have more weight if you'd actually read the books.'

'So it would.' He looked entirely too pleased with himself, as ever. And not in the least bit shamed by his own ignorance. 'But what would be the fun in that?'

We moved into the family room again, and the conversation kept going as we settled into the worn and comfortable couches. He propped his feet up on the coffee table. He told me about his years in Africa: the heartbreak, the struggle, the slender hope that the small bit of good he was doing might somehow balance out what sometimes seemed like far too much bad, like a kind of avalanche there was no hope of stopping.

'Aren't you afraid you'll burn out?' I asked. I was drinking coffee now, in a desperate attempt to combat my dizzy head, but it didn't help. And I was perfectly aware that it was not the wine that had gotten to me this way; it was Alec.

His expression then was something close to sad. Or was it merely fatalistic?

'I burn out at least three times a month,' he said, his low voice gruffer than before. 'Burn-out isn't relevant. It can't be. You keep going, because no matter what state you might be in, you're some of these people's only hope.'

I looked at my coffee, and my bare fingers clutched around the mug.

'That sounds terrible.'

'It's not.' He was sitting on the couch opposite me, his arms stretched out along the back. 'It's really not. It's . . . worth it. Hard and demanding, but no one ever said it would be anything but that. Challenging. But not everyone can do it, and I can. And I think the rewards of that make up for the rest, however hard it is to see them sometimes.' He shrugged. 'I guess that when that changes, I'll stop.'

The fire danced against the grate, and outside, the dark night had grown windy. It bumped against the old house, making the windows jump.

'How do you recharge in between burn-outs?' I asked softly, wondering what he saw then, his dark eyes focused on something so far away. Distant. On continents I could hardly imagine. When I thought of Africa I thought of a great big sky, safaris, the cliffs of Cape Town. I had a sense of immensity. I doubted that was what he saw.

'There's a beach I like in Namibia,' he said after a moment. 'Sometimes I camp there for a few days. Just me and the waves and the occasional seabird.'

'I hope you're not responsible for any promotional materials for your clinic.' I shook my head at him. 'You're not exactly selling it.'

He laughed at that, and rubbed his hands over his face, as if scrubbing it clean of whatever dark things lurked within him. If only it were that easy, I thought.

'It's been a tough few months,' he said. His mouth moved into something a little bit too self-deprecating to be a smile. 'I'm feeling a little more down about things than I usually do, I guess. You're catching me at a bad time.'

'Well,' I said, meeting his gaze and finding it too raw, too much. I looked down again. 'That's going around.'

The conversation twisted and turned, from books to politics to war and then back again. Alec told me what it was like to stand in a supermarket for the first time after living in a tiny village in Africa – how that always seemed to be where he felt the culture shock the most. All those options! All that food! We talked our way from food to wine to what it was like to defend idiots like Benjy Stratton from the consequences of their own behaviour.

'But he deserves to lose his licence,' Alec argued, as if baffled that there could be another side. Which there wasn't, really. Except in the technical sense.

'How I ended up defending drunk drivers is one of life's great mysteries,' I told him, as if I were confiding a great secret. 'I guess it turns out I'm good at it.'

But was it enough to be good at it? Shouldn't I want more from my career, too? At the moment, tucked up in a Vermont farmhouse a lifetime away from Benjy Stratton and the rest of my over-entitled Rivermark clients, I didn't want to think about what I should do instead. *Something better than DWI cases*, I told myself. *Which means* anything *besides DWI cases.*

We had moved on to talking about some old friends of ours that neither one of us had seen in years when I let out a huge yawn, surprising myself. Alec sat up and looked over at the clock, and I did too. It was just before midnight. I had to blink and look again, not believing what I saw the first time.

'Shit,' I said, completely taken back. 'I didn't even notice how late it was. I have to get out of here.'

Alec looked at me for a long moment, and I felt the heat between us swell again, brighter and hotter, like some kind of crescendo. I put my mug down on the coffee table in front of me, very carefully.

'I have to go,' I said again. Maybe a little bit desperately.

'How long is the drive?' he asked in that quiet, intent way of his that made my stomach clench. 'Four hours?'

'Five.'

'Come on.' He smiled slightly, and it was like throwing gas on an open flame. 'Stay.'

Stay.

What a host of images that simple syllable conjured up in my head. Memories mixed with fantasies mixed with entirely too much longing. I felt his mouth against mine again, so hot and hard, and his hands against my face. I remembered the slick thrust of him inside me years ago, the taste of his skin, the way he pinned my hands over my head, grinned down at me, and dared me to match him. And I always had. I sighed, and shifted in my seat, pretending I didn't know why I suddenly felt so restless. So close to undone.

'Alec . . .' But I couldn't seem to continue. I didn't know what I wanted to say.

That was a lie.

But I wasn't going to say it.

'I will, of course, make every effort to protect your virtue,

Sarah,' he said, all that laughter in his voice and in his eyes, though he didn't smile. 'I'm not a teenage boy.'

He hadn't been a teenage boy the last time I'd stayed here either, as I recalled, and that hadn't prevented him from taking me in hot, breathless, heart-stopping silence with my back against the wall and my legs wrapped tight around his waist, his parents sleeping peacefully down the hall as we both managed, somehow, not to scream.

Good lord. Where had *that* come from?

I could only describe the way he was looking at me then as *wolfish*, very much as if he was accessing the same memory. Which, I told myself, he wasn't. Of course he wasn't. I felt slightly feverish, and told myself I was acting like an idiot. Alec was many things. Annoyingly argumentative. Intense. Dedicated to his pet causes in ways I didn't believe he would ever be devoted to people. He was endlessly fascinating to me, still. But that didn't make him psychic.

'Tomorrow's Christmas Eve,' I pointed out. As if that were either relevant or necessary for us to note. That crook of his mouth only deepened.

'Which is why you shouldn't drive off in the middle of the night, fall asleep at the wheel, and splatter yourself all over I-91,' he said.

He got to his feet then and stretched, which was really just unfair. It was late and he was gorgeous. Too lean, and far too tanned in the swathes of skin I could see when he raised his arms up over his head like that. He lowered them, bringing my temperature down slightly, and then raked his hands through that wild mess of his hair. It stood about in spikes and looked ridiculous and I wondered how it was possible to want anyone this much.

'Okay,' I said, feeling hushed. Reverent. Even scared. But I didn't want to leave him yet. I knew that was true, if nothing else. 'I'll stay. If only to keep myself from becoming roadkill.'

And Alec smiled.

I helped him clean up in the kitchen, and then stood around feeling awkward and somehow obvious while he shut down the house, putting out the fire and locking doors. I crossed my arms over my chest, then stuck my hands in my pockets. I felt like the teenager he'd assured me he wasn't. He led me up the stairs to the bedrooms, and I was sure I could hear my heart pounding like a kettledrum as we walked – so loud that I thought he could probably hear it too. If he did, he was polite enough not to mention it.

The upstairs of the farmhouse retained its original flavour – the rooms weren't huge, but cosy, and the halls were uneven and tight. It was hard to remind myself why all of this was a bad idea when the cold wind howled outside and I was standing in a tiny, breathless space with Alec, who seemed to be entirely focused on acting like the perfect host. I stood in the doorway of the cheerful yellow guest room and he handed me a small stack of sage-green towels from the nearby linen closet that squealed in protest when he opened and closed the door. Which was pretty much how I felt. I gripped onto the soft towels as if they were life rafts and I'd suddenly found myself adrift on the high seas.

For absolutely no reason at all, except maybe to torture me, he lifted his hands high over my head and braced them on the doorjamb above me. So he could look down at me from that delicious and inappropriate angle. So he could mess with my head. So he could make it all that much worse.

I could have stepped back, further into the room.

I didn't.

'I don't know if you remember the bathroom's down there,' he said, nodding toward the other side of the small hallway. 'And I'm in there.'

This time he indicated the doorway that was catty-corner to mine. Through it, I could see the pile of his bags at the foot of his bed, the unmistakable reminder that he was not a man who stayed put. I stared down at the stack of towels in my hands.

'Um,' I said. I couldn't seem to banish all the images in my head, of Alec spread out across a bed like a pagan sacrifice for which I would very much like to be the reigning priestess, naked of course, tossing and turning with all of that golden skin on display ... *Not helpful*, I snapped at myself. 'Thanks,' I said inadequately and when I looked up at him again, those dark eyes of his were gleaming. With far too much knowledge and wicked delight.

'Do you need a nightlight?' he asked, his voice that sexy drawl. 'I think my sister left one in the attic room upstairs.'

'I think I'm good,' I replied, with far more bluster than I felt, as if that could banish all my inappropriate thoughts. He was so close, all that lean muscle arrayed before me, hanging there on display . . .

'Okay, then,' he murmured, his voice much too low. It reverberated in me. Through me. It made me . . . *ache*.

'Okay.' I could barely speak.

'I'll see you in the morning.'

I could hear the smirk in his voice, even if it wasn't on his face.

'You will,' I said. Stupidly. I wanted to put myself out of my own misery. I wanted . . . God, the things I wanted. I was punch-drunk on them all, so inebriated with his closeness that I was tempted to pretend I didn't remember why this was a bad idea. Why *he* was a bad idea.

The reason why I'd left him in the first place – which hadn't changed in all this time. And never would.

He reached down and brushed my hair back from my face with one hand, his eyes so intent, his mouth so serious, all of that focus and attention that made him so formidable riveted on me. I caught my breath. I could hardly do anything else.

For a long moment there was nothing but the wind outside . . . and this. Him. This winding coil of tension.

The sweetness of it, the heaviness. I could feel it shaking me, rattling my bones and making my skin seem to prickle in response. Would he kiss me again? Would I kiss him? Did I want either one of those things to happen? Both? More?

'It's so easy to forget,' he said, his voice so low it was barely a ribbon of sound, almost carried away by the wind against the windows.

But I heard it. I felt it like heat.

'Forget what?' Did I move towards him then? Or was he simply bigger, somehow, looming over me in that tiny hall, all smooth muscles and that concentrated power that was pure Alec? I felt hectic and out of control, as I always did around him. As if anything could happen. And might.

'All the things I should remember,' he said, something dark and almost sorrowful in his voice then, and he drew his hand away, and I wasn't the only one of us who felt bereft when he broke that connection. I knew I wasn't. I could see the echo of it on his lean perfect face.

I wanted to throw the stupid towels on the floor, reach for him, and wrap myself around him until there was no question any more of remembering or forgetting. Until there was nothing at all but the fire I could feel crackling and building between us, in us, around us, consuming all the air in the house, making all these decisions for us.

But I didn't. I would make my decisions for myself now. I wouldn't hide behind anything. Not even him.

'Goodnight, Alec,' I said instead.

And impossibly, I stepped back into the room, smiled, and closed the door in his face.

Then spent the rest of the long lonely night lying wide awake in that cosy little room with Alec only a few feet across the hall, within reach if I wanted him, wondering what the hell was wrong with me.

14

The next morning, I felt as awkward and oddly vulnerable as if we'd actually had the wild one-night stand that I'd cleverly averted the night before. I woke entirely too early from the restless sleep I'd fallen into shortly before dawn, and found myself staring around the happy little room in hollow-eyed confusion, as too-vivid images chased each other through my head.

'Dreams,' I whispered to myself, my whisper seeming to fill up the little room and clash with the pale-yellow wallpaper. 'Those are nothing but dreams.'

And then I had a small panic attack. Well, maybe not so small. It was a heart-pounding, head-spinning, high-octane *panic* that made me believe that I really might pass out, or, worse, vomit all over Alec's guest room, a prospect which panicked me even more. Which really didn't help.

When I could breathe again, I seriously considered getting up and sneaking out of the house to make my escape, in the time-honoured Walk of Shame style that I hadn't employed in more years than I could count. Since I was all dressed up to kill in one of Brooke's photo albums, in fact. I plotted exactly what I would do, up to and including putting my car in neutral and letting it roll out of Alec's driveway on the off chance he was up early communing with nature. Why I thought I required spy-like manoeuvres to avoid him was another issue alto-gether, and one I didn't feel up to confronting while my heart was still beating too fast in my chest and I was lying there in the foetal position in a tiny twin-bed that made me feel like a child again. I left so many times in my head that it was almost a surprise to discover that I hadn't moved from the bed at all. And only the fact that I was pretty sure that there was some kind of alarm on the front door that I wouldn't know how to disarm kept me from actually getting up and launching myself into action.

I lay there for a long time, caught somewhere between fuming and worrying. It was becoming my natural state.

In the cold light of morning, my actions from the day before seemed completely incomprehensible to me. As, no doubt, they would to anyone. To everyone, in fact. A quick glance at my phone showed a whole list of texts from Lianne and Brooke, and I was too ashamed of myself to read through them. What would I say? Lianne would not be impressed that I'd driven all the way up here and thrown myself on a man's doorstep. Brooke would not be impressed that, having done so, I'd failed to sleep with him.

Meanwhile, I kind of thought I needed to start thinking about my life less in these crazy Goldilocks terms and more in *my* terms. What did *I* want? What life did *I* want to build for myself? Good questions, I thought – and not ones that could be answered while I was taking an extended tour of my past. It had to stop. *I* had to stop. Tim and Carolyn had slept together because they'd wanted to sleep together. I hadn't done anything to make that happen. I hadn't set all of it in motion all those years ago by making choices that had nothing to do with either one of them. There were no clues here, and I knew it. I wasn't going to find some kind of secret treasure lying on the side of Memory Lane – at least none that would give me any clarity on what was happening, right now, in the life I kept trying to leave behind in Rivermark.

This had all been part of my breakdown, when I thought about it like that. My necessary end-of-marriage crisis period, which surely every woman was entitled to experience. This had been a productive breakdown, sure, but still. It was my little personal pageant of craziness. And the truth was, I was tired unto my very soul of being broken.

I swung out of the bed and picked up one of the towels Alec had given me the night before. I pulled my jeans back on, because this wasn't a sorority movie and I was not the sort to scamper about random houses in my underwear. I thought about putting my bra back on under the longsleeved T-shirt I'd slept in, but decided I could forgo it if I was only going to the bathroom. I eased my door open, and then froze there in the significantly chillier hallway, listening.

There was nothing but quiet. The usual sounds of an old house in winter; creaks here and there and the far-off sounds of old radiators doing their work. But nothing else. Alec's bedroom door was closed. For a moment, I found myself lost in one of those dreams again, tangled limbs and that serious, talented mouth hot on my body . . .

Not helpful, I barked at myself. Just as I had the night before, and with about as much success. Annoyed at myself, I charged down the hallway and wrenched open the bathroom door, determined to shower and say my goodbyes like the mature adult I'd thought I was before all this and then get the hell—

'Oh, shit.'

I didn't realize I had said that out loud – squeaked it, really, in a pitch only dolphins might consider appropriate – until Alec's eyebrows crooked upward in a lazily amused sort of response.

But who cared about his eyebrows?

He was in the process of wrapping a towel around his waist, and that meant there was nothing in front of me in the little farmhouse bathroom but skin. Glistening, hot, tanned and perfect male skin, wrapped around that mouthwateringly lean and athletic body of his.

Oh my God.

All of the carnal images that had haunted me since I'd

laid eyes on him again taunted me now, and I could *feel* him as if he were touching me, as if he'd moved, as if he was doing every one of the things I could see him promise with that dark gaze of his.

'Careful,' he said in that low, knowing way of his that echoed through me and seemed to *hum* beneath my skin. 'You're getting drool on the floor.'

'I'm not drooling,' I shot back at him, even though I felt winded. Or was that dizzy? 'I'm disgusted.'

'Yes.' Was that a smirk? It was. 'I can see that.'

He stepped toward me and I decided it was absolutely crucial that I betray no sign that he might be intimidating me in any way. That I stand up for myself. Just because something was tempting didn't mean I had to sample it. Just because my breasts seemed to swell and I could *feel* him between my legs in an insistent pulse, well, there were worse things.

There had to be. I just couldn't think of any of them right now.

'Sleep well?' he asked. He'd brought all of that absurdly hard-packed male flesh so close now that I literally lost the will to drag my gaze from his naked chest up to his face, and when I finally did, his eyes were laughing at me.

'Like a baby,' I said, with a good deal more bravado than was strictly necessary.

'So up every five minutes, then, frantic and wailing,' he said, still in that amused sort of drawl. He leaned down and stopped my heart when he put his hands on my cheeks, one on each side, holding me there. Killing me. 'In other words, you didn't sleep at all. You spent the entire night tossing and turning and remembering. Or was that just me?'

'Alec.' I was all heat and heartbeat, and I couldn't seem to catch my breath. Or care. Last night's determination had slid into this wildfire of need, and I thought I might die from it. And it sounded like a great idea. 'Please shut up.'

His mouth curved slightly and his dark eyes gleamed, and I wanted him so much it actually hurt.

'Why don't you just kiss me,' I ordered him, because I thought I might die if he didn't.

And Alec, ever the gentleman, obeyed.

Everything got crazy.

White-hot and wild.

He hauled me into his arms, and then up, so he could hold me pinned against the door frame as he angled his mouth against mine again and again. Tasting. Drowning. Pouring fire on fire and then burning alive.

I wrapped my legs around his waist and wished I hadn't put on any clothes before I'd left the room because if I hadn't, he could have dropped that towel and slid inside me and *that*, I thought in a frantic haze of need and lust, would have made everything perfect.

But it was close enough.

I tasted his warm skin, reacquainted myself with the

span of his chest, the width of his shoulders, the artistry that was that lean torso of his. I felt how hard he was against me, how soft I was in turn. He caught my mouth with his, and I believed him. I believed that he'd been up all night, as cranky and thwarted as I'd been. I believed that he wanted me as much as I wanted him, even now, even all these years later, even though this fire should have sputtered out whole lifetimes ago.

God, how he tasted. And the things he could do with that grave mouth of his, the way he could light me up. I couldn't get close enough. I couldn't taste enough, touch enough. I felt greedy and desperate and *more*.

He shifted back, leaning against his side of the door frame so he could slowly pull my shirt up and then over my head, baring my breasts to him. His face tightened; his eyes glittered, and then he lifted me higher so he could fasten that hot mouth of his to my nipple. I made a soft little noise I didn't recognize, but he did. He laughed, and then moved to the other breast, and then I was out of my mind, I was insane with this wild heat, I wanted him more than I could handle – when he froze.

He went completely, utterly still.

'What?' I asked, completely dazed, as he let my legs slide back down to the floor. He cocked his head as if he were listening to something, which made no sense to me, and anyway, I couldn't hear anything over the racing of my heart and my own laboured breathing. He held up a hand, urging me to be quiet.

'Alec?' came the voice. The female voice, sing-songing up from what sounded like the bottom of the stairs directly below us. 'Are you up?'

'Yeah,' he called, his gaze on mine, dark and frustrated. 'I'll be right there. Why don't you make yourself useful and start the coffee?'

'Up yours!' came the breezy voice, almost making me smile, had I been capable of something like that at a moment like this, and I heard footsteps retreat toward the kitchen.

'My sister.' He sounded so close to mournful that I nearly laughed.

'Oh,' I said, keeping my voice low. 'Well.'

'Shit,' he muttered. He rested his hands against the wall on either side of my head and looked down at me for a long moment, and then he repeated himself. And I couldn't help but agree. *Shit*. And then he pushed away.

I grabbed my shirt from where it had landed, almost in the toilet, and pulled it over my head. When I looked around again, Alec was across the tiny hall in the doorway of his room, pulling on those old jeans and shrugging into one of those button-down shirts that made him look like a particularly edible lumberjack. He didn't bother to button the shirt, he just fastened the jeans and ran a hand through the thick wet mess of his hair, that dark hot look eating me up from across the small hall.

'This is probably for the best,' I said piously.

For a moment he didn't react, and then he rolled his eyes.

'Of course you would say that,' he said, sounding somewhere between disgusted and amused. 'That's just perfect.'

'It really is,' I continued, darting a glance toward the stairwell and trying to keep my voice low and under any sisterly radar from below. 'There's no need to confuse the issue.'

Alec let out another short laugh. He started toward the stairs, but stopped when he was right in front of me. For a moment, we only stared at each other. I told myself my heart wasn't even beating too hard any more. I'd shifted from my own feverish dreams to a gorgeous half-naked man in the bathroom too fast. Anyone would have jumped all over that. Him. It didn't mean anything. It wasn't even relevant.

He reached out and grabbed a handful of my shirt and then hauled me toward him, up on my toes, making me laugh slightly in some hectic mix of surprise and that sudden jackknife of desire that would have knocked me over if he hadn't had his hands on me.

'I'm not confused,' he whispered, and then he proved it with a carnal, masterful kiss that made tears come to my eyes and my knees weaken beneath me when he finally let go. I staggered backward and had to grab the wall to keep myself upright.

Alec, meanwhile, looked smug. He practically glowed with hot male satisfaction, and I was too busy fighting my own response to him to take as much issue with that as I should have done.

'I wanted to make you come, but I guess I'll have to make you breakfast instead,' he said in a growl. 'How does that sound?'

'Jesus Christ,' was all I could manage to get out.

'He's the reason for the season, Sarah,' he said, mocking me.

Which made him laugh, and then keep on laughing, all the way down the stairs.

'You remember my friend Sarah,' Alec said in what no one would ever call a particularly polite tone of voice when I walked into the kitchen on still-rubbery legs a little while later, having helped myself to the basket of guest supplies I assumed his mother, not he, kept stocked in the bathroom. He was standing in the corner of the kitchen, his back to the sink, looking even grumpier than usual, though he had managed to button that shirt. Sadly. He bared his teeth at the woman sitting on one of the kitchen stools. 'Sarah, my sister Jennifer. You have no reason to remember her.'

'Of course I do,' I said, smiling at her. 'It's great to see you again.'

'And you,' she said warmly, not even trying to hide the speculation in her gaze as she looked from Alec to me and then back again. 'It's been how long?'

'Years,' Alec said shortly. 'Lifetimes. Thanks for bringing that up, Jen.'

If his rude tone of voice bothered her, his sister didn't show it at all. If anything, her smile widened.

'I came over to remind Alec to swing by for our little Christmas Eve get-together tonight,' Jennifer told me. She was what Alec would look like if he were a normal person, I thought then, a little too enchanted by the notion. She had thick, mostly dirty-blonde hair and the same dark eyes, only nothing about her was either grim or bad-tempered. 'He likes to pretend he doesn't know what day it is if I don't come and personally remind him, and we see him so little that we can't let him sulk around in this house the whole time he's home—'

'I can't think of a single reason I would crave solitude,' Alec muttered, rolling his eyes. He raked impatient hands through his wild hair, which only made him look more unruly. Not a bad look on a dangerous man, it had to be said.

'Anyway,' Jennifer said, ignoring him. Pointedly. 'You should come too, Sarah. You're more than welcome. It's an open house, so the more the merrier. Everyone in town swings by if they can, and I'm sure they'd all love to say hello to a friend of Alec's—'

'Appealing, but I think Sarah would rather die.' Alec interjected again, grumpily. 'I know I would.'

'To prove that he actually has a friend?' I asked his sister sweetly, unable to help myself. 'I can see how that might be a subject for debate.'

Jennifer snorted with laughter. Alec only eyed me from

his position near the far counter, where he was lounging and looking as disreputable and misanthropic as possible. What was wrong with me that I found him so appealing?

'Exactly,' Jennifer said, all but winking at me. I got the sense she would have hugged me if it was later in the day and she'd loosened up with some spiked eggnog. Or maybe if I had. 'It would be like our very own Christmas miracle! Alec in the company of another human being who isn't one of his patients!'

I had a vague memory of liking this woman well enough all those years ago. This morning, however, I loved her. Which immediately made me sad, of course. Because it didn't matter how nice she was, or how funny she was, or how tempting it was to erect whole, complicated fantasies around the things she said and the rich imaginary life I could make out of them. Alec didn't do anything that stuck, that held. He was temporary. His inability to really commit to a relationship was the one thing that would always be true about him.

And I knew that. His mouth on mine didn't change that; if anything it only made it that much more poignant.

'I don't think I'm going to be around tonight,' I said then, and the regret in my voice was real. 'But if I was, I'd love to come.'

Jennifer smiled at me again, and then faced her brother. 'I want you there,' she told him. 'No arguments.'

'I'm coming for Christmas,' he retorted, in a tone that

suggested this was the latest round of this particular battle. 'You can't get blood from a stone, Jen.'

'But I should be able to get my only sibling to a party during the one tiny window of time he's home all year,' she threw back at him. 'Don't be such a baby, Alec. It's a party, not a pit of snakes. I know you like to spend social events with your back pressed to the wall, making snide comments to yourself, and that's perfectly okay. We expect nothing less from you. Just come and be your delightful self and give the neighbours something to talk about until your next trip home. Please? Can you do that?'

'I'll think about it,' he said, in a voice that said *no, I will not.*

'Merry Christmas Eve, then,' she said, beaming as if he'd actually agreed. She turned that smile on me. 'I hope to see you again tonight, Sarah.' She waved a hand towards the big kitchen window, looking back at Alec. 'If you see any arterial blood down there, call. Or perform whatever surgery you think is necessary. I trust you.' She laughed. 'Medically, anyway.'

She headed for the door while I turned and looked out of the window. Down on the pond, a group of kids in bright puffy parkas were engaged in what looked like a particularly rowdy game of ice hockey in the sparkling winter sunshine, which explained why Alec had been shovelling the ice clear of snow yesterday. It suggested he was maybe a little bit less surly-to-the-bone than he acted. I didn't know what to do with that possibility.

'Nice to see you again, Sarah!' Jen called over her shoulder, and then the heavy front door slammed behind her.

'Why would you encourage her?' Alec asked. I couldn't decide if he sounded a little bit appalled or if he was about to start laughing again. I decided the latter wasn't very likely. This was Alec, after all. Mr Grim and Resolute at all times.

'I was completely unable to help myself,' I offered freely. I was still staring out of the window, though I quickly admitted that I was really trying to see his reflection in the glass. It seemed safer than turning around.

'You've created expectations,' he said then, and I realized there really was laughter there, lurking around in his voice. 'You'll have to stay and fulfil them.'

I laughed myself, and turned then to find him watching me with that same dark, fulminating look he'd had trained on me in the upstairs hallway. I had much the same reaction now as I had then.

Heat. Fire. Holy shit.

'Are you talking about your sister or you?' I asked breathlessly.

'Does it matter?' He shrugged. His eyes never left mine. 'For the first time in at least three decades, Jennifer and I want the same thing. Talk about Christmas miracles. How can you refuse?'

I meant to. I really did. I tried.

But Alec decided to turn the day into the re-enactment

of some kind of Christmas carol, and I was helpless to resist his version of a winter wonderland. We went ice skating – or he did, with his usual careless athletic ease, while I hobbled around stiff-legged and wobbly and did several highly ungraceful headers into the snow banks around the pond. We warmed up afterwards with hot chocolate complete with marshmallows, which he made a big production out of continually feeding into my mug, so that there would never be a marshmallowless sip.

'You have to consider the precise proportions and, of course, symmetry,' he told me, his expression completely serious when I laughed, forcing me to nod as if I, too, had given a great deal of thought to the marshmallow situation.

'Yes,' I agreed very soberly. 'Proportions and symmetry. You make a very good point.'

And he rewarded me with that flash of light in his dark gaze, which was even warmer than the hot chocolate.

We made a big lunch of ham sandwiches on thick bread with delightfully spicy wholegrain mustard and then we crashed out by the fireplace, dozing in our chairs like an old, comfortable married couple.

Though I couldn't think about him like that, I reminded myself when I jerked awake later, dizzy and overheated from another aching sort of dream that I couldn't allow to sink its hooks into me now that my eyes were open. This had always been the problem with Alec. He felt like forever, but he wasn't. He didn't have *forever* anywhere in him. And I knew that my wanting him to suddenly transform into someone he could never be was the very worst kind of wishful thinking. This was the man who could never, would never, so much as consider changing his plans. Not for me, not for anything. Did it matter if he was wonderful to be around if he was only ever around on his terms? That wasn't a life. That was *his* life.

'Come with me to this party,' he said some time later, when we'd both woken up and dealt with our inevitable post-nap crankiness to some degree. 'It will be awkward and embarrassing. You'll love it.'

The sun outside was inching down toward the hills and I couldn't stay. Of course I couldn't stay. There was nothing for me here. But I couldn't seem to get up from my chair and start for the door, either.

'Stop waiting on me,' I snapped at him as he tried to hand me another cup of coffee. 'It's making me feel crazy.'

'The coffee is not what's making you feel crazy,' he contradicted me, completely unperturbed.

He put the mug down on the small table next to me and then squatted down in front of the chair, which, of course, brought him way too close to me. I sucked in a breath and tried not to move, afraid my body would simply *explode* into him, regardless of my instinct to be cautious. To hold back.

'You're right,' I said. I eyed him. I did not look at how easily he squatted there, or how gorgeous he looked, all mussed up from his nap, narrow-eyed and a little bit ornery. Just the way I liked him. I did not look at any of that. 'It's probably not the coffee.'

'What are you going to do if you drive home now?' He craned his neck around to look at the clock on the wall, then back at me, a faint hint of challenge in his voice. Or maybe not so faint. 'It's 4.30. You won't even get home until almost ten. Probably later if it starts snowing, which it's supposed to. You really want to spend Christmas Eve on the road?'

'Alec.' I tried to sound admonishing. Adult. *Aware* of how foolish it was for both of us to play around with a fire we had no intention of letting burn. Not really.

'Sarah.' He mimicked my tone perfectly and then he slid his hands on to my legs. His hands were too warm. Long, elegant fingers, but strong. A doctor's hands. I tried to act as if I didn't notice he was touching me. As if it didn't affect me in the slightest.

'If you'd wanted to leave you would have,' he said. 'You know you want to stay longer. I think you should. Do you want me to beg you?'

That was far too intriguing. 'Would you?'

'I might.' He smiled, slowly. Dangerously. 'But I don't think you'd like the way I beg. By which I mean, you'd like it too much and we'd never leave this house.' His dark gaze burned. His hands didn't move, but I could still feel them everywhere. All over me. 'Works for me.'

'Um, no,' I said, but my voice was weak. Almost as weak

as my willpower where he was concerned. 'I don't think that's a good idea.'

'Of course you don't.'

The moment stretched out. Got hot.

It was go to his sister's holiday party or go to bed with him, right then and there, and I couldn't do it. I took the safer road. I told myself I had no choice. A party was a party. Sleeping with Alec, on the other hand? That was crazy. *Really* crazy.

'So,' I said into the taut silence. 'Um. Is that what you're wearing to your sister's?'

His smile deepened, and his hands tightened against my legs and then let go.

'Your loss,' he whispered.

And I couldn't help but agree.

Alec drove us over through the quiet, snowy streets, brooding the whole way, as if Christmas Eve were a torture designed specifically to hurt him and his sister's house was his personal Guantanamo Bay.

'You're scowling like the Grinch,' I told him mildly from the passenger seat. 'Not that I mind necessarily, but you run the risk of scaring small children away. Maybe that's your goal?'

'You're hilarious.'

But his expression lightened.

Jen's house down in the village was cheerful and bright, and was overflowing with holiday spirit. Holly garlands, ropes of pine, and two separate Christmas trees. Mistletoe in every doorway. Fat stuffed Santas, mischievous elves, and blinking reindeer arranged just so on the front lawn. Carols poured from the speakers and the tables were laden down with piles of holiday delicacies. Children and dogs charged through the happy rooms, and everyone inside greeted Alec with a warm smile. It was like stepping into a living, breathing Christmas card. I couldn't decide if I loved it or hated it, or if I had a whole host of far more complicated reactions altogether, so I helped myself to a cup of thick, rich eggnog liberally laced with rum and decided not to ask myself questions that had no right answers.

'Are you happy?' Alec muttered at his sister when we found her in the kitchen, her cheeks red and hair curling as she wrestled with something in a giant pot on the stovetop. 'I'm here.'

'I'm so proud,' she told him, reaching up and patting his cheek, clearly just to annoy him – and just as clearly, succeeding. 'If you hadn't turned up, I was sending Mike over with the pickup truck and a tranquillizer gun. I think you made the right call.'

Was that a slight smile I saw on Alec's mouth? I stood a little bit apart from him and his sister and the genial, grinning man I assumed was Mike, her husband. This was Alec's family. This was the life Alec claimed not to want any part of and acted all grumpy about and yet returned to, if what they were saying was true, every holiday season without fail. Something about that made me ache.

And then he glanced towards me, as if making sure I was still there, and my heart squeezed just that little bit tighter in my chest.

He looked wild and impossible tonight, in a black sweater that did remarkable things to his already fascinating torso, and a slightly less battered pair of jeans. I had done what I could with the few things I'd thrown in the car with me when I'd left Rivermark, which meant nothing more than a different, marginally more festive sweater, and I'd tried to do something with my hair.

Alec's hair, of course, all but stood on end, and I realized as I watched him interact – or not – with the townspeople that he did that deliberately. It marked him as the mad doctor, always off saving the world, or as a bad-tempered curmudgeon years before his time when he was home. Yet none of his friends, neighbours, or family members seemed to take his crankiness amiss. If anything, they seemed to encourage it; laughing at his snarky little comments as if he were trying to be funny.

Maybe he was, I thought then, with a sense of something like wonder that I'd never considered that possibility before. Like most realizations where Alec was concerned, however, it almost immediately made me feel maudlin. Sure, that could have been the eggnog, but why was I doing this to myself? Why was I exploring the mysteries of Alec Frasier when I already knew how this would end? How it had already ended? Why was I torturing myself?

'You should eat something,' he told me at one point, frowning at the glass I'd refilled with a little more holiday cheer.

'Are you telling me that as my friend or my doctor?' I asked, filled with bravado in the centre of such a pretty little party. And definitely feeling a little more irrationally irritated with him that I was willing to admit. I mean, why did he have to be so ... *him*? Why hadn't he become boring and unattractive in all these long, intervening years, like normal people would have? Like I had.

'Am I either one of those things?' he retorted, taking me by surprise, his gaze hard on mine.

I didn't know how to answer him, and so I didn't, smiling instead at the matronly woman who came up to us then, her round face kind and beaming. If I was relieved at the interruption, I told myself she didn't know me well enough to see it. I knew Alec did.

'I taught him in the tenth grade,' she told me after delivering a kiss to Alec's cheek which made him redden slightly, though he grudgingly submitted to it. 'He was horrible.'

'I think you mean entirely too gifted and smart,' he corrected her.

'Horrible,' she repeated, but she was still smiling. 'If he could have led the entire class in a revolt, he would have. I'd never been so happy to see a student leave my class in all my years of teaching.'

'I was very intelligent,' Alec told me, as if he were telling me a secret, but his dark eyes were bright and fixed on his teacher. 'I was just bored. Constantly, terribly bored.'

'He was a holy terror,' the woman told me. She also patted Alec's cheek, which I noticed had gone faintly red again.

'They really like to pat your cheeks,' I noted, when she'd moved on and Alec was leaning back against the wall in the corner again, looking cool and remote and on the verge of snide, as his sister had predicted he would.

'They're convinced that if they keep touching me, it will humanize me,' he said in that mild tone that made me grin despite myself. 'I think they saw it on some wilderness show. It's that or throw raw meat at my feet. To be honest, sometimes I think I'd prefer the steak.'

'You really are completely antisocial, aren't you?' I asked. 'I always thought that was a doctor thing. But it's a *you* thing, isn't it?'

Alec gazed at me for a moment then. I understood, somehow, that if we'd been alone he would have touched me, and that he didn't because we were standing in the middle of a crowd, all of whom were watching us as closely as possible from the corners of their eyes. *She's not his girlfriend, I don't think,* I'd heard Jen tell someone in a stage whisper earlier. *But I know she* was *his girlfriend a long time ago, so . . .*

So, I echoed in my own head. *So what?*

'One feeds on the other,' he said gruffly. 'At the end of the day, I'm more interested in healing people than getting to know them. I guess that makes me an uncomfortable dinner date.'

'Who would want to *date* you?' I asked, in such a deliberately insulting way that he actually laughed. I caught a series of surprised looks from the people clustered around the baked brie.

'I told you,' he said with a certain edge to his voice, like he was throwing down some kind of gauntlet. 'I'm no monk. An arrogant asshole most of the time, yes. But not a monk.'

'I never said people didn't want to sleep with you, Alec,' I said with an exaggerated sigh. I waved my glass of eggnog at him and very deliberately did not think of the *Audreys* and the *Madelines* and the *Elises* of the world, all of whom, I felt sure, knew exactly how monkish he wasn't. 'I mean, look at you. You're hot, sure. But a dinner date? I don't think so. You'd probably mortally offend everyone in the restaurant, including the cook.'

'Oh,' Jen's husband Mike said, coming up next to us and grinning at me, then at Alec, wearing a jolly sort of red-and-green sweater that should have looked sad and silly but on a happy guy like him just looked like fun. 'She's been out to dinner with you then, huh?'

Alec only shook his head, but I could see the smile he tried to hide, and it made something shift inside me. Too hard, and too fast, like heavy furniture on a steeply tilting boat, about to lose itself to the waves. I was capsizing right there, in full view of an entire Vermont town, Alec himself, an oozing platter of baked brie, and a life-sized stuffed version of Frosty the Snowman, complete with corncob pipe, grinning maniacally at me from the corner.

And that was the moment I realized, once and for all, that I was a complete and utter fool. That I should never have come here. And that I needed to go home immediately.

Before it all got even worse.

15

'Why are you so quiet all of a sudden?' Alec asked in his gruffest voice as he aimed the Jeep back toward his discordantly cheerful house up on the rise on the other side of the frozen river.

I stared out of the front windshield and I could see it up there ahead of us, that warm and affable sprawl of a farmhouse, the few lights he'd left on shining out proudly against the thick night. Like some kind of beacon. Or in my case, probably more of a lighthouse, warning of the rocks dead ahead.

I had to get out of here. I had to get away. It felt like a physical necessity, not a decision.

It was sometime before midnight on Christmas Eve and all I wanted to do was cry. I wanted to curl up into my tears and let them dissolve me. Everything felt too big, too unwieldy, too impossible. Too wrong. I felt small and insignificant, and not in a good, properly awed sort of way, the way I sometimes did when I stared at the ocean.

I felt as if the searing cold of the sky above and all the millions of stars were witness to this petty and broken little life of mine, and yet I had nothing to show for myself. Not even after these forays into the past. There was only my doomed marriage and my broken family I was trying to pretend didn't exist tonight. And this *thing* between us that felt so alive in the Jeep with us now, that kept me trembling slightly, deep inside, like my muscles wanted to fling themselves apart. I didn't know what it was. What *this* was. Much less what the hell I was doing here, now, when I already knew how this story ended. I felt like I was made of glass, about to shatter, and the next faint breeze or dark look from Alec might send me right over the edge.

'This has been so great,' I said hollowly, woodenly. Desperately. I stared at my fingers fiercely as I laced them together in my lap. 'Really. You didn't have to spend all this time with me. I descended on you with no warning, and you hardly see your family as it is. You didn't have to take my little breakdown so seriously. Anyway, I appreciate it.' I cleared my throat in the tense silence. 'More than you know.'

'Oh, are we making speeches now?' His tone was acidic. A lash. 'I forgot to write mine.'

'It's been so good to see you, Alec,' I said in the most friendly tone I could manage, looking over at him. The intermittent street lights played over the stark, lean lines of his face, making him appear far more beautiful than he should. Than anyone should. 'I hope we really can be friends this time. I'd really like that.'

His jaw moved then, but he didn't speak, and I thought he seemed to grip the wheel tighter than necessary. I worked my interlocked fingers all the tighter in my lap.

'Are you about to burst into song or something, Sarah?' he asked in a clipped voice. I felt the way he *didn't* look at me like a slap. 'Or is this your shitty way of saying goodbye? Again?'

'I'm just going to jump in the car when we get to your place,' I said, as if I couldn't hear everything seething in him that made him talk in that way. As if I weren't perfectly well aware that his temper was heating up. As if I couldn't tell. 'It makes sense. You have Christmas morning with your family and I should get home anyway. It should be a really easy drive tonight.'

'What the hell are you talking about?' he asked, as if he hadn't heard a word I'd said. As if he didn't want to hear any of it. As if I were a raving lunatic.

'Come on.' I was frustrated suddenly – and furious, just like that. Like some switch flipped in me. 'You're temporary, Alec. That's all you ever were, or want to be. And that's not what I want. It never was.'

'Define "temporary",' he gritted out. 'Because I seem to remember that we were together for a year.'

I shifted in the seat, turning to glare at him. Hard at that lean cheek nearest me, like I could bore holes into it, through it, with my eyes alone.

'When does your plane leave?' I demanded. A muscle moved in his jaw, and I knew he was clenching it. 'I know you already have your ticket. You always do. When?'

'January.' He looked as if he were biting back other words. Harsher words. Or maybe he really didn't want to answer. 'The fifteenth.'

'So.' I didn't know why I'd wanted confirmation of that. It turned out, I really didn't. 'Don't pretend you're someone you're not, Alec. I never do.'

He stamped on the brake then, bringing the Jeep to a sudden, slippery stop in the middle of the empty street. And then he . . . did nothing. The headlights poured over the road before us, looking rich and somehow thick against the night. I could hear the engine chugging along. The heater churned at my feet, not yet warm. He stared out ahead of us for what seemed like a very long time and then he turned his head to look at me, much too slowly and deliberately, and my skin prickled in reaction to the glittering look in that too-dark gaze of his.

'Don't look at me like that,' I whispered. 'You know I'm right.'

'You are so full of shit, Sarah,' he said in that low, furious tone that I hadn't heard in a long time. But I remembered it. It was as if I'd been waiting for it to reappear. To remind me of those last, terrible days with him. 'Always have been, always will be. You think you're digging around in your past? Is that what you call it? You show up married and weepy and suddenly wanting to talk about the relationship *you* walked away from years ago, but I'm the one who's pretending?'

'Just take me to my car.' I bit the words out. 'Can you do that? Or are we going to have a stupid fight right here in the middle of the road?'

He threw the car back into gear then, skidding slightly, and drove. Too fast, but I didn't care. I stared out the window and wondered why I felt so rough and unfinished inside. Like such a disappointment to myself. Like I'd just torn something apart, really ripped it into pieces irreparably, when that was the last thing I wanted. Wasn't it? Or was the real problem that I still didn't know what I wanted, even after all of this?

Alec pulled up to the farmhouse and slammed out of the car. I followed more slowly, annoyed that I'd left my other clothes in the house and had to fetch them now. I wanted to leave. I wanted to just . . . leap in the car and drive. For hours. Like somewhere out there, on that dark highway, I would finally find what I was looking for. In that miserable little moment as he wrestled with the lock, I was sure I would. I had to. Didn't I?

Inside, I went up to the guest room and grabbed my things, ordering myself to calm down and *breathe* so I could get out of there as smoothly and easily as possible, and then as far away as possible – but I stopped when I heard the creak of floorboards behind me. I didn't turn around.

Maybe, I admitted to myself, I was afraid to.

'What are you doing?' he asked, and the worst part was that his voice was so much softer than I expected it to be. Like this wasn't a fight at all. Like he was as disappointed in me as I was.

But I had to shove that aside. 'I told you already.'

'That doesn't make it any less stupid,' he said, and that was the voice I knew. That dark kick to it. That addictive hint of all his brilliance, his eternal impatience.

I turned then, and there he was, standing in the doorway with his arms crossed and that considering expression on his face; everything I'd thought I'd wanted once and as frustratingly out of reach as ever.

But he's here, now, a treacherous little voice whispered. *And so are you. Temporarily. Together. Maybe it would be crazy not to do this.*

And when I thought about it that way … what *was* I doing? Or really – why was I walking away from this now? It wouldn't last. It couldn't. But if I already knew that, why not enjoy it – him – while I could?

He felt the shift in me. Or maybe he saw it on my face. I didn't know. But I watched his gaze darken as I dropped my extra sweater on the bed and roamed closer to him. Experimentally. To see if all that heat and lust was still there when I was kind of mad at him, too.

And it was. *God*. It was worse.

'I'm married,' I said. Because I felt as if I had to say it, even though I'd taken off those rings. Even though I had no plans to stay that way for long. Even though I understood that I was finally done with that big mess. Because despite all that, it was true. I knew what that made me. He should, too.

He shrugged. 'Barely.'

'Everyone knows you shouldn't sleep with your exes.'

He shifted his stance slightly, and his dark eyes turned to fire.

'And yet,' he said in that sexy voice of his that made the kind of promises I knew he could keep, the kind he was best at, 'everyone does it anyway.'

I moved that final, suicidal, step closer.

'You're temporary, Alec,' I whispered. I slid my hands onto his chest, and shivered when his arms came around me, pulling me flush against him. 'You can't even help it.'

'You need a new definition of the word "temporary",' he said quietly, bringing that serious, impossible mouth so close to mine, as his hands found their way to the small of my back, the curve of my hip. *So close.* 'Yours sucks.'

'Because it's true?' I taunted him. I couldn't seem to help myself.

But I didn't let him answer. I closed that final distance between us, arched against him, and licked my way into his mouth.

And this time, I had no intention of stopping.

And neither, I could tell, did he.

It was as if we were possessed – like we thought someone might come busting in again and stop us. We stripped each other where we stood, our hands tangling in our shirts, laughing when we lost our balance, leaving what we took off of each other wherever it fell.

He kissed me again and again. I clung to him. I reacquainted myself with the hot male scent of his skin, its smoothness and strength. And then, somehow, we were on the floor in a mess of inside-out clothes and hastily kicked-off shoes, and he was moving over me and then into me.

And it was just as good as I remembered. Just as hot, just as flush and sweet, and he braced himself there like he wanted to look at me. He smiled, that beautiful smile of his I hadn't seen in so very long, untainted by any hint of the darkness and sardonic inflection he usually carried around with him, and I felt it like a new heat at the back of my eyes.

He whispered something that might have been my name. And then he began to move.

And that's when it really went crazy.

Later, he carried me into his bedroom and laid me down on the bed. It was wider and more comfortable than my little guest twin, and the pillows smelled like him. I buried my face in the nearest one and breathed deep. My body was still humming with the after-effects of what we'd just done. My mind was perfectly, happily blank.

I could only feel. And I felt everything.

I didn't remember falling asleep, but when I woke Alec was tracing patterns over my skin with his talented hands, bringing me from a vaguely erotic dream into a white-hot reality without missing a beat. His fingers moved along my arms, the line of my neck, spreading flames wherever they touched. He tested the shape of my breasts against his palms. I sighed, and the sigh turned into a moan, and the moan was his name.

I never wanted this to end.

'What are you doing?' I whispered when he shifted to crouch over me, kissing his way from my navel to my hip, then inward, toward the molten core of me. I arched into him, unable to stop myself. Not that I wanted to stop either one of us.

'Ruining you for all other men, if possible,' he replied, laughter heavy in his voice, and then he shifted again and took me in his mouth.

And when I exploded all around him, again, he came to lie next to me and pulled me over him, to straddle him. I tried to catch my breath as I braced myself against his hard chest, meeting those dark eyes of his, and then I rolled my hips back and took him deep inside of me.

Still holding his gaze, I began to move.

'Good thing you're not a monk,' I teased him in a hoarse whisper.

He laughed, his hands coming to rest on my hips as I set the rhythm. Slow. Sweet. And all of it an exquisite madness.

'I may take it up after this,' he said like it was torn from him. 'I think I just found God.'

And then neither of us could speak again for a very long time.

It took me a long moment or two to understand why I woke next, my heart already racing wildly in a chaotic, frightening beat. I sat up, gasping, trying to figure out what was happening.

Next to me, his arm falling away from me when I moved, Alec opened his eyes and was immediately wide awake and clear, in the way he'd once told me he'd learned in medical school.

'Phone,' he said matter-of-factly. 'Not mine.'

I lurched out of the bed and into the cold hallway, completely naked and my feet therefore uncomfortably bare against the frigid floorboards. The phone kept ringing. I slapped the light on in the guest room and then squinted against the glare of it, my brain refusing to work as it should. The phone stopped ringing, and I rubbed at my eyes, waiting for them to adjust to the brightness. Waiting for my body to recognize that I was not, in fact, in the middle of a nightmare, and calm itself accordingly.

'Here,' Alec said behind me, even as warmth enveloped me. I pulled the comforter he draped over my shoulders tighter around me, and then leaned into the kiss he pressed to my temple. I took a moment to watch him move down the hall toward the bathroom, still gloriously, carelessly naked. I needed to investigate my own body, take stock of what and how I was feeling, both physically and emotion-ally. There were so many layers here.

Or maybe I needed to take advantage of the fact that we were both awake at this godless hour and save the stock-taking for daylight.

But then my phone started ringing again, and I frowned, as that now familiar little arrow of fear worked its way through me. I moved over to the bed that I could now see without being blinded, and dug around in the purse I'd left there. My phone was at the very bottom of the damned thing, of course, and a quick glance told me it was my mother. At 5.42 on Christmas morning.

Somehow, I doubted that she was calling to see what Santa had left me under the tree.

'Mom,' I said by way of a greeting. 'What's wrong?'

'I won't even ask you where you've been,' she said.

'Vermont,' I told her anyway. Because her *not asking* was, of course, asking. 'I'm with a friend. Is that what you called about? At this hour?'

The irritation felt good. Better and cleaner, I thought, than what had to be coming next.

'Vermont!' She sounded horrified, as if I'd said some-thing like deepest Siberia. 'That's hours away!'

'Mom!' I didn't bother to control the snap in my tone. I heard my mother sniff as if I'd wounded her. Of course. With all her wounds, she could have been a saint. I'm sure she'd considered it. 'Tell me what's happening.'

'It's Tim,' she said, as she had once before, though it

seemed so long ago and far away to me now.

And everything froze. Again. *I'm afraid it's Tim*, she'd told me then, on Thanksgiving night. It was like another life. Was this it? Was this the call I'd been dreading all this time?

Was it finally over?

I didn't know how long I stood there. It could have been hours. It was probably seconds. I felt too many things to name. I saw that fucking blouse again, as ever. I remembered the way he'd kissed me at our wedding, his blue eyes so bright and happy, and the way his lips had seemed to buzz against mine, as if he were laughing. As if we'd really found joy, the two of us. As if it were meant to be ours to keep. *Was it really over?*

'Is he ...?' I didn't know how to ask the question. I didn't *want* to ask the question. Whatever came next, I didn't want it. I didn't want any part of it. But I pulled in a breath and braced the hand that wasn't holding the phone over the rest of my face, like a shield, and asked it anyway. Because it was mine to ask, whether I wanted to or not. Whether I wanted the answer or not. 'Is he dead?'

The silence seem to last for centuries.

'Oh,' my mother said, as if surprised I'd asked such a thing. 'No! No, not at all.'

Was that relief that poured through me then? Nausea? I couldn't tell. 'Then what ...?'

'He woke up,' my mother told me, a wondering sort of note to her voice. As if she thought it were magical.

She would no doubt credit this to fucking Christmas and get wildly pious about it, I thought, and then wondered why my reaction at such a time was so grumpy and uncharitable. Was that Alec's influence? But I couldn't let myself go there. Not now.

She sighed, and I forced my head back into the game. Back into reality, like it or not.

'He woke up, Sarah,' Mom said again. Pointedly, even. 'And he's asking for you.'

16

It was almost noon when I made it to the hospital in Rivermark and by that point I was just a zombie. I accepted it. Hell, I welcomed it.

Zombies did not feel. Not that I knew a great deal about them outside of the usual horror movies, but I thought that part was probably universal. Of course they didn't feel. In particular, I felt sure that zombies did not relive horrible parting scenes with their ex-boyfriends while sobbing their hearts out all the way down to the Vermont state line. Oh, no. Zombies simply drove. They stopped only to pick up more supplies of caffeine and sugar and to gas up the car, they left extremely rambling and incoherent messages on their friends' voicemails at still dark o'clock on Christmas morning about how upset and worried and whatever else they were, and they kept right on driving.

Merry fucking Christmas to me.

The good news about such a long drive was that I really couldn't muster up much in the way of emotion when I finally got there. I was wiped out. I walked into the hospital lobby and toward the elevator on autopilot. It was only when I pressed the UP button that I remembered the way I'd left things with Carolyn the last time I'd been here. Meaning, not good. Had that only been the day before yesterday? It felt like years to me. Long, Alec-filled years.

But I had to stop thinking about him. There was no point in it. It had been over for years. This had been nothing more than revisiting an old memory in a not very smart and entirely too tactile way, and I had to simply pack it back into the depths where it belonged. I never should have taken it out in the first place. I understood that now.

Not that understanding it made it hurt any less.

This is how you always leave, he'd said, all that pain and fury in his dark eyes, so much I'd had to look away. *Out the door without a backward glance – but I'm the one who's 'temporary'?*

And the worst part was, I knew I deserved it. I'd never stopped to consider Alec's feelings in any of this. It had been *my* journey, *my* breakdown. I hadn't given a thought to what my reappearance might do to him. What had I thought would happen? And what kind of person did that make me, that I could toy with someone else's feelings like that? I'd spent that endless stretch of road across Massachusetts wondering that very thing. I still didn't have an answer, and now it was too late. My time was up. This limbo, in-between life I'd been living was finally over, for good or ill.

'There you are.'

I couldn't make sense of Brooke's voice, not here and not now, and certainly not cutting through my memories of Alec's hard-hitting words. Of the pain that I'd caused. I turned, convinced this was likely the start of the hallucination portion of my extended breakdown, but even when I blinked a few times, she was still standing there. And so was Lianne, right next to her, both of them looking unaccountably fierce. They looked like the best surprise Christmas presents I could have imagined.

'I hope it's okay that we came,' Brooke said, her gaze moving worriedly over my face. Having glimpsed myself in the reflection in the glass doors on the way in, I knew that *zombie* was actually a kinder description of my appearance at the moment than I deserved. I raised a hand to deal with my hair, but gave up before it got there. I was beyond caring.

'You should both be having Christmas with your families.' I rubbed at my face, my gritty and still-swollen eyes, feeling even more dazed and bleary-eyed, suddenly. Or maybe I was simply exhausted. 'No one should have to be in the hospital today if they can avoid it. I should have said *Merry Christmas* on your voicemail and left it at that.'

'The kids were up at six,' Lianne said with a shrug. 'Christmas was over by 8.15. Billy can handle them for a while.'

'And it's not like I need an excuse to get away from my family,' Brooke said in agreement. 'There's a reason I moved to New York and never went back, you know. My mother overserved herself on the Irish coffee and was sleeping it off by 9.35. A personal record.' She smiled. 'I took her car as soon as I got your message.'

If they'd been singing me my very own personalized Hallelujah Chorus it couldn't have touched me more.

'I'm so glad you're here,' I whispered, and let them hug me. I kind of . . . leaned into them, and let them prop me up for a moment. Just for a second, I let nothing matter but my two best friends in the whole world, together, in the last place on earth I would have expected to see them. Just for a tiny little moment I let someone else – two someone elses – help me stand up in all of this.

'Of course we're here,' Lianne said in an undertone, her arm tight around me.

'Friends don't let friends cope with the aftermath of a cheating husband's coma alone,' Brooke said staunchly, as if she'd dealt with things like this so many times she'd put together some kind of Guide to Cheating Husbands and Comas. It made me smile to imagine it. As if it were a chapter in something she edited, something brightly lit and fun, and maybe we would all go out for fruity cocktails afterward. Instead of the harder fact that we were standing in the lobby of the Rivermark hospital, with who knew what waiting for me upstairs.

I'd thought about that a lot on my drive, in between other bombshells and unpleasant realizations. This was the end of everything, wasn't it? Tim was now awake and could make his own medical decisions. He could look me in the face and tell me all about the baby he'd made with Carolyn, and what that meant, and what he wanted. And then I could walk away. I'd have to, wouldn't I?

That should have made me happy. I told myself it did. Or anyway, it would. I was sure it would, eventually.

'All right,' I said now, before I started sobbing all over them, something I would have thought impossible after all the day's weeping – but no, my eyes were wet again. 'Let's get this over with.'

And for the first time in the weeks since Thanksgiving, I wasn't all alone as I made my way to Tim's room to face whatever came next. It was amazing how much of a difference that made. It was as if I could somehow breathe a little deeper, a little better, simply because they were here.

'You look terrible,' Lianne said, frowning at me as we stepped into the elevator and let the doors close behind us. 'What the hell were you doing in Vermont?'

'Please God, let it be Alec Frasier,' Brooke replied fervently.

I stared at the plate above us as the elevator clicked through the lit-up floors, one by one. I thought about Alec and that impossible, stubborn mouth of his that so bewitched me I did things I never imagined I would. I thought about Tim reduced to that still, small body in his hospital bed, unaccountably helpless. I thought about what I wanted, and how odd it was that such a simple question seemed to have nothing but murky answers the harder I looked for them.

'I can't even process how inappropriate this conversation is right now,' I said after a moment. I wasn't angry. Not even annoyed. It was just a simple statement of fact. 'On every conceivable level.'

We all stood there quietly. I sensed more than saw the two of them exchange a glance, but I didn't mind. Or react. And still the elevator rose.

He woke up and is asking for you. I still didn't know what that meant. I hadn't called back for clarification. I hadn't wanted to give my mother the opportunity to upset me any further – and, of course, I was afraid that I already knew. Tim had been so clear about what he wanted. A divorce. Carolyn. Was he asking for me so he could reiterate that? To my face? Or was he angry at me for how Carolyn undoubtedly felt she'd been treated – as my mother had predicted he would be? I didn't want to spend all those hours in the car knowing *that* was coming at me. It had been an act of self-preservation.

Which looked a lot like cowardice, I could admit.

Once again, I saw the way Alec had looked at me as I headed for the door. Those last, harsh words. That empty place in my chest where I knew my heart was supposed to be beating. But I'd walked into that situation, that whole night, *him*, with my eyes open, hadn't I? I'd known what I was doing, however unfair.

This is what temporary means, I'd thrown at him, hardly

knowing who I was angry with. Or why. *And it's not like you'd ever dream of changing your plans for anyone, would you?*

Is that what this was, Sarah? he'd asked so quietly. Too quietly. *Revenge?*

But I hadn't been able to answer. And I knew that was cowardice, too. It was funny, I thought then, staring at the lights before me in this familiar elevator that I never wanted to ride again, but I'd never seen myself more clearly than I did today.

'The important thing,' I said out loud, mostly to cut through the noise in my head, the rush of all those images, 'is that Tim's awake. And therefore better. That's what we need to focus on.'

There was a brief silence.

'I'm still punching him in the face,' Lianne mused, as if to herself. 'I don't care if he's been in a coma for the past few weeks, he's still a slime ball.'

'I'll help you,' Brooke said in the same tone. 'And Carolyn too, let's not forget.'

'Don't worry,' Lianne replied, with an evil note in her voice that reminded me exactly why she'd been my best friend through all those terrible teenage years. 'I haven't forgotten.'

And that was why I was smiling when the elevator doors slid open to reveal my entire family waiting on the other side. Just . . . standing there, in the elevator bank. All three of them. Looking markedly unhappy.

There was a pause.

I felt as if everyone were staring at my smile, then – as if it were the physical equivalent of a very inappropriate mariachi band crashing a funeral or something. I tried to wipe my expression clean, but it was too late. The tension was already much too high, and mounting. I could practically taste it.

We all stared at each other. Everyone looked awful, which made me feel better about my zombie impression but was also a bit alarming. My father appeared to be wearing the largest, most ill-fitting orange sweater of all time. My mother's hair was uncharacteristically frizzy and her face looked slept on. Carolyn, meanwhile, looked hollow-cheeked and haunted. None of these were the reactions I was expecting. This was not the way they should have been celebrating Tim's awakening – which, of course, made me wonder what had happened.

'What's going on?' I asked briskly, diving right into what scared me the most. 'Why are you all standing here? Did something happen?'

'You could say that,' Carolyn snapped. She glared at me as if I'd done something to her. I let my gaze drop to the faint swell of her belly and couldn't imagine what that might be, relatively speaking, even as relief trickled through me. If she was angry, Tim couldn't have died. If she was angry, it had to be something else altogether.

'Head injuries are very strange things,' Lianne said into the coiling tension. 'Recovery can be very—'

'You should see him,' my mother told me, interrupting Lianne. 'Alone.'

I knew better than to view that as a gesture of support. Not from my mother. Which meant it kind of terrified me.

'Tell me what's happening,' I said, looking from her to my father and then back. They were a wall of grim, with beetled brows and tired eyes. My father kept shaking his head, which was never a good sign. 'You're scaring me.'

And then I looked at Carolyn, because I figured she would know, and she certainly wouldn't go out of her way to spare me the blow. And what I'd learned since That Day was that there was always, always, a blow.

'Did he slip back into his coma while I was driving?' I asked, hearing the uncertainty and the beginnings of a new panic in my voice. 'Is that what you're not telling me?'

'No.' Carolyn's voice sounded almost strangled. She couldn't meet my gaze. Were those tears glinting in her eyes?

I felt someone grab onto my hand from behind – Brooke or Lianne, I couldn't tell – and I was absurdly grateful. I held on. Tight. Carolyn held one hand over her heart, like it hurt her from within, and I was too freaked out to even think the usual sardonic thought about that. Much less express it.

'He's awake,' Carolyn said in a very odd voice. As if she were trying to be formal. Or careful. But that didn't make any sense. 'The thing is, he doesn't remember anything.'

'Anything?' My mind raced. Because I wasn't even remotely as mature as I wanted to be, I thought first of television shows, not real life. *Alias*, for example, as Brooke and I had already discussed. 'Are you talking about amnesia?'

'It's a kind of amnesia,' my father chimed in then, in his lecturing professor voice. 'Did you know that some people have to relearn all their motor skills? Language?'

'Tim can't speak?' I asked numbly. My mind wouldn't accept that. I couldn't make sense of it. Whoever was holding my hand squeezed it.

'No, no.' Dad sighed. 'He's one of the lucky ones.'

There was another silence. I heard Brooke mutter something behind me, and I couldn't blame her. I was about to kill somebody myself.

'What doesn't he remember?' I demanded, frustrated and afraid. 'Will someone just *tell—*'

'Me,' Carolyn blurted out, her face twisting, her hazel eyes nearly black with unshed tears. 'He doesn't remember *me*. The last six months are just . . . gone.'

'Six months?' I echoed stupidly.

'Six months,' she threw back at me, with what felt like more aggression than the moment called for. 'The last thing he remembers is your birthday party.' She let out a hollow laugh. 'But not the most important part of it.'

It took me a moment to understand that she was, in fact, confirming the fact that she had hooked up with my husband at my own birthday party back in June. I blinked, but couldn't quite bring myself to summon up the necessary outrage. I felt ... empty. And the truth was, I didn't want to imagine it. Them. How it all began. I didn't want to plot it all out in my head and use it to torture myself. There was quite enough in there already.

I realized that I had absolutely no idea how I felt about any of this.

'You should go talk to him,' Carolyn said then, much more quietly, and her voice shook. My stomach twisted, and then lurched when she reached out as if to touch me. Whatever she saw on my face made her drop her hand. 'I know that you hate me, and probably him, too—'

'I don't hate anyone, Carolyn,' I said, interrupting her. And it was true. 'I'm numb all the way through.'

She looked at me for a moment, and then nodded, as if she'd talked herself into something. Or, knowing her, out of it.

'He's scared, I think,' she whispered. Her face twisted. 'And all alone. He needs you, Sarah.'

I snuck up to the entrance of his room and stood there, uncertain, before peeking around the curtain. When I did, it was hard not to make a noise – to gasp or cry out or otherwise react.

He was propped up in his bed, his blonde head turned toward the window. The winter light poured in and he looked thin. Drawn. Cold in such an antiseptic room. It felt so strange, now, to see him sitting up at all. To see him with far fewer machines connected to him. He looked tired. Sick.

But he looked like Tim again. I told myself the strange feeling creeping through me then was gladness – that he was alive, awake, *him* – but it wasn't quite that simple.

I hovered there, not sure what I wanted to do, not sure what I was supposed to do. And then he turned his head on his pillow, not without difficulty, and saw me.

For a moment, we only looked at each other.

His eyes were still so blue. Wide and confused now, but still that same summer-sky blue that I'd always loved so much. Even thin and pale, he still had the look of the friendly, focused man I'd always known, if reduced somewhat today beneath those thin layers of hospital blankets. I felt a sharp pang, deep inside.

He looked like the man I'd married.

The one who would never do the things he'd done. The one I'd trusted to adhere to our plans, to believe in this life we'd built. The one I'd chosen, deliberately and purposefully, because he'd made me believe that he could be trusted in the first place. That he would be safe. Permanent. Easy. There was such a riot inside me as I looked back at him. Pain and betrayal, yes. But something deeper and richer, running like a deep vein beneath. Grief, I thought, and felt it twist through me in some kind of dark confirmation. But surely I should be happy he was awake? That he wasn't dead? That was what mattered here, didn't it?

It was a pity I was still so small inside, I thought then. That I couldn't help but think about myself at a time like this, when if I was any kind of person, I would be more concerned about him. What did his memory loss mean *for me*? For us? What would it do to this tragic little triangle we were in? A better person would have waited before entertaining such thoughts. I was disgusted with myself.

I had to acknowledge, again, the part of me that had seen this accident of his as an opportunity to hold onto him a little bit longer. To keep us from being as over as we'd seemed before his car had spun out on that icy road. That part of me was deep in grief today, and I understood it. Some part of me would always grieve for what we'd lost, long before the accident. Him. Our marriage. Whatever happened now, whatever had happened while he was in his coma or in those six months with Carolyn, I'd loved him.

It didn't matter what he remembered. I would always mourn the loss of the way I'd loved him, all the way up to the moment I stripped that blue blouse off of my body and everything changed.

'Sarah—' he began, but his voice was raw, unused. It was little more than a croak, and it spurred me into action.

'Don't talk,' I managed to get out past the lump in my throat, rushing inside the room and making my way over to him. 'Don't say anything now. You need to rest, Tim. You've been through a horrible ordeal.'

And what was funny was that I meant that. I had no

urge to yell at him here, in this state, while he looked at me with all of that confusion and panic on his face. I had no desire at all to punch him in the face, as Brooke or Lianne would have done. I didn't want to think about any of the things that loomed here with us in this tiny room, elephants dancing in circles all around us, demanding to be named and noticed. I didn't want to think about the things he'd done, or the things I'd done, or even the conclusions I'd come to when I'd assumed he would wake up with his memory intact. I didn't want to think about anything at all. I wasn't sure I could.

I'd given all of that up. I'd moved on. But that was before – before it turned out he didn't remember any of it. It was one thing to walk away from the guy in the hospital who didn't want me, but what if he didn't feel that any longer?

If he didn't remember what he'd done, did I have to?

'I don't . . .' He shook his head as if his mouth wasn't working the way he wanted it to. 'I don't know . . .'

He reached for me when I got to the side of his bed and I didn't think. I sat down on his bed with him and hugged him. I pulled his head to my shoulder and wrapped my arms around him, and I felt him breathe, ragged and a little bit wild, against my collarbone.

It had been so long since I'd held him. Longer still since he'd held me. Something that felt like stone inside of me seemed to melt a little bit.

'I don't understand what's happening,' he told me, his

voice the smallest whisper of sound, the words more garbled than not. It wasn't Tim's voice at all. It wasn't his easy, confident way of speaking. But it was Tim. *Awake.* I let it wash through me, over me. I held him tighter and rocked him a little, stroking his hair with my hand. Soothing him. Soothing myself, too. Reminding us both that he was alive, and conscious, and everything outside of that was a detail. Just a tiny detail. And maybe the fact that he couldn't remember his own details meant we got some kind of do-over here. A chance to live as if none of this had happened.

And who wouldn't want a do-over?

'It's okay,' I whispered. 'You're okay.'

I stared past him toward the window, where the world waited, cold and harsh and unforgiving. There would be no escaping what we'd have to work through. There was a baby on the way, innocent of all of this despite what its parents had done, but a complication all of its own, nonetheless. And I had no doubt that Carolyn had every intention of fighting her way back into Tim's memories, his life, however she could.

But none of that mattered today. Now. It couldn't. I wouldn't let it. He might not have protected us when he'd had the chance, but I could. I would. Didn't I have to?

'You're awake, Tim,' I murmured to him, holding him close, letting myself love him the way I had for all those years, as he clung to me the way I knew he wouldn't if he'd had access to his own history. I let myself do it anyway.

Once upon a time he'd kept me safe, I thought then, my eyes drifting closed, my cheek on the top of his head. Now I could do the same for him.

And I wanted to.

I did.

17

But it turned out that his dramatic awakening wasn't quite the Christmas morning miracle I might have been a little too tempted to imagine.

The real story came out later, after Tim was transferred to a rehabilitation centre for the rest of his recovery and I was forced to interact entirely too often with Carolyn, who Tim said he didn't want to see but who lurked daily in the clinic's lobby or outside my house so she could prise information from me. She was remarkably consistent. Determined, even.

Today, I realized with some surprise as I pulled into my driveway to see Carolyn's car already there, engine running and kicking up clouds in the late-afternoon cold, was New Year's Eve. It felt as if much more than a week had passed since my Christmas Eve in Vermont – but I couldn't let myself think about that. Not when there was so much else to do. Like watch Tim work so hard to recover all of his speech, his ability to walk, parts of his memory. Like be the proper wife he'd asked for the moment he'd been capable of asking for something. As if we could erase the past few months, just like that.

I was clinging to that. Maybe more than I should. It was easier to simply fall back into my old role. I knew it so well it hardly required thought. It even felt good. *Right*, I told myself. *It feels right.*

'How is he today?' Carolyn asked, climbing out of her car after I parked mine and started toward the front door. She looked defensive and miserable, and yet I couldn't seem to take any pleasure in that the way some part of me wanted to do. If anything, looking at her made me feel sad. For all of us.

'Better,' I told her. I outlined the progress he'd made today, the steps he'd taken, both literal and more metaphorical, and the doctors' new thoughts on his prognosis. I did this as quickly as possible. There was no point holding things back; she would find out eventually and anyway, I wasn't her. I didn't have anything to hide. 'If he keeps going at this rate, he should be back home in a couple of weeks.'

'That's great!' she breathed, more to herself than me. Then she frowned up at the house. 'Will you move him back in here?'

'This is his home, Carolyn,' I pointed out as I unlocked the front door and pushed my way inside. Maybe a little bit testily.

I let her follow me into the house and shut the door

behind her. I didn't even complain when she slumped into one of the chairs around the little table in the eat-in kitchen with entirely too much weary familiarity. My knee-jerk reaction was to toss her out into the cold, but I contained it. For one thing, barring Carolyn from my house after finding her with Tim in my bed seemed way too much like making a big production of slamming the barn door long after the horses had galloped wild and free. And for another, this was actually the rare occasion when I *wanted* to talk to her. Possibly the first time I'd wanted such a thing since September.

'When's the earliest they think he might be able to leave that rehab centre?' she asked me now. I shuffled through the stacks of mail, an assortment of catalogues and bills, then tossed it all on the kitchen counter. I didn't go over and sit with her. That seemed far too civilized for the mood I was in.

'Earlier than you might think.' I studied her for a moment. Her jet-black hair was showing a hint of grey at the roots. Her eyes seemed to sport permanent bags. She shrugged out of her coat and sat there, looking listless and sad, her hands rubbing her belly. I decided it was an unconscious gesture on her part, that it wasn't for my benefit. But that didn't change what I suspected she'd done, did it? 'Earlier than I would have thought, certainly. But then, Tim didn't suddenly wake up in a searing burst of clarity on Christmas morning, did he?'

I watched Carolyn flinch. She shifted in her chair, almost

as if she were nervous. She was slow to meet my eyes.

'That depends on what you mean, exactly,' she said. Much too carefully.

'I mean that he was twitching and thrashing a little bit before I went to New York,' I said, keeping my voice cool and very nearly prosecutorial. 'But apparently, while I was away, he started opening his eyes and seeming to track conversations. He grunted responses. All signs that he was coming around. He started *talking* on Christmas morning, but he'd been waking up for days.'

She didn't have to answer. I already knew. And even if I hadn't been sure, I could see the truth written all over her face.

'That was why you were so angry with me when I came back from New York that morning.' I shook my head, still trying to take it in. I'd cried when I'd finally understood what Tim's doctors were telling me. I was finished crying now. But that didn't mean it didn't hurt, or that I wasn't stunned by what further depths she was willing to go to. 'I thought it was because you knew I'd seen a private moment between you and Tim, but that wasn't it, was it? You didn't want me to know he was coming out of it already.'

'Sarah . . .' she began, her hands reaching out like some kind of supplicant. Except that wasn't Carolyn's style, was it? She wasn't *beseeching* me about anything – she was trying to get me to calm down. Same gesture, different meaning. It was a crucial distinction and I needed to heed it. Carolyn wanted Tim. I was in her way. That was the whole story, the end.

'What I have to ask myself,' I said slowly, staring at her, wondering how she'd turned into such a monster right in front of me this past year without my ever noticing it, and how I'd managed to be so incredibly oblivious for so long, 'is whether you were ever going to tell me. What was your plan, Carolyn? How long were you going to keep it a secret?'

She wrapped her arms around her waist, and blew out a breath. She didn't try to argue. 'I didn't think it would matter.'

'How can you possibly think that's true?' I was flabbergasted – more that she would admit it than anything else. 'What kind of sociopath are you?'

'Well, I didn't.' She lifted her chin. Defiantly. 'The fact is, if Tim could remember the last six months, he would want me with him, not you. I'm not trying to be mean. It's the truth. So why tell you that he was waking up? You would have found out eventually. And he would have gone ahead and divorced you, the way he planned.'

'Do you listen to the things you say?' I asked her, in some kind of amazement. 'I get that you think that you and Tim have some magical connection, and who knows? Maybe you do. But I'm still married to him. I've *been* married to him for years. What makes you think you're the only person who cares about him?'

'I'm in love with him,' she said, and it was the way she

said it that set off some kind of air-raid siren inside me. She was so matter-of-fact. So calm, as if there was no room whatsoever for debate. I had to repress a shiver. She met my gaze, and there was no shame in hers, only that strange directness, like she didn't care what the consequences were. Or maybe it was only strange because I'd never owned anything like that in my life. 'Are you?'

'Of course I love him,' I snapped at her.

Because what did it matter what she *owned*? This was about me, too. This was my life she was playing with. I had the passing thought that being back here, playing the wronged wife, felt something like good – it was black-and-white, anyway. It was easy. And Carolyn had no leg to stand on, did she?

'That doesn't change because he did something horrible,' I continued, my voice warming. '*I* wasn't the one who had the affair, Carolyn. *I* wasn't the one who wanted a divorce. I didn't get the *option* of deciding whether to love or not love Tim, the two of you *took it* from me.'

'That's not the same thing as being in love with him,' she replied immediately, and I remembered, then, that she'd thrown something like that at me on That Day. It was hard to recall her exact words; they were still buried in all the screaming. Most of it mine. 'I think you're comfortable with Tim, Sarah, but you don't love him. Not really. Not the way I do, and not the way he deserves to be loved.'

I scraped my hair back from my face and tried not to

scream bloody murder. Much less commit it. I told myself that seeing red got no one anywhere they wanted to go and waited, therefore, for my vision to subside to something a bit more calmly orange before I replied.

'Thank you for your incredibly patronizing and self-serving analysis of my marriage,' I managed to grit out.

'Is it patronizing?' she asked, her voice smooth. Untroubled. I wondered if these were the conversations Carolyn practised in her bathroom mirror. 'Or is it true?'

'What makes you think you have the right to comment either way?' I realized my hands were in fists. 'It's none of your business. Even if Tim regains all of his memories tomorrow and never wants to lay eyes on me again, you don't know a single thing about our marriage. All you know is what you wrecked.'

She hugged herself again, and started rocking, slightly, in her chair, which made me think she wasn't quite as calm as she wanted to appear.

'You can't wreck something if it's already broken,' she said, and her voice was a little rough then, as if there were some emotion buried in there.

But not, I was sure, for me. Never for me.

And that was the part I couldn't seem to understand, not even after all of this. Especially after all of this. Sure, my relationship with my sister had always been a little bit rocky. We had never dressed in matching outfits or called ourselves best friends. We had never shared secrets or whatever else the world fantasized sisters did. She was never my first call when something went wrong; most of the time, in fact, we didn't talk much at all between major holidays. And not because there was some kind of falling out between us, but, I'd always thought, because we didn't have anything much in common besides our parents. The house we grew up in. The remnants of a shared childhood. We were two very different people who happened to be sisters.

We didn't have to be close, I'd always thought, but that didn't make us enemies, either.

She'd had her wild-child Portland years, and then she'd moved to Boston, claiming she needed a complete change. She'd pursued that goal the same way she did everything else: with 150 per cent total commitment. Damn the torpedoes, etc. The last few years or so she'd been in what Tim and I had called her *elite goth* phase, which involved the dyed black hair and severe lipstick she'd suddenly seemed to prefer, but also her perfectly unobjectionable marketing career. She'd seemed happy in Boston. And that life had made more sense to me than her self-righteous, hemp-clothed communal existence in Portland, all Burning Man and medicinal weed. I'd actually wondered if maybe, with her laid off all those months and living with my parents, she and I might reconnect the way that people claimed adult siblings sometimes did. And the crazy part was, I'd thought we had. We'd seen so much more of each other, and it had been pleasant enough. No scenes, no drama. I even remembered thinking at some point over the summer that it was nice that Tim was so much more accepting of her than he had been . . .

I was such an idiot.

But it had never occurred to me that my older sister might not care about me. Not really. Not *enough*. That she might weigh up her options and decide that hurting me was an acceptable risk. That had never crossed my mind until I'd walked into my own bedroom and seen the proof of it. It was still so hard for me to accept, to really believe, and yet here she was in my house, telling me so from her own mouth.

'I don't understand why you're okay with this,' I said finally. Painfully. 'Why doesn't it give you any pause at all that you're sitting here debating with me – *with your sister* – about the way you broke up my marriage? About whether or not I love Tim the way *you* think I should? Where's the shame, Carolyn? The regret? Do you think the way you've hurt me is more noble somehow because you did it for love? You have to know that's ridiculous.'

She looked away for a moment and when she looked back, her eyes seemed darker. Her mouth trembled. But it still wasn't enough. I wasn't sure what would be.

'I didn't do any of this to hurt you, if that's what you think,' she said in a low voice.

'Sometimes I think you must not have thought of me at all,' I whispered, giving voice to the things that moved in me, the things that kept me awake on that sofa in the den all hours of the night, 'and sometimes I assume the fact that I was the wife whose husband you were stealing made it that much sweeter for you. And I don't know which is worse, to be honest.'

Carolyn stared at me. I watched her swallow. I imagined I saw regret there, then, washing over her face. But if it was, it was gone too quickly for me to be sure.

'It just happened,' she said, her voice cracking slightly. 'It was an accident and then . . . we couldn't help it.'

I thought about Alec, then. Alec who I could never really have. Alec who was impossible to hold on to, and oh, how that made me wish I could. Alec who was profoundly unsafe; demanding and never easy and so much *work*. I thought about how I'd driven all the way up there, and stayed there, and jumped back and forth over that fire between us as if begging it to burn me alive. As if I'd wanted it to. I thought of all the times I could have stopped him, stopped myself, stopped the whole thing. But I hadn't wanted to stop it. I'd wanted to see where it went. Where we would go. I'd wanted to know how it felt, again; if I was remembering it right. If I was remembering *him* right. I'd wanted whatever came next, even if there would be a price to pay for it, and for that long night I hadn't cared about that price. I hadn't even considered it.

'You're lying,' I told Carolyn now, with more weariness than accusation. 'You could have helped it. You just didn't want to.'

The kitchen was silent for a long while. Outside, freezing rain began to fall, lashing the windows with the year's last storm. I didn't know what Carolyn saw as she looked at me. Happy memories from our childhood, whatever those looked like for her – like maybe stealing my Halloween candy in preparation for far greater thefts later on? Or maybe that air of sadness that both of us seemed to wear now, mirror images of each other, like the hazel eyes we'd inherited from our maternal grandmother? Or did she only note, as I did, how empty this all was – how little there was to yell about after so much had happened. There was only surviving whatever came next.

'You're right,' she said eventually, meeting my gaze and holding it. 'I didn't want to. And I guess I'll have to live with that.'

'So far you seem to be doing pretty well,' I observed.

'Appearances can be deceiving,' she said softly. 'I do love you, Sarah. You're the only sister I've got.'

'But you love him more.' It wasn't a question.

'I do.' She shrugged, helplessly. 'I'm sorry, but I do.'

I was surprised to feel tears prick at the back of my eyes, and had to blink hard to keep them at bay. I pulled in a deep breath somehow, then another, and somehow, seemed to turn into some kind of stone. Because she'd admitted it, maybe. Finally. Because she'd actually said it to my face.

'And what are you going to do if he never gets those memories back?' I asked her then. 'Some people with his type of head trauma never do.'

'I can't let myself believe that,' she said, in a tone that

indicated she'd spent a lot of time worried about it herself. 'I have to focus on the future and the baby and hope everything will work out the way it should.'

'Okay,' I said, feeling outside of myself. As if I danced around the outskirts of this remarkably quiet conversation, somehow the more painful for its lack of fireworks. 'But let's be realistic, here. Let's say his memories don't come back. He and I don't divorce. He doesn't remember you as anything more than his sister-in-law. You have his baby. What happens then?'

She cocked her head slightly to one side, as if she were searching my face for clues. Her hands clenched over her belly, betraying a level of agitation I didn't see anywhere else in her.

'Are you just going to live here in town with the kid?' I asked, my voice entirely too reasonable. I wasn't sure why I was painting this particular picture for her. But I could see it so easily. It would be such an obvious outcome here. We could end up there with so little effort that it seemed almost preordained. 'What about if Tim and I have kids, too? Will they all go to school together and swap lunches as well as DNA? How do you see this all playing out?'

'Wait a minute,' she said, shaking her head slightly, as if baffled. As if I wasn't making sense. 'What are you saying?'

'I'm just wondering what the future looks like.' I crossed my arms over my chest. 'Right now he doesn't want anything to do with you. That may never change, Carolyn. Are you prepared for that possibility?'

Her mouth actually dropped open slightly, and I could see the colour high on her cheeks. She pushed to her feet, pulling her coat back over her shoulders, and it looked like she was shaking.

'I keep forgetting,' she said in such a low voice that I almost couldn't hear her, 'that you would do anything to maintain the status quo. That all you want is for everything to go back to how it was. Even now.'

'It's not about what I want,' I said then, feeling, it was true, ever-so-slightly self-righteous. And *good*. Like what a great person I was for even caring what Tim wanted should have been shining off of me, blinding the world around me. 'It's about what Tim wants.'

And, maybe, about winning. About beating Carolyn at this game. I didn't really want to admit that, but I knew it was in there.

'Of course it's about what you want!' she said with an outraged sort of laugh. She raised a hand then, taking in the kitchen, the open-plan design that flowed out into the great living room. 'Jesus Christ, Sarah. What is so great about your life – about this stupid house – that you would live in it *knowing* that it's fake? Knowing that he could get his memories back at any moment and when he did, he'd hate you? But you think *I'm* the sociopath here?'

'Why should I give up my marriage if he can't remember that he wanted that?' I asked her. I hadn't necessarily thought about it in such stark terms, but there it was. And so what if there was a hollowness to that? There would be a satisfaction, too. The satisfaction of the life we'd led. It had been a good life, no matter what Carolyn thought. No matter how unlike the other lives I might have had it was. It could be good again. Smooth. Easy. Sensible.

Of course it could, I thought wildly. And then all of these months would simply be a bad dream, easily forgotten once the light of day came. Maybe this was the answer, after all. Maybe all those other lives I'd tried on didn't fit me because I wanted the one I'd had, even if it was a little more imperfect than I'd imagined it. Maybe this was where I was meant to be after all. *It could be.*

'Why would you want to hold on to your marriage if you know that it's only the *head injury* that makes him think he wants it any more?' she asked me then, sounding appalled. As if I were the monster here. 'Why would anyone want that?'

'Why does anyone want anything, Carolyn?' I threw back at her, and maybe I was more angry, still, than I'd thought. Maybe the weariness was only the outer layer of the things I felt. I rocked back on my heels as I regarded her, feeling unduly powerful. In control. And I realized how long it had been since I'd felt that way. 'You wanted your sister's husband. Maybe I want him back, and I don't care how. Maybe it's not any deeper than that.'

*

But that wasn't precisely true.

Later, I sat by myself in my favourite spot in the den and watched the ball drop in Times Square on the big flat-screen TV that Tim had been so excited about. Finally, this long fall was over. Finally, we were at the end of this terrible year. I should have been jubilant. I ate cheese and crackers from one of the pretty china plates we'd put on our wedding registry, drank my champagne straight from the bottle, and told myself I was perfectly fine.

I was fine.

I could have spent the night at Lianne's. She and Billy threw a party every year, and I knew I would have been more than welcome there. I could have mingled with our old high school friends and drunk too much of Billy's famous holiday cocktail – it involved a very doctored version of mulled wine and was vicious – and woken up sometime on New Year's day on the floor of Lianne's guest room. I'd done it before. Alternatively, I could have gone down to New York and gone out somewhere glittery and fabulous with Brooke.

How glittery? I'd asked in response to her texted invitation.

As glittery as possible, she'd texted back. *You'll love it. Nowhere near Times Square, of course! We glitter elsewhere, thank you.*

But in the end, I'd chosen my couch. I had too many ghosts to sort through, and I was old and experienced enough now to know that this kind of thing was best done in private, rather than in the middle of someone else's party. There were too many loose ends that seemed to flutter around me, tripping me up, choking me, even as I sat still. That conversation with Carolyn had unsettled me. Deeply. I'd spent the whole first part of the evening vehemently denying it, but now, sitting cross-legged in the dark while the entire nation partied elsewhere, glittering and oh so freaking happy, there was no avoiding the truth of it.

Are you upset that you lost Tim? Lianne had asked me a hundred years ago. *Or are you upset that Carolyn took him?*

How could I still not know the answer?

I reached over and picked up my phone like every teenage girl in the nation, scrolling through the old list of calls and messages, looking for something that wasn't there. That wouldn't be there. Alec wasn't the kind of guy who called, and even if he were, he certainly wouldn't call *me*. Not the way we'd left things.

Because he hadn't been mad at me for leaving that morning. Of course not. He wasn't a jealous lunatic; that had always been more my style. He'd helped me pack the car. He'd made me more of his perfect coffee and put it in a travel mug for the road.

Call me when you have a minute, he'd said, and that had started it. *When things settle down a little bit.*

Come on, Alec, I'd replied, feeling helpless and something else, too – something much closer to furious, though I'd thought I'd shoved that down deep. *I'm not going to call you. What's the point?*

He'd stared at me, and I'd hated imagining that I wouldn't see those dark eyes of his again, that clever mouth. That I wouldn't get the pleasure of talking to him again, of following the twists and turns of the way he thought. That I wouldn't get to laugh like that, feel like that, *be* like that again, because I felt free with Alec in a way I'd never felt free anywhere else. But he wasn't staying around. He already had his plane ticket out. And I'd lived through all of that before, hadn't I? This time, I hadn't let myself fall too far. This time, I'd kept myself safe.

Even if I'd realized in that grocery store that Tim and I had never connected like that, had never moved in concert, had never felt so close – well, Tim also never hurt me so much, so badly. Not even by sleeping with Carolyn, which I could already see my way to overlooking if that would preserve the marriage.

Meanwhile, everything about Alec hurt. He called that *honest*. I called it too much.

He hadn't much liked it when I'd said that. He'd lost it, in fact.

He'd even called it *revenge*.

I took another swig from my champagne and grimaced against the sour taste.

'Buck up,' I told myself, my voice way too loud in the quiet of my den with the TV on mute. 'This is fucking festive.'

What did Carolyn know, anyway? It wasn't like she didn't have a vested interest in this situation. It wasn't like it wasn't to her advantage to make me feel bad about wanting to save my marriage.

If I'd had pompoms, I might have dragged them out then, to cheerlead my own thought process.

But I was no cheerleader, and anyway, I didn't believe my own rationalizations. Not even when I was sucking them down with a bottle of champagne, alone and unchallenged. The fact was, I couldn't deny that Carolyn had a point. I could hate her all I wanted, and hell yes I wanted, but that didn't make her wrong.

What is so great about your life – about this house – that you would live in it knowing that it's fake? she'd asked.

Alec had said something similar. Loudly.

It careened around inside me, leaving cuts and bruises wherever it hit, and I couldn't answer that one, either. I didn't know.

I saw that blue blouse of mine, coffee-stained and still warm from my skin, hanging in the air in front of me, frozen forever as a marker of what I'd thought my life was versus what it *actually* was. How long had I been so wrong about my life? For at least six months, certainly. Probably longer.

And who was to say Carolyn was Tim's first affair, for that matter? Why had I blithely assumed that? For all I knew, he'd never been faithful to me at all. Our entire relationship could have been a sham from the start. He didn't even have to be particularly evil for that be true, I knew; there were far too many men who seemed to believe that they shouldn't have to give up sleeping with as many women as possible simply because they'd acquired wives. Maybe Tim was one of them. Given that I'd missed the fact that he was sleeping with my own sister, how could I be sure that I knew anything about him at all?

And if I accepted all of that as possible, the question remained: why would I want to hold on to a marriage that was *that* fake? This was just a house, after all. Just a quiet little life, maybe even a good one, but nothing spectacular.

It's really pretty here, Brooke had said Christmas night, when she'd stayed over after the day's revelations. She'd gazed around the great room and had seemed almost sincere. *Really.*

You're not convincing at all, I'd said with a snort.

It's the prettiest suburban house I've seen, she'd said, grinning at me. *But I'm not cut out for the suburbs, Sarah. You shouldn't pay any attention to what I like or don't like. It's what you* like *that matters.*

But . . . what did I like? Why was that question still so hard to answer?

The fact was, I was all Goldilocksed out. There was no *just right*. I didn't want Brooke's life, much as it made me nostalgic for the one I'd left behind. I didn't want whatever life was with Alec, where it was so great when he was around and then I could wait for him to come back to me as if from the wars, doing God knows what with myself in the meantime. And here I was back in my marriage, playing the dutiful wife to a husband who, for all I knew, would hate me the way Carolyn said he did when he fully recovered from his accident.

It was all borrowed time and hand-me-downs. None of it was mine. None of it fitted. I was paralysed. Still. Waiting around for someone to notice how well-behaved and *worthy* I was, and reward me for it. As if that were likely to happen.

It was well after midnight on New Year's Eve. I was all alone, and I still had no idea what to do about it.

18

'Carolyn was here today,' Tim said.

I looked up from the foot of his bed, where I was busying myself by unnecessarily folding and refolding his blankets as he sprawled there, catching his breath. He had just returned from another gruelling session with his physical therapist and was still sweating, but he looked like the Tim I remembered, coming home from a workout at the gym and throwing himself on the couch in sweats and a T-shirt. Only the fact that we were in this rehab centre rather than our house indicated that he was anything but healthy. That and his spotty memory.

And, of course, all the small details about his little love triangle that we hadn't discussed until today. Until now. Because he hadn't let Carolyn in to see him before today – or so I'd thought. But it wouldn't be the first time I'd been the last to know something, would it?

'Oh?' He wasn't looking at me when I glanced at him.

His attention was focused on his hands, as if there were secrets tattooed there. 'How was that?'

Tim looked at me then, and my heart lurched slightly. Or maybe it was my stomach. Those blue eyes, so very bright. That open, trustworthy face. For some reason, I remembered then how much I'd loved it on the rare occasions he'd danced, because he did it so badly, and with such glee. I remembered how I'd used to laugh and laugh . . .

Everything can't be a lie, I assured myself. *Not everything.*

'Is it true?' he asked, his voice quiet. But his gaze stayed steady on mine. 'Everything she said . . . The baby. Is it . . . Did I do that?'

It had been two weeks since I'd last seen Carolyn. Two weeks since we'd had that quietly shattering conversation, and I'd worked overtime to convince myself I'd forgotten all about it. Tim was doing so well, recovering so quickly, that it was easy to get wrapped up in that and act as if that were all that mattered. It was easy to live in crisis mode; it was easy to arrange my life around his schedule, to play the doting wife. It wasn't even an act, entirely. The doctors had advised us to let him ask the questions rather than bombard him with information he wouldn't be able to remember and which might upset him, and maybe I'd gone too far with that. Maybe I'd tried a little too hard to climb back into my marriage and hide there.

Just as I'd told Carolyn I wanted to do. Why was I surprised that she'd taken matters into her own hands?

'Yes,' I said now. 'I think you did.'

'Okay,' he said. He shook his head slightly, which made me notice that the blonde hair he liked to keep short was longer now. Bordering on the very far edge of unruly. The Tim I knew would have hated that. 'Wow.'

'Yeah,' I agreed. 'Wow.'

I stopped pretending that I was accomplishing anything with the blankets, and sat down in his visitor's chair. A little heavily. The rehab centre was much roomier than the hospital, and his entire windowsill was cluttered with flowers and cards, a whole town's worth of *get well soon* wishes. I reached over and straightened one of the cards. And then I accepted that I was nervous. And that I wasn't sure I wanted to have this conversation.

And as I sat there and waited to see what he would say next, I wondered why. Why was I waiting for him? Why was I even here? Why was I floating around my own life, waiting for other people to solve it?

'I know I can't remember everything,' he said slowly. He laughed slightly, like he was aware of the understatement there. 'But I'm kind of shocked. I always thought that if someone was going to cheat, it would be you.'

Um. What?

'What?' I scowled at him. 'What did you say?'

'I don't know, I kind of thought you'd be the one to cross that line,' he said again, in that conversational way, as if what he was saying wasn't completely fucked up. As if it didn't make a mockery of everything I'd suffered these past months.

'Sorry.' My voice was definitely on the hostile side. 'It was all you. Doggy-style – did she mention that part? I saw it with my very own, until-that-moment-totally-faithful eyes.'

The room was silent.

'Until that moment?' Tim asked. He laughed, and it sounded rusty that time. Or, possibly, a little bit forced. 'Does that mean that afterward you weren't faithful?'

I immediately felt guilty. And was then furious with myself. If anyone should feel guilty, it certainly wasn't me. No way.

'I can't believe I'm having this conversation,' I said, squeezing my eyes shut for a second as if that could contain the sudden blooming headache. 'I don't even know what you're talking about, Tim. Why don't you tell me what you remember? Because you really did have an affair with Carolyn and she really is pregnant with your child, and any line-crossing in our marriage was done by you, not me. Is that clear enough? Does that help?'

'I don't want to fight with you,' he said. 'That's the last thing I want. Really.'

He settled back against his bed, and folded his arms beneath his head, and I couldn't help studying him as he lay there. He was a good-looking guy. A little scrawnier at the moment than he usually was, and a bit more pale.

But still attractive. It wasn't so much his individual features but the sum of them put together. He had charisma. He was the kind of guy who made you *want* to do things for him – *want* to please him. Notably unlike Alec, who was hostile and often rude. If not downright surly.

Not that I was making comparisons.

'Good,' I said now, feeling annoyance like adrenalin pulsing through me, making me feel jittery and wired. 'Let's not fight.'

'You look different,' he said after a moment, studying me. He pointed at his hair, as if to indicate mine. 'I mean, you look the way you did when I met you.'

I didn't know if there were layers of meaning there that I should attempt to excavate. I decided against it. I reached up and ran a hand along my hair, which grew like a weed and was now nearly to my shoulders, every new inch making me feel less like the wife he'd betrayed and more like the woman who'd chosen him very deliberately all those years ago. A crucial distinction.

'If that's your way of telling me I look younger,' I said, 'thank you.'

'You've been so good to me,' he said quietly. 'You were all I wanted when I woke up. I was completely delirious and you were the only thing that made me feel any better.'

'I'm glad I could be here for you,' I said, and that wasn't a lie. It was perfectly true. It was just that there were complications surrounding that. Shouldn't it mean something that I was willing to put it all aside at a time like this? Shouldn't that prove what a good person I was, unlike Carolyn – what an excellent and longsuffering wife? I shouldn't be the one he left. It was so unfair.

It wasn't that I wanted a medal. But a kinder word or two wouldn't hurt, either.

'Sarah . . .' He rubbed his hands over his face. 'I don't think we were happy.'

I felt myself deflate. I wondered if it was visible. And when I was small again, I felt the rest of it: shame. Regret. Humiliation. And that panic.

'Did Carolyn tell you that?' I asked, battling to remain calm. 'It seems a little convenient.'

'She told me a lot of things,' he said. 'But the part about us, the things I remember . . .' His blue eyes were intent on mine, and perfectly clear. 'Do you think we were happy? Really?'

'I was happy,' I said simply. Wasn't I, back then? Or anyway, I'd never been *unhappy*. What was the difference? I raised my hands slightly and let them fall to my lap. 'I know it would be so much easier if I could say everything was terrible, but it wasn't. Not for me. And if you weren't happy, you never told me. You let me walk in on you. And then you raced right ahead into the divorce like it was a foregone conclusion.'

'Carolyn says you refused to listen,' he said. 'To even entertain the conversation when I tried to have it with you. She thinks you wanted—'

'Carolyn is, to put it mildly, an unreliable source,' I

pointed out, interrupting him, and trying not to bite his head off. He was still a patient. He was still recovering. He looked weak, and I had to remind myself that this was all a mystery to him. He wasn't trying to hurt me – he honestly couldn't remember. But it was hard. 'And I'm not sure you should use your pillow talk with her as evidence against me when you're the one who can't remember anything.'

He let out a breath, as if it hurt, and I was so angry with him and trying so hard to keep it locked inside that I didn't even ask him if he was okay.

'Why are you here?' he asked, frowning like he was truly confused. By me. Carolyn struck again. 'Why are you helping me, if it's not out of some kind of guilty conscience?'

I stared at him, shaken. More shaken than I wanted to admit, much less share. I knew I didn't have a guilty conscience. Not even about Alec, not really. But I wasn't exactly pure of heart, either, and that was the part that was getting to me.

'Because you're my husband.' I shook my head, realizing only then that I was much too close to tears. Again. 'That meant something to me, Tim. Even if it didn't mean anything to you. Obviously.'

I met my father for coffee in the cute little independent coffee shop in the village a day or so later, at his request. He looked ill at ease and severe, scowling at the selection of pastries in the glass case as if he suspected a trick.

'They're just croissants, Dad,' I said, trying to be reas-suring, and ordered one. 'They're not going to hurt you.'

He ordered plain coffee, black, and closely monitored the barista behind the counter as if he anticipated some kind of bait and switch, as if he suspected he might be given a latte instead and be expected to make do. We settled down at one of the empty tables and marinated for a moment or two in the familial awkwardness. I thought about the meetings I'd had to have with the local lawyers still handling our case load, and with the ever-loathsome Annette. I'd finally admitted the truth to myself: the law I practised at Lowery & Lowery bored me. I had no desire to defend drunk drivers. In fact, I kind of hated them. I'd have thought that revelation might have come with a trumpet or two, at the very least. Instead, I was having a notably non-Parisian croissant in a Rivermark coffee house with my remarkably uncomfortable father. *Six of one, half dozen of another*, I told myself.

'I'm sorry you won't come to the house,' he said after a while. 'I wanted to see how you're doing. Your mother's feelings are very hurt, you know.'

'I'm sure they are,' I said. Not nicely.

'She's doing the best she can,' Dad said, that stern note in his voice. Defending her, as ever. Well, maybe he had to. 'This situation between you girls is very tricky.'

I should have expected that. The *tricky situation* bullshit that people trotted out because they didn't want to tell me to get over it to my face, and they were uncomfortable that I couldn't seem to do it on command anyway. That I had *feelings* about what Carolyn had done to me. Very tricky, indeed.

'It's not that tricky,' I replied. I wasn't even angry this time, or not very. I sounded well-rehearsed to my own ears. Or maybe that was real weariness with all of this, finally taking me over. 'All you and Mom had to do was try to be a little compassionate to *both* your daughters. And maybe a little less openly supportive of the one who caused this whole thing. I get that you couldn't do that. It's fine.' I fiddled with my cup. I drank so much coffee these days, sitting in hospital rooms and trying to combat my largely sleepless nights, that I wondered if it was running in my veins instead of blood. 'But I'm obviously going to have a lot of feelings about that, Dad. I'm going to feel abandoned. And that's not something a lasagne dinner is likely to cure.'

'This bitterness can't be good for you, sweetheart,' he said gently.

You would know all about that, I thought but kept myself from saying. My mother had made a career out of her own bitterness. She let it infuse every last part of her life. She had never so much as voiced a single syllable that didn't drip with it, as far as I knew. And she seemed perfectly fine with her life, didn't she? So did my father, for that matter. And on some level, I got it. There was a grandchild in the mix now, or would be soon enough. I was sure they told themselves they were taking the long view, and maybe they were. If I squinted, I could almost see where they were coming from.

And maybe, in time, I would get to a place where that stopped hurting me so much. But I wasn't optimistic.

'Don't be so sure,' I told my father then, and I even smiled. 'Some days I think it's all I have left.'

'Oh, come on,' Lianne said, scoffing. We stood in her cosy kitchen, basking in our Wednesday afternoon coffee date. Or anyway, I was basking. She was mad, and rapidly getting even madder. 'You can't keep waiting on him hand and foot while he's lounging around musing about what *you* did to the marriage. What the hell?'

'I feel like that's where I need to be right now,' I said with perfect calm. Because I really was calm. Possibly psychotically calm, but I didn't like to judge. 'I think there's probably a really limited amount of time left where I can be his wife, Lianne. I don't think there's anything wrong with taking advantage of that while I can.'

'That's maybe the single most depressing thing I've ever heard you say,' she retorted, her voice thick with feeling. 'What are you thinking?'

But I wasn't thinking. I didn't want to think.

'I spent months and months doing nothing but thinking,' I told her, my voice shaking, the myth of *perfect calm* shattered that quickly, 'and what good did it do, Lianne? What came of it? So I'm not thinking anything.

I'm living through this. One day after the next.'

'Sarah.' Her voice was something like worried, like she'd lost me. I didn't want to hear that tone in her voice. I didn't want to see that expression on her face. I wanted all of this to be over. I wanted the decisions to be made already, and dealt with. I wanted to fast-forward to the end, wherever that was.

'I'm fine, Lianne,' I said. 'I'm perfectly happy.'

Or I was close enough for it to count, and who cared if that wasn't all the way there? I ignored the face she made.

'Why is the way I'm happy never good enough for other people?' I demanded. 'Why doesn't the fact that I say I'm happy, or was happy, ever matter? Maybe this is the exact amount of happiness I'm capable of.' I spread my arms out, taking in the world, this situation, my life. Everything. 'Maybe this is exactly what I want.'

'Then congratulations,' Lianne said dryly. And a little bit sadly, which I chose to overlook. 'You sure have it.'

When I got home I stood in the kitchen for a moment, feeling unbearably restless. Like there was a drumbeat underneath my skin: an impossible itch. Like I was breaking out in hives, except no matter how many times I inspected my skin, I wasn't. I didn't want to know what it was, I told myself. I didn't want to know what it meant.

And yet I found myself in the attic, digging through old boxes and strange parcels I couldn't identify, getting dusty and dirty, and I kept right on going. Finally, I found it. I dragged the big box out into the upstairs hallway, and ripped open the cardboard without caring that my hands looked chapped and grey from the cold and the dust.

There they were. My old travel journals and guidebooks. All the notes I'd taken about the places I'd wanted to go, the things I'd wanted to see. Botswana and Budapest. Prague and Sydney. All of those dreams of mine, hidden away in a cardboard box with my backpacker's pack at the bottom. I pulled it out, smiling slightly. It was a dark green and had all of those clips and buckles, all of which seemed strange but all of which worked beautifully when you were living with the pack on your back. When it was your moveable home and you had a hundred different needs for each and every clip, depending on where in the world you found yourself. I picked it up and carried it downstairs and laid it out on the coffee table in the centre of the living room. I had wanted to carry what I needed with me, and find what I wanted in the places I wandered. And instead I had chosen to nail myself into place. To stand still. To represent drunk drivers and fill a house with pretty things that anyone could buy in the same stores I'd visited. I wanted more. I wanted . . . *bigger*.

I fingered the shoulder straps of my once-beloved pack, and I understood that I had felt more like myself while I was lost somewhere in the world than I ever had when I was here, being dutiful. That I had put myself aside to be this very specific kind of adult, adhering to a very specific set of rules. Lawyer hair and appropriate clothes. A polite smile.

Maybe Brooke had been right. Maybe *smooth* and *sensible* really was settling.

Maybe I'd been wrong about that, too.

Later, I wrapped myself up in my thickest comforter and stood out on the deck that jutted out into our barren, wintery backyard. It was dry and cold, and the wind picked up as the sun set. But still I stood there, watching the stars come out and the moon rise. Watching the night settle over the world.

It got colder and colder, and I didn't move; I pulled the comforter tighter around me. As if I were keeping my own quiet vigil far up here on this ridge, where no one could see me. Where no one would know. And it was fifteenth January, and even as I stood there, shivering and teeth chattering, Alec was on a plane somewhere. Over the ocean maybe, or all the way to Africa already for all I knew. But gone. Always gone.

And that was that.

That was who he was. This was what he did.

He'd never promised me anything, not then and not now. That was Alec.

So I had no one to blame for that hollow, wrenching feeling inside me but myself.

19

When I walked into Tim's room in the rehab centre the next day, I stopped short. He was on his bed – but so was Carolyn. They were curled around each other, kissing. It wasn't wild and passionate. It was almost sweet, I thought. If they'd been other people. If I hadn't been married to one of them and related to the other.

It was also déjà vu.

There was no blue blouse this time. No scales fell from my eyes as I was confronted with a terrible new reality I didn't want to accept. There was no awful sense of a *before* and *after* that I had to come to terms with.

No, this time I simply stood there, watching my husband make out with my sister.

It could be worse, I thought philosophically. This could actually be a surprise. Or it could hurt. But it didn't.

And the fact that this sickening tableau aroused absolutely no response in me was the telling bit. The fact that I felt little more than empty, that I once again felt like a zombie, that my overwhelming urge was not to *do* anything but to turn around and simply walk out . . .

'What is the matter with you two?' I asked. I didn't yell. I didn't freak out. Unlike the last time, I didn't scream.

Carolyn did. She screamed and she jack-knifed up and then she scowled at me, her hands clapped over her heart.

'Sarah! My God!' she cried.

I ignored her. I glared at Tim instead. He looked a little bit dazed. Uncomfortable and kind of guilty, if I was reading that pinched expression right. Neither of which, I felt, was the appropriate response.

'You knew I was coming,' I said quietly. 'Did you stage this?'

'Of course not.' But he wouldn't meet my gaze, and I wondered.

'Listen,' Carolyn said, pulling her drapey sweater tighter around her and sitting up straight, her tone suddenly businesslike. It was jarring, to put it mildly. 'We need to talk to you, anyway. Tim will be getting out of here soon and going home. And I'm not living apart from him. I'm pregnant, and I need to be with the father of my baby.' Her frown wore deep grooves into her forehead. 'And it's half his house, anyway.'

'I would say I couldn't possibly have heard you right,' I said slowly, not really wanting to look at her but not able to look away. I sighed. 'But I know I did.'

'Maybe it's time you thought about reality,' Carolyn suggested, her eyes narrowing. It was a deliberate call back to the conversation we'd had, and we both knew it. She was challenging me.

'And the reality you'd like me to think about now is you moving into my house?' I asked. I actually laughed then. How could I not? 'I think that's taking the concept of *sister wives* to a whole new and horrifying level, to be honest.'

'You're getting divorced, Sarah,' she said, and I had to admit that she wasn't saying it in a particularly nasty way. It was the words themselves that were nasty. It was the fact that she was sitting on a bed with the man who was still married to me while she was saying them.

'And you're leaving this room,' I told her. Not unkindly, to my credit. 'Right now.'

'Uh, no, I'm not—'

'You are.' I let my bag drop to the ground and crossed my arms. 'I'm not having this conversation with you, Carolyn. If Tim wants to tell you all about it later, I can't control that. But you already broke up my marriage. You don't get to sit in on the conversations he and I have about that.' She looked mutinous. 'This is non-negotiable,' I snapped.

'Carolyn.' I realized I'd never heard that particular tone of voice from him. My stomach rolled a little bit. It was like that tender moment I'd witnessed in the ICU. I didn't want to know their private language. Nor should I have to know it, I felt.

Carolyn looked at him, but she dropped her head slightly

in silent acquiescence. And then she pushed herself off the bed and onto her feet.

'I'll be down in the lobby,' she said. To Tim. I expected her to jump on him and kiss him again, to prove a point, but I supposed even she knew she didn't need to do that.

She glanced at me as she walked by, and her mouth moved as if she might say something. We looked at each other for a long moment, and then she bowed her head again, and left. I told myself I was relieved.

And so I just stood there by the wall, arms still crossed, and looked at Tim. He lay there on his industrial bed, probably a bit weaker than he appeared. He'd cut his hair – had Carolyn trimmed it for him? I bet she had, and hated the images that inspired – and he'd shaved. He looked exactly like my husband. Like the man I'd lost.

I couldn't pretend I wasn't still grieving that. Him.

I noticed that he did not leap into the silence that stretched between us to apologize for what I'd walked in on today. Or to attempt to excuse himself in any way.

'Did you get your memories back?' I asked.

'No.' He studied me. 'But the fact that's your first question makes me think Carolyn is right. That I really did want to leave you – this marriage – that badly.'

I shook my head. And recognized that finally, *finally*, I was angry. At him, as he deserved.

'I understand that this must be a difficult time for you, Tim,' I bit out. 'I can't imagine what it must be like. But you're still married to me. And I've cared for you throughout this whole ordeal, when a lot of people might have walked away and left you to it.' I didn't try to hide what I felt. I didn't try to control the way I glared at him. 'If you can't muster up any kind of respect for the five years we've been married – if you think I somehow deserve less consideration than you would give to one of the nurses here who you don't even know – at least have some respect for that!'

It only occurred to me then that the door to the hallway was open, that anyone could hear and that this was Rivermark, where people were certain to be listening, but I couldn't let myself focus on that. Tim sucked in a long breath.

'You're right,' he said after a moment. 'I'm sorry.'

I sighed then. I slumped back against the wall behind me, stared at him, and had no idea what to do. The apology was nice, but anticlimactic.

I could remember, so vividly, standing in Brooke's apartment before Christmas and vowing that it was time to unclench my fist from around this marriage, from this man. I'd thought the same thing in Vermont when I'd finally taken off my wedding rings. I'd been ready to move on, whether Tim woke or not. And yet the slightest indication that I could get back in, that I could dive back into this little life of ours no matter what I had to swallow and hide to do it, and I'd leapt right in.

What was that about? What was I so afraid of?

But I knew.

Given the choice, I wanted simple. Easy. Smooth. I wanted the things that didn't require work. The easy way out. It was hard to be honest with yourself, much less with a partner. It was hard to choose to do the right thing when the right thing hurt and the other option wasn't *wrong* so much as it was *not really as good*. Black-and-white choices were always so much easier to make, weren't they?

My God, I thought, in dawning realization and no little horror, *I am such a coward.*

'I want more,' Tim said then, with heartbreaking simplicity, and it didn't matter, then, what I was afraid of facing because it was right there in front of me whether I liked it or not. 'I want to be with someone who loves me so much it would kill her to lose me. I want to be with someone who would risk everything for me.'

My throat was dry. 'That's very romantic.' I couldn't help the bitter little laugh that came out then. 'Maybe a little less romantic than it would be if you weren't saying that to the woman you're still married to. The one who, presumably, is not the one—'

'I loved you so much,' he said then, struggling to sit up straighter and reaching out to pull himself up on the side rail of his bed, like it was a fight against gravity and he wasn't sure he'd win. 'That's what I remember, Sarah, and it has nothing to do with Carolyn. I didn't care that you didn't feel the same way about me. I thought I'd win you over. That's what I do. I'm the guy who can sell anyone on anything. I figured it was only a matter of time.'

'I loved you too!' I threw at him. 'I trusted you. I trusted you more than I'd ever trusted anyone, Tim. I *believed* you.'

'I know,' he said in that same way, that *determined* way, 'but we're not talking about the same thing, are we? Do you think I didn't know you were hung up on that guy when I met you? I didn't think it would matter. He was gone. I was there. I thought you would figure out that I was much better for you than he ever could be.'

'And you succeeded,' I said, very distinctly. Because he had. How could he not know that? Brooke knew it. Hell, even I knew it. 'Did you miss the part where we moved out here? Where we bought a pretty house and opened a practice and built a whole life together? What part of that was me pining away? What part was me not loving and trusting you?'

'Sarah,' he said, like my name was a sigh, deep and sad. 'Please don't do this.'

'I'm sorry that I didn't love you the way you think I should have,' I said stiffly. 'I guess I should have asked my sister for pointers.'

He looked like he was biting his lip. Biting back words. It made me wonder what he thought would qualify as *too harsh* in this scenario.

'It isn't your fault,' he said, but there was a chill in his voice and I suspected he wanted to defend Carolyn. *See? I* told myself. *He's still the man you married, the great defender of the innocent and protector of all he can. That just doesn't include you any longer.* 'I shouldn't have done it the way I did. I can't pretend I'm not the shithead here.'

'I don't think anyone's pretending that,' I agreed. I was not biting back my words. Clearly.

'We weren't happy,' he said quietly, and I could see he meant that. That he wasn't confused. That this was his truth, however unfair or unpleasant I thought it was. 'I think on some level, you know that.'

I wanted to throw something back at him, but instead, I thought about the photographs I'd seen of Prague in my guidebooks last night, and on the postcards I'd collected from various bookstores over the years. The fairy-tale city, that beautiful bridge bristling with artists and statues and a different kind of life than anything I'd find here. It was only one of the magical places I'd wanted to go to, but I'd given that up as one of those childish daydreams that real adults like me didn't get to hold on to any longer. I'd given up everything because I'd thought that's what I was supposed to do.

I thought about what *happy* really was. I'd thought for so long that it was a choice between *temporary* and *permanent* and Alec had been such a clear, self-proclaimed temporary situation, and he'd hurt me so terribly when he'd left. When I'd been too scared to go with him, because I'd known that I wanted things he couldn't give. I'd known better than to force that issue on a different continent. I'd been right back then, for a variety of reasons and because I couldn't possibly have handled him, but that didn't change how badly it had hurt.

And I'd thought that the permanence Tim offered could save me from that. From the hurt, from the part of me that wanted to ignore the things I felt and follow Alec around anyway. I'd believed Tim knew better than me – that he had a reason to be confident enough to propose *forever* on the third date. That he was *right*. And I'd done whatever I'd had to do to make sure that forever worked. Drunk-driving cases in my safe suburban hometown. Cutting off Brooke, who challenged me and my brand-new fascination with the status quo, to preserve that sense of safety. Whatever it took.

But what would happen if I decided I could . . . be happy? If I let that take whatever form it took? If finally, once and for all, I just let go and let whatever happened, happen?

How fucking revolutionary.

'Say something,' Tim urged me.

'I don't see why,' I said after a moment. When I could speak without all that emotion in my voice. He didn't deserve to hear any of that. Not any more. It was mine, I realized. Not his. 'There's not really anything left to say, is there? It's not like I'm going to debate you into being happy with me if you weren't.'

I pushed away from the wall. I scooped my bag up by its strap.

'I wish I hadn't handled all of this so badly,' he whispered. 'If I could have done this without hurting you, Sarah, I would have.'

'You've said that before, Tim.' I shrugged. 'That's actually kind of a meaningless and shitty thing to say, if you think about it.'

'That's not how I mean it,' he said, rubbing at his face. 'Really.'

I inclined my head as if I understood, and maybe some part of me did. But none of it mattered. I finally got that.

We looked at each other then, for what felt like a long time. I didn't know how I was supposed to feel. I knew how his mouth tasted. I knew what noises he made when he was sick, when he was being silly, when he was about to come. I knew what he liked to eat on Sunday afternoons in front of the game, and how he liked his toast. I knew what he smelled like without a shower. I knew what he was afraid of, and what he regretted from his childhood years. I remembered how he'd held me close on our honeymoon, and the things he'd whispered in my ear. I'd soothed him as he sobbed over the deaths of his parents. I'd stroked his forehead through fevers, even held him when he'd woken from this coma and had known no one in all the world but me.

Did all of that disappear now? Did it matter less because it was over? I didn't know how this worked. I didn't know how to shift into a space where we weren't intimate, where we weren't close, because we knew too much about each other. Maybe that was what I'd been fighting all this time. I didn't want to give this up. Because whatever else it was, whether it was as happy as it should have been, as I'd thought it was, it was ours. It was real.

'I really did love you,' I whispered. 'Whatever you might have decided since then.'

'I know,' he said. 'I know you did. As much as you could.'

And when I left, when I finally turned and walked away the way I should have done in September or maybe long before that, he let me go. He didn't even say goodbye.

But then again, he'd been saying goodbye for a long time. I had only just learned how to listen.

It was snowing again when I got back into my car, and it annoyed me.

Snow was lovely and picturesque in December, when everything was some kind of extended, interactive Christmas card, and there were whole radio stations dedicated to playing endless loops of carols telling us all how wonderful winter was.

Snow in January was nothing more than cold. And spoke of the endless, gruelling, impossible winter months laid out before us, with spring the barest hint of possibility in the far-off future.

But that was fine, I told myself now, glaring at the flurries that dusted my windshield, because I had a plan.

My plan.

It was funny how clear everything had become. How much sense it all made all of a sudden.

I didn't want this. This marriage. These choices. This

life. I didn't want any of it. And I certainly wasn't going to fight for it any longer.

I was going to do something much better. I was going to go home and buy a plane ticket to somewhere far, far away. So far away it was already summer, like in Australia. And then I was going to very carefully pack up that backpack of mine, and I was going to simply . . . go.

I was going to open my hands as wide as they could, and I was going to let all of this flow through them and disappear. I was going to stop looking back. I was going to let life find me, instead of imposing my plans on it out of fear and heartbreak and a knee-jerk reaction to what I *ought* to do. I was going to let go, starting right now. I was going to make room for whatever came next.

I drove carefully through town, and then started up the hill towards the house. I would have to make some phone calls. There was the question of what to do with the stuff I actually wanted from this old life of mine, and what to do with it while I was travelling, but that was what storage facilities were for. There were also the legal issues to work out – the divorce and all our assets – but I didn't really think there would be a fight. Tim had a baby on the way, after all. I suspected he would want it all over as quickly as possible.

And I wanted to be free. I wanted to see what I found out there, and then, when I was done with that, I wanted to spend my life helping people who needed help – not tending to the kind of people who risked others' lives in so cavalier a fashion and then complained about it afterward. The Benjy Strattons of the world were not my problem. Not any more. Not ever again.

I went down lists in my head. Tim and I had always maintained three bank accounts: his, ours and mine. I would be more than fine, and if he bought me out of the practice and the house as I expected he would, I would be even better. In a way, I thought a bit ruefully as I turned down our street, it was as if we'd been planning for our divorce since the day we met. I hadn't thought that then, of course. I'd thought we were so practical, so clear-eyed and unemotional about things like assets and worst-case scenarios. I wasn't sure that meant the things Tim thought it meant, but there was no denying the fact that would make all of this that much easier now.

I had come full circle. I understood my life in a way I hadn't before – because I'd been actively hiding from myself. All my depositions had led me to one inescapable conclusion: I'd created my own prison. I'd put up these bars and locked myself away in *safe* and *easy*. And that was sad, but the good news was, I was the one who could walk free of it whenever I wanted. Maybe Tim had always known that, on some level.

And now I did, too.

I pulled into the driveway, frowning at the car that was already there, engine running and wipers slapping back and forth. What now? My money was on my mother, the only one who hadn't weighed in recently on my life choices.

That was very unlike her. I braced myself for her eternal woundedness, her martyrdom, as I climbed out of my car. I even cautioned myself to be kind. After all, who knew what her prison looked like? Who knew what she was hiding from herself?

But it wasn't my mother who swung out of the driver's seat and faced me across the snow flurries. It wasn't my mother who made me stop still and stare.

It was Alec.

20

'Impossible,' I said flatly, as if I thought he were an apparition brought on by stress. Which he very well could have been. 'You flew out yesterday.'

'I was supposed to fly out yesterday,' he agreed, the familiar kick of temper in that low, commanding voice of his. 'I made it to JFK for the New York to London leg. I was all ready to go. It's a long flight, Sarah. *Flights*, in fact. London to Johannesburg and then on to Windhoek. It takes forever. And I didn't get on the damned plane.'

'You don't change your plans,' I said, like I was arguing. 'Ever.'

'No, Sarah, I don't,' he muttered dangerously. 'Yet here I am. In your driveway. In the snow.'

He looked surly and delicious, all dark eyes and his bone-deep crankiness. He wore a ridiculous fuzzy hat with a pompom jammed down on his head, no coat and those same ancient jeans that *did things* to his legs. He should have looked foolish. Or at least cold.

'I don't understand,' I said. But I'd seen so many movies. I knew what I wanted this scene to mean. Was this where he swept me off my feet and carried me away? Was this where the curtain fell over a happily-ever-after kiss? There was a part of me that wanted that – him – desperately. Maybe I always would.

But I didn't want that *now*. I didn't know if I believed in happily ever after any longer, and I had only just realized all the things I had to do.

It didn't matter that he was here. It couldn't.

I opened my mouth to tell him so.

'I'm not the marrying kind,' he gritted out at me, shocking me into silence. 'I don't see that changing. Why should a piece of paper or a religious ceremony mean more than what two people know they feel? That doesn't make any sense to me, and I don't think it ever will.'

'I didn't propose to you, Alec,' I pointed out, rocking back on my heels as if he'd accused me of clinging to his pant-leg. 'And I don't need a run down of your objections to something I don't even—'

'Please shut up,' he said, through his teeth. He waited for a moment, as if to see whether or not I would, that lean body of his seeming to vibrate with some kind of electric current, some kind of charge. I shoved my freezing, gloveless fingers into my pockets, let the snow flurries fall on my face, and shut up.

'Here's what I promise you, Sarah,' he said, moving closer, looming over me right there in the driveway, in front of the house and the life I was abandoning. At last. 'I will never forget you. I never have and I never will. I will always miss you when you're not with me. I always do. I have two photos of you that I carry with me everywhere, like an obsessed person. But I accept that.'

I stopped caring that it was cold, that I was already running on empty, that I was exhausted from all the different layers of grief I'd been slogging around in for so long. I stopped noticing anything but that grim, resolute mouth of his that never made promises he couldn't keep.

Never.

'I will annoy you with coffee and other food you don't want every morning you wake up with me,' he continued, moving even closer. 'I will irritate you. I will probably drive you crazy, and I'll probably think that's pretty funny.'

'You don't have to do this,' I told him, though there was a lump in my throat. 'I don't need you to do this.'

'I promise you that I will never lie to you, even if it would be easier,' he continued, as if I hadn't spoken. 'I'm not a cheater. I don't see the point. I promise that I will treat you like my equal in all things, even when that gets uncomfortable. I promise to expect nothing less from you.' He was standing directly in front of me then, looking down, his expression one I'd never seen before. Solemn, but lit from within. As if these were vows. 'I promise that I will listen to you, and try to understand you, and try to give you the benefit of the doubt when the things you say make me angry. I promise never to ask you to hold my scalpel, unless it's a medical emergency and I need your help. I promise to treat you like the smart, fascinating, capable woman that you are. And I promise to listen to you if you feel like I'm not giving you what you need.'

'Alec.' I could barely speak. 'Come on. Stop. What do you think this is?'

'I think this is long overdue,' he retorted, his voice gruff, but that odd light in his gaze. 'A necessary clarification. I promise not to ask you to follow me anywhere unless I think it's somewhere you'd want to go too. I promise not to act like my career is more important than whatever you choose to do, even if I secretly think it is, because I am, after all, an arrogant asshole. I promise not to get too pissed when you call me that. It's true.'

'Am I going to call you that, do you think?' I asked, reluctantly enchanted by this. The man, the snow. The things he was saying. What they meant. 'Often?'

He only smiled that specifically Alec smile, little more than the curve of his mouth.

'I promise to count every single one of your freckles, all over your body, because they could change, and those are important facts that I need to be on top of,' he said, his voice dropping then, becoming husky. 'I promise you that you are the most interesting woman I've ever met, that you haunted me for years, that I blame you for my inability to really move on with someone else, and that I'm not at all sorry your marriage isn't working.'

'That's the most romantic one yet,' I managed to get out, but I was smiling despite myself.

'I promise that I won't hold it against you if you decide you can't handle me – at least, not too much. And I promise you that if you give me a chance, I will celebrate you,' he said fiercely, running his cold hand over my cheek, then using it to hold my face up to his. 'I will spend every minute we have together making sure you know that in every way that matters, I will always choose you. I will always want you. I will. I promise.' His eyes searched mine. 'There's nothing temporary about the way I feel about you, Sarah. There never was.'

I don't know how long we stood there, gazing at each other, breathing the same air, soaking in all those promises. My hand snuck up to cover his. For a long time, I didn't even notice the chill. I was too off-balance. Too wild inside. And I understood, at last, that this particular kind of out-of-control was a good thing. This was where life happened, this feeling. It couldn't be regimented or regulated. That was prison. This was . . . joy.

Eventually, I led him inside, to stamp off the snow. To pull that silly hat from his head. He looked dishevelled and disreputable as he prowled around the big open floor plan of the house's first floor, frowning at all the things I'd collected, few of which, I told myself, I would even remember once I left here. And even fewer that I would miss.

Alec roamed over to the couches set around the coffee

table, and sat down, leaning forward to run his hands over my old pack. He picked up one of the guidebooks that lay beside it and flipped through it.

'I'm taking a trip,' I told him. I felt almost bubbly with nervousness, as if I were carbonated. I drifted over to the couch across from him, considered sitting there as if this were an interview, but thought better of it. I circled the table and dropped down next to him. Close enough to feel the heat of him, to smell the snow against his skin. But not quite touching him. 'A long one. That one I always talked about.'

He looked sideways at me, then back at the books. He picked up China, then New Zealand. He ran his fingers over India.

'How long?' he asked.

'I don't know. A year?'

He nodded. 'Alone?'

'That's the plan,' I said.

But that didn't seem sufficient. It was non-committal. It didn't do justice to the things I wanted – and I was afraid it sounded like some kind of invitation. Which it wasn't. If these last few months had taught me anything, it was that I needed to take some time on my own to figure out who I was. What I wanted for myself. I never wanted to feel like Goldilocks again, trying on other people's lives for size. I wanted my own.

'I mean, yes,' I corrected myself. 'Alone. Just me and whoever I happen upon along the way.'

He leaned back then, stretching that rangy body out next to me, his long arms along the back, and his gaze was so bright it made those bubbles inside me seem to fizz over.

'Good,' he said, matter-of-factly. 'You should.'

Because to Alec, dreams were never crazy, no matter how big or grand or out there. It would never be a question of *why*. It would always be *when*.

'Well,' I said after a moment, trying not to grin like a fool, and not even really knowing why I felt so giddy. This wasn't a magical moment. This wasn't the kiss to build a dream on, or any of that nonsense. But then again, maybe that was why. Tim had kissed me. Tim had flattered me. Alec understood me. 'It's been a long time coming.'

He reached over and pulled a strand of my hair between his fingers and tugged on it, very gently.

'A year is a lot longer than it seems,' he said, studying me. And close. So close. 'You might want to see a friendly face every few months. To get your bearings.'

I let myself grin then the way I wanted. 'Would this friendly face be located in Africa, by any chance?'

He dropped my hair and traced a gentle little pattern along my jaw instead.

'It would,' he said. 'You should think about dropping by. Maybe even making it a base of operations. The clinic could always use another good brain, you know. Especially a lawyer.'

'You're talking about work,' I pointed out. 'I'm talking

about a long-overdue journey to *find myself*. And I could end up anywhere, Alec. The Russian steppes. Machu Picchu. Possibly not in Africa at all.'

He shifted then, and stroked my hair back from my face, with so much tenderness that I thought for a moment I might weep. But I didn't. I found myself smiling instead, even wider, and twisting around so that I faced him, one leg drawn up on the sofa cushion between us, touching him.

'Wherever you are out there,' he said, and his voice was strong and sure, 'you'll find what you're looking for. I don't have any doubt.'

'That's good,' I whispered. 'Because I do.'

He smiled then, a genuine smile. 'You're the only one.'

He didn't want anything from me, I realized then. He had said all of those things, made all of those promises, and he wasn't going to push me into making any declarations in return. As if he trusted me to make the decisions I had to make. As if he believed in what I was doing, whether that fitted into his plans or not.

Of course I had loved this man so much that losing him had set off a seven-year chain reaction of questionable choices and assumed identities. Of course. It wasn't that I regretted Tim, or our marriage. I didn't. But suddenly, I understood it better.

And in understanding it – and me – I was that much closer to free.

'Maybe I will stop off in Africa at some point,' I said.

He let his fingers trace over my lips, and his eyes burned, but he was still smiling.

'Promise?' he asked.

And I smiled back, because I trusted him, and I knew that this time, I would make sure to trust myself, too.

'I promise,' I said softly, knowing that to him, this was the only vow that mattered.

'There's this beach in Namibia,' he said, his hand sliding around to cup the nape of my neck as he leaned closer, that serious mouth so very close to mine. Close enough to kiss. 'Someday I'll show it to you. I think you'll like it.'

And he was right. I did.